The Dream snatcher

Abi Elphinstone

SIMON AND SCHUSTER

For Edo,
who named Gryff and is like him in so many ways

The Dream snatcher

First published in Great Britain in 2015 by Simon and Schuster UK Ltd
A CBS COMPANY

13

Simon & Schuster UK Ltd
1st Floor
222 Gray's Inn Road
London WC1X 8HB

Simon & Schuster Australia, Sydney
Simon & Schuster India, New Delhi

A CIP catalogue record for this book
is available from the British Library.

PB ISBN: 978-1-47112-268-2
EBook ISBN: 978-1-47112-269-9

Printed and bound by CPI Group (UK) Ltd, Croydon, CR0 4YY

www.simonandschuster.co.uk
www.simonandschuster.com.au

TANGLEFERN FOREST

THE DEEPWOOD

THE ANCIENTWOOD

Prologue

There are footprints in the snow, sunken marks picked out by the moonlight. They weave a path through the forest, round the ring of ancient oak trees and on towards the wooden hut. But there they stop, and the smoke curling out of the chimney is the only sign that anyone is inside.

Seven cloaked figures sit round a table, their hoods pulled up despite the fire crackling in the grate. At first, they whisper together, their voices low and guarded. And then the whispers fade, heads drop and lips curl back. A chant begins. There are no words, just grunted sounds scratching at the back of throats.

One of the figures pushes back her hood and long grey hair falls about her shoulders.

'Not this!' she cries. 'You said it wouldn't be this . . .' She shakes her head and makes as if to stand. 'I – I won't do it. It's not right!'

But the others surround her, closing in like hungry shadows. They force the old woman towards the fire and,

1

though her legs scrabble beneath her and her arms grope for the table, the flames loom closer.

'Not my hands!' she sobs. 'Please, no!'

But the flames are already licking her knuckles, shrivelling her skin black. She shrieks in agony, again and again, but the others only grip her harder, joining together in a crooning chant:

> 'A curse we seek, we call it near,
> To brand this hag who turned in fear.
> Follow her close, all through her life,
> Let her never escape our curse full of strife.'

The old woman falls to the floor, whimpering, but even she cannot stop the charcoal mark that seeps through the skin on her forehead. She rocks back and forth, cradling what is left of her hands.

The other figures turn back to the table and, when they are seated, repeat their wordless chant; it gathers pace, throbbing with a rhythm all of its own, and then shadows twist up from behind each figure, swelling in the air to form a cloud of darkness.

The figure at the head of the table stands, beckoning the darkness closer with long, thin fingers. It settles in the outstretched hands, a black shape shifting up and down, as if breathing gently. The figure withdraws a hand, reaching inside its cloak for a small glass bottle. Flicking the lid back, the figure tips the clear liquid into the darkness. The shape shudders, then there is a brittle sound like frost crunching underfoot and the darkness hardens into something long and black.

The figure draws back its hood and in its hand is a shard of black ice. 'So it begins,' the figure says.

And, from somewhere deep in the forest, an owl hoots and snow starts to fall.

Chapter 1
Trespassing

Ten years later

Moll woke with a start, her eyes wide, her body drenched in sweat. She spun round on her hands and knees. Her bed, her wagon, the camp: gone. She was alone in the forest with the darkness and it swelled around her like misted ink.

Heart thudding, she waited for her eyes to adjust. Brambles twisted up around her, closing over her head, curling round her back. Moll tensed. To get inside the bramble tunnel, where the forest was knotted and wild, she must have run past the Sacred Oaks, climbed over the sprawling creepers, then crawled through the undergrowth. Not difficult for Moll usually, but – her heart raced faster as she realised – she'd made this journey *in her sleep*.

She scrambled back down the prickly tunnel – away from the darkness, away from where the nightmare had taken her. Brambles tore at her skin and thorns sank into her bare feet, but she struggled on. The nightmare – the one that came for her every night with the drum and the rattle and the masked figures – was growing stronger. It had pulled her out of bed before now, but Oak, the head of her camp, had always found her, always brought her home. Until tonight. A bramble snagged Moll's long dark hair and yanked her backwards. She twisted free and blundered on.

'It's over,' she panted into the night. 'The nightmare's not real . . .'

But the sound of the drum and the rattle was still pulsing inside her, roaring like an untamed animal. She burst out of the tunnel, gasping for air, her feet scored with cuts. The forest around her was still, a tangle of moon-lit trees. Barely drawing breath, Moll bounded over the creepers and darted between the ferns – back towards the safety of her camp.

And then a shiver crept down her spine as she remembered. She stopped suddenly. On any other night she would have been safe there. But tonight was different. How could she have fallen asleep? Tonight was the night she had planned to break her promise to Oak and that meant 'safe' was the last thing she'd be.

She snatched a glance around her, beating back her fear. Somehow her nightmare had lured her from the camp without waking the watch and now she was exactly where she wanted to be – just moments from the river boundary she'd promised Oak she would never cross.

Moll hugged her cotton nightdress to her. She wouldn't be beaten by her nightmare, by something that wasn't even real. She ducked beneath a yew tree and gave the trunk a sharp punch.

'I'm needing protection tonight, tree spirit, and a bit of that pig-headedness Oak says is bubbling away inside me. None of this falling asleep and wandering off into brambles or who knows what. I've got a plan to carry out. You hear me?'

A breeze sifted through the ivy, brushing Moll's skin like a whisper. Taking a deep breath, she turned and ran. Back towards the river.

And that's when she heard it.

A noise threading through the trees towards her. A low, rolling sound, only metres away, like an engine throbbing deep in the bowels of the earth.

'*Brrroooooo.*'

A smile flickered across Moll's face. She wasn't alone now.

'Gryff,' she panted, leaping over a tree stump and squinting into the undergrowth. She couldn't see anything. But she knew he was there, racing along just metres from her – silently, like a faster, stronger shadow. Then she spotted him, springing out from behind the cluster of alder trees that lined the banks of the river.

Gryff was large, even for a wildcat, with a muscular body and long banded legs. His coat was thick and grey with jet-black stripes and his tail long and bushy – ringed with perfect bands of black – and ending in a blunt tip.

Moll skidded to a halt before him, gasping for breath. She crouched down, level with Gryff, and gazed into his eyes.

They were yellowish green and large, like her own, but with vertical pupils. Wild pupils.

'It's all right, Gryff. It's all right ...'

Gryff's hackles rose and he arched his back. '*Urrrrrrrrrr.*' He was so close to Moll the growl felt like it rumbled inside her body.

She fiddled with a stick by her foot, then looked up. 'I'm crossing that river, Gryff. Skull's camp have been raiding our clearing for too long. They've taken chickens, dogs, firewood ... And now they've gone and thieved a horse! And not any old horse. They've stolen Jinx – *my* cob.'

Gryff didn't move, didn't even blink. Moll wanted to reach out and touch him, to stroke his thick, soft fur. But there were rules, even in the wild, and she wasn't about to go breaking them.

'*Never touch a wildcat; they're the only animals that can't be tamed,*' Oak had told her when Gryff first appeared at the camp.

No one knew where he'd come from. The wildcat just showed up one day, as animals sometimes did. Oak had said there were no wildcats left in the southern part of the country. But he was wrong.

Gryff had showed himself to Moll first, out of everyone in the camp, and not even the Elders could explain the bond that had grown between them over the years. It was with Moll that Gryff ran through the forest and it was Moll that he seemed to trust and even understand. No one else.

'*He probably doesn't feel threatened by you because you're so small, not much bigger than him really*,' her best friend Siddy had said.

But Moll didn't think it was that. Not really.

She tossed her waist-length hair over her shoulder and huffed impatiently. Gryff flinched, backing away several steps. Moll dipped her head, an apology for the sudden movement. Communication with Gryff had to be slow, measured and calm – everything Moll was not.

She rested her elbows on her knees and looked deep into Gryff's eyes. 'The Ancientwood here belongs to us, Gryff; Skull's camp aren't frightening us away by thieving and I'm going to let them know it. They've got the Deepwood and that's where they should stay!' She looked towards the river and her face darkened. 'And besides this'll show them back at camp that I'm no *half* gypsy.' Moll narrowed her green eyes – eyes that were almost the same colour as Gryff's, but that marked her out as different from the rest of the dark-eyed gypsies in the camp, and had earned her snide comments in the past that she'd never forget. 'This'll show them,' she muttered.

Gryff didn't move, but his claws sprang out from beneath him and sliced into the earth.

Don't go, he seemed to say. *The Deepwood's not safe.*

Tanglefern Forest was vast, with some trees so old and tangled that few had passed beneath their branches. But there were places you went and places you didn't. The Ancientwood in the north of the forest was safe: there was the glade of brilliant spring bluebells and yews beyond Oak's camp, then a grove of crab-apple trees, and beyond that, after the forest, the farm itself and Tipplebury village. But south ... Well, south was another place altogether. So she'd heard. The Deepwood was rumoured to be full of shady trees and rotting undergrowth and, when it ended, the heathland, with it sinking bogs and soggy marshes, began.

But south was where Moll had to go if she wanted to get Jinx back.

Gryff was growling now, his warning deep and throaty. Moll scrunched up her nose and hurried to the riverbank. Only yesterday Oak had said that one day he'd get his revenge on Skull. Well, to Moll that was a sign, possibly even an order, for her to cross the boundary and make things right – as quickly as possible. She grabbed the catapult she'd hidden in the hollow of an alder the day before, then clutched at the chain around her neck. Every person in the camp had a different talisman to bring them luck, and hanging from Moll's chain were two boxing fists joined at the wrist. Her initials had been engraved on them: MP – Molly Pecksniff. She gripped themtightly – for further protection against evil spirits and bad luck – then slipped into the gurgling river.

The cold nipped at her ankles, but she stooped to pick up a pebble; no point carrying a catapult if she didn't have a stone ...

'PAAAAH!'

Gryff was behind her on the riverbank, bracing and stamping his forelegs. And he was spitting now, which was never a good sign.

'It's rude to spit, Gryff,' Moll said. 'I don't go spitting at you when you're off hunting in the dead of night.'

Gryff cocked his head, considering. Then he hissed and spat again.

Moll clung to a branch for support, then she edged further into the river. The stones beneath her feet were slippery and she stumbled forward. She whispered a quick prayer to the water spirit who she'd heard could twist up whirlpools and conjure rapids against those who stomped in her river for no good reason. Then Moll carried on, bracing her legs against the current, feeling a path through the stones with the soles of her feet.

She looked up. She was nearing the banks of the Deepwood now, closer to Skull's camp than she'd ever been. Fumbling for her catapult and swallowing back the thud of her heart, she waded on.

Chapter 2
Into the Deepwood

Clutching at reeds, Moll hoisted herself up the far side of the bank. She glanced around.

The same tangle of trees she'd grown up with in the Ancientwood: beech, birch, ash, yew, holly, hawthorn. The darkness couldn't muffle their bark and leaves and she could almost hear Oak's wife, Mooshie: '*All trees have a spirit, Moll, and they lend it to us if we listen hard. Silver birch – its spirit protects against evil beings, and the sap's good for sugar when you're making beer and wine . . . Holly berries – the greatest fertility charm there is . . . Ash – pass a naked child through a split ash tree and you'll find rickets and broken limbs all cured . . .*'

And yet there was something about the air this side of the river. It felt different, as if the night might be full of watching eyes and brooding shadows. Moll's heart beat faster still and a shiver prickled down her spine.

Branches swished above and Moll jerked her head backwards, towards the river. A split second later, Gryff landed on the bank beside her. He nodded towards the forest, his eyes narrow.

Moll dipped her head, grateful that he'd decided she wasn't going on alone.

Somewhere nearby a twig cracked. Gryff's ears swivelled to the sound and he grunted. A deer perhaps.

Moll shook herself. 'We've got to be quick. Soon as dawn breaks we'll be seen; the summer nights aren't ever long.'

With Gryff at her heels, she ran further into the Deepwood beeches, her anklet jangling in the dark. '*Over the river . . . Straight through the beeches . . . Past the glade . . . Then you're in Skull's camp – God help you . . .*' She'd overheard the Elders talking enough times to know the way.

Gradually, and so slowly that at first she didn't notice, the beech trees began to change. Their bark was no longer silver; it was flaky and grey and it peeled back like dead skin. Moll and Gryff wove in and out of them, but the trees were not strong, like the ones surrounding Oak's camp; they were withered and holed and they curved overhead like the bars of a cage. Moll jumped as a bat shot out from a tree. Its leathery flaps crumpled into the distance. Gryff's ears flattened to his head.

It was darker this side of the river somehow, as if the moonlight chose not to come here. And it was quiet – just the tired creaking of branches stirring in the gathering wind. Eventually they came to the glade, but the grass was dead and brown, smothered by fallen branches and fungi. Moll shivered and kept running.

And then Gryff stopped, his neck craned towards the far end of the glade.

'Urrrrrr,' he grumbled, whiskers twitching.

Moll knew what that meant: he was picking up vibrations of sounds that fell beyond the reach of her own ears. They must be near Skull's camp. She clenched her fist round her catapult and made as if to move on.

But Gryff remained where he was and Moll realised that it wasn't only sounds that the wildcat was picking up on. His tail was flat to the ground and he was crouching. He'd seen something too. Moll scrunched her eyes into the night, but Gryff could make out things in the darkness that not even gypsies could see.

Moll crept closer to him, her face sharpened with fear.

'Urrrrrrrrrrrr,' Gryff growled.

Moll heard its creaking before she saw it, just like Gryff had done.

Some metres ahead, hanging from a decaying branch, was a birdcage. They crept closer until they were footsteps away. The cage was huge, several metres high and wide, swinging gently in the wind. Only there wasn't a bird inside. It was littered with bones.

Moll gulped. Gryff growled again.

And there was something else. Nailed to the trunk of the tree below the cage was a creature with a bald tail and a knobbly skull. A dead rat.

Moll swallowed again as they stepped out of the glade back into the trees. Then Gryff tensed. Hanging from another branch by a piece of tattered string was an owl: dead, eyeless.

'Just an owl,' Moll whispered to herself.

But she knew the signs; every gypsy did. Caged bones. Dead rats. Hanging owls. These were witch doctor omens. She and Siddy had laughed at the stories of Skull being a witch doctor, but Oak had been telling the truth all along. And if Oak knew the truth about Skull no wonder Skull's gang wanted to force Oak's camp out of the forest.

Moll glanced behind her; it wasn't too late to turn around. But Jinx ... She couldn't leave Jinx in a place like this. She clenched her teeth.

Then the whispering started.

It was a strange kind of whispering – scratched and guttural, like muttering – as if it was coming from deep within someone, right from the back of their throat.

And it was close, too close.

Moll's body stiffened and fear settled around her neck. And yet she edged closer, somehow drawn to it. Gryff followed. It was louder now and there was a rhythm to it – strong and pulsing. And slowly, like a frosty breath, a feeling slunk into Moll's mind. There was something familiar about those whisperings. The feeling lingered in her mind, breathing quietly.

Then a movement caught her eye. Cloaked figures were stirring between the trees. She edged closer still, hiding behind a tree, and there, just in front of her, was Skull's camp. Four figures were circling a fire in the clearing, moving like a dark wave.

Moll's breath caught in her throat. The whisperings were

getting louder and faster now, growing like an untamed wind. And they were words that didn't belong to Moll's world: strange, rasping words that—

The thud of a drum.

The hiss of a rattle.

Moll's blood froze. Her nightmare was unfolding before her.

· Chapter 3 ·
Dark Rituals

She was so close that the drumbeats thudded through her body and the rattle hissed in her ears. Gryff was absolutely still beside her, his eyes locked on to the cloaked figures. They were moving faster now, a whirl of faceless black. But there was one figure who wasn't stirring; instead he squatted by the fire like an enormous spider, making something from a ball of wax.

Suddenly the figures stopped, their heads bent, the drum and rattle silenced.

Unfolding his body, the squatting figure stood upright. Firelight fell upon his face which was hidden completely by a white mask. A shiver tore through Moll's body. And then a horrible feeling seeped into her. She'd *seen* that mask before, *heard* that drum and rattle, not just locked inside her nightmare, but outside it too – *in real life*.

The mask was white and it shone in the firelight like polished bone. Dark holes marked the eyes and two lines of jagged bones jutted out below in a grim smile. Moll knew right away that this was Skull, his mask a sign of the witch doctor's name. And, although Moll could see the mask had been carved from wood then painted white, it shone out with all the horrifying sickness of a skull.

Skull held up the wax, now moulded into a shape: the unmistakable outline of a person. The chant began to grow again, pulsing in time with the drum and the rattle, and an eerie coldness rippled through Moll. Skull raised the wax figure into the air and squeezed it in a clenched fist. The wax, still warm, squirmed between his fingers like glue.

Moll felt the breath drain from her body, as if an iron fist was crushing her lungs. Beside her, Gryff shivered. A laugh slid out between Skull's teeth, coiling its way between the trees. The chanting rose and once more Skull gripped the small figure, punching his fist into the air. The wax squeezed through his fingers until it was a mangled lump once more.

Then Skull's voice came, slithering and cold, seeking them out like a chill. 'Come, beast, come, child. Come, beast, come, child . . .'

Moll felt it, as if he'd called them by their names. The chant was for her and Gryff. She was sure of it. But stranger than all of that was the feeling growing inside Moll. She almost *wanted* to step forward into the clearing towards Skull. She clutched at her talisman.

'Keep me safe,' she murmured. 'Keep me safe.'

Then a horse brayed, snapping her from her trance. She drew breath sharply and staggered backwards.

'Jinx . . .'

She knelt down by Gryff, but he stared ahead, his body shaking, as if the chant was holding him prisoner.

Moll's heart raced. 'Come on, Gryff!' she whispered.

Gryff jerked his head back behind the tree. His eyes were wild and his hackles wet with sweat.

Moll breathed deeply. 'Skull – he's – he's calling me – he's calling us both! We've got to move!'

She scanned the trees around the clearing, trying to block the chant from her head. To her right, beyond the fire and battered wagons, was a canvas tent propped up against a tree. Gryff skirted round towards it and Moll followed. Behind the tent was a huddle of larger shapes and she'd know those silhouettes anywhere: they were gypsy cobs.

Like a shaking fledgling, Moll pressed her body into the trees, and Gryff slunk through the shadows beside her. They crept past the canvas tent and there, just metres away, was Jinx.

She was easy to spot – smaller than the rest of the cobs – her palomino coat glowing in the darkness. And she was edging forward in tiny, fragmented steps, her eyes wide with fear. Moll's heart hammered. Had Jinx seen her? Her halter was still on and her tethering rope trailed on the ground. Why hadn't they tied her up? Why hadn't she run off? Moll tiptoed forward until she was behind the closest tree, clutching her catapult tight.

She stopped sharp. Jinx wasn't coming towards *her*; she hadn't even seen Moll. Emerging from the shadows, just metres in front of the tree Moll was hiding behind, was a boy. And he was tiptoeing towards Jinx with his hand outstretched. He was taller than Moll, with a tattered waistcoat and a faded blue shirt stained with saddle polish and dirt. But he looked about her age – twelve, thirteen at most.

Moll frowned and squinted at the boy through the darkness. He was no gypsy … He had fair hair and a pale complexion. What was an ordinary boy doing in Skull's camp? And yet beneath the scruffy blond hair was a bright feather earring, blue and black striped. Only one type of person wore a jay feather earring: a Romany gypsy.

A ball of jealously grew within Moll; Jinx was *her* cob and this boy was beckoning her. And he had no right.

Jinx paused, her ears pricked, her tail stiff. She looked straight at Moll whose heart quickened. Jinx *had* seen her but the boy hadn't realised.

'Here, girl, come on then, a little more,' he urged, taking a step closer in his scuffed leather boots. He stretched out his hand as far as it would go. 'I'm not going to hurt you.'

His voice was softer than Moll had expected and she could hear the pieces of carrot turning over in his hand. But Jinx was no longer interested because she knew that Moll had come for her.

Like a shadow to the unknowing boy, Moll raised her own hands. But they were not filled with carrots; they were clasping the catapult. Gryff crouched low beside her – ready, like a hunter. The pebble was in the pouch and she raised it to her chin. Closing one eye, she placed her thumb on the

Y-frame and pulled back. The rubber strips stretched until taut and then she took aim at the back of the boy's head.

Everything was still beneath the chanting.

For a second, Moll wavered. She'd never used her catapult on a person before. There were rules back in the Ancientwood. But Skull's camp was a place without rules and she needed to get away, fast.

She drew the pouch back, a notch further.

Then fired.

Chapter 4
Flight

The boy doubled over in pain, clutching the back of his head. 'Argh!'

In the next fraction of a second, Moll was charging towards Jinx.

'Argh!' the boy yelled again, rocking his head in his hands. He struggled up in disbelief. 'Skull! There's – there's someone here!'

He staggered to a tree, unable to piece together what was happening. Moll grabbed hold of Jinx's mane and leapt up on to her back. Digging her heels into the cob's flanks, she spurred Jinx on.

The chanting had stopped and the camp was silent.

'It's a girl!' the boy cried behind her. 'And a button-sized one at that!'

There were a few guffaws from the fire.

Then a voice, cold and loaded: 'After her, Alfie.'

Guiding Jinx with only her legs and voice, Moll urged the cob on, away from Skull's camp.

'Go, Jinx, go! Faster than you've ever run before!' she

cried. It didn't matter that her nightmare had come alive any more. Now it was just about the chase – and she had to win.

If the boy was in pain, he no longer showed it. Placing his fingers to his mouth, he whistled. The smouldering body of a black stallion cob appeared from behind a tree, its eyes as dark as night, its nostrils steaming. Yanking the tethering rope from the cob's halter, the boy hoisted himself up on to its back.

'After them, Raven!' he yelled, kicking hard.

Weaving between trunks and dipping beneath branches, Moll raced back towards the glade – past the giant cage, past the rat, past the owl, leaving all of that behind. Jinx's neck was stretching forward now as she darted between the trees, reaching the full speed of her gallop. And every now and again Moll glimpsed a flash of grey and black stripes as Gryff ran alongside them.

'That's my girl! Go on, Jinx! Go on!'

But there was a thundering of hooves behind her now, churning up the deadened glade. Moll twisted her head for a second. The boy was there, some metres behind, on his stallion cob. Whoever he was, he rode fast.

'Go on, Jinx!' Moll urged.

The boy and his stallion, Raven, continued to gain on them. Moments later, they were side by side and the boy was crouching up on his feet on Raven's back, ready to leap towards Moll. His eyes were blue and intense, like his jay feather, and his teeth were set. Moll's eyes widened and she kicked harder.

The boy steadied himself, about to leap, but Moll leant forward, pulling Jinx's halter hard. They sidestepped his grasp and, from somewhere nearby, Gryff growled.

The boy looked around – alert, on edge – but there was nothing there, only dawn needling through the darkness, pricking the night sky blue. The boy slid back to a seated position, cautious now.

Moll breathed again. 'Just to the river, Jinx. We're safe past there!'

'Come back here, titch!' the boy yelled, spurring Raven on.

Moll scowled, her face hot with fury at the insult. She leant forward towards Jinx's ears. 'That's my girl. Keep going, Jinx!' They leapt over stumps of trees and fallen branches. On, on, towards the river.

'You thieved from us, spudmucker!' Moll cried over her shoulder. 'I'm taking back what's rightfully ours! Oak's camp is never leaving the forest, however hard you try to force us out!'

Jinx galloped even faster, but the thunder of hooves behind them didn't stop. Like cogs in a monstrous machine, they charged on, closer and closer.

'You wait till Skull gets his hands on your scrawny neck!' the boy shouted.

Foam was dripping from Raven's mouth, flecking his chest white. Again the boy crouched on the cob's back, swinging for Moll's halter. But Jinx burst away. The river was in sight, sparkling in the moonlight like a promise. Moll leant forward and stroked the soft, downy hair behind Jinx's ear, the place where sensitive cobs keep their souls. They were within strides of the water, racing towards the alder trees.

'Now, Jinx, jump!'

Jinx lifted from the ground, knees bent, hooves tucked beneath her stomach. They soared across the river and landed, panting, on the other side.

Moll bent low to Jinx, whispered in her ear and, as Jinx surged forward, Moll leapt from her back into the branches of an alder overhanging the river. She scampered upwards as Jinx's hooves faded towards the clearing of the camp.

On the other side of the river, Raven came to a skittering halt. He paced by the bank in tight circles. And, from beneath a mop of fair hair, his rider cursed.

Safe in her aerial world of branches and leaves, Moll glowered down.

'One shout from my pipes and the whole camp'll come running,' she hissed. 'The Ancientwood is Oak's territory so you can go back to your den of thieves and wipe your backside on a tree root!' She drew out her catapult and brandished it at the boy. 'And they say girls can't fight!'

The boy scowled. His cheeks were flushed and he was breathing fast.

Moll crouched in the tree, tucking her feet into its branches. 'You've no right here; beat it.' She looked Raven up and down, then spat through the leaves. 'Your cob is nothing in a race with Jinx!'

The boy's body stiffened. 'Don't you insult Raven,' he replied, stroking the stallion's mane. 'You saw how he outdid your *pony* in our glade. Raven would win a gallop and you know it!'

'*Pony?*' Moll cried, leaping up a branch and hissing. 'Jinx isn't a pony! She's quick as lightning!' She paused. 'You're daft, you are. Tree spirits have eaten your brains.' She picked at a leaf casually. 'I've also got a wildcat,' she said, 'and you're not going to top *that*.'

At the mention of the wildcat, the boy shifted on Raven and then went very, very still. His eyes narrowed.

Somewhere nearby Gryff growled, low and deep, like the groaning of a faraway glacier. And suddenly Moll felt as if she'd betrayed a terrible secret. She coiled her body into the alder and scuttled further up its branches.

The boy's face relaxed slightly. 'A wildcat?' Then he scoffed. 'Raven's one of the only animals who can recognise himself outright in a mirror. Beats an imaginary wildcat.'

But there was something about the boy's voice now. Something which made the hairs on Moll's arms stand on end.

Again Gryff's growl came, even deeper than before, warning her to stay back. But why? There was no drum, no mask, no chant now – only the rippling of the river winding downstream. Skull was far away in the Deepwood and this was just a boy. Not even a real gypsy boy if his colouring was anything to go by.

The boy turned away, tugging at Raven's halter and

gripping his talisman, a knot of his cob's black hair tied to a string round his neck. Moll remained silent, watching them leave. And then, nonchalantly, she slipped backwards, catching her knees on the branch so that she was hanging upside down above the water.

'And don't come back!' she shouted.

A sickening lump formed in her throat; the boy and his cob were coming back. The boy was kicking Raven in the flanks, hard, and they *were* charging back towards the river. Towards *her*.

Moll flipped her body back into the tree. She'd have to jump, then sprint to the camp to get there first. She gasped. Her foot was caught, jammed between two branches. She couldn't move, couldn't breathe. And the boy was charging towards her, just metres from the bank.

There was a rustling from the undergrowth beneath her as, like a ripple of silk, Gryff sprang up into the branches, pounding at the one that trapped Moll's leg. And when that didn't work ... he touched her. For the very first time. Actually *touched* her. She felt his soft, warm strength pushing against her, and it filled her with courage. She yanked her foot harder and harder until it slipped free. Then she leapt to the ground, landing in a crouch, and sprinted several paces away from the river. She turned.

Gryff was still in the branches, hissing, growling and stamping his forelimbs. His eyes glowed green and his hackles rose, as if he was growing in size, and, as he snarled, he bared rows of white fanged teeth.

27

The boy yanked Raven's halter and they skidded to a halt, centimetres from the riverbank. The soil beneath Raven's hooves began to crumble and they retreated backwards.

The boy stared at Gryff, blinking in disbelief. His voice was altogether different now: half curious, half afraid. 'It – it can't be …' he stammered. 'The beast – the child from …' He looked Moll straight in the eye.

But at that second a hand clapped down on Moll's shoulder.

The boy turned sharply, then galloped back into the Deepwood.

And Moll whirled round to face Oak.

Chapter 5
Questions

Oak didn't ask where she'd been; he could tell from the look on Moll's face: guilt mingled with fear. She'd crossed the boundary into Skull's camp – that much was clear.

Oak pulled a chair round to the foot of Moll's wooden box bed, brushing the red velvet curtains wide. Oak was a strong, sturdy man, but, as he ran a hand over his stubbled jaw, Moll saw that he looked tired. She glanced at his large gold ring set with obsidian stone – the mark of his role as head of the camp. It glowed under the lamplight and a flicker of guilt wavered inside Moll. She looked away and focused on her wagon: at the stove with its shiny copper pans, at the pinafores strewn on the pine floor and at the small wardrobe with gigantic fir cones and kingfisher feathers scattered on its top.

Oak sat forward, fiddling with his talisman, a lump of coal in a leather pouch he kept in the pocket of his waistcoat. But he didn't speak yet. He had his ways.

Moll pushed her patchwork quilt back to her knees. 'I got

Jinx back, Oak. I did it – all by my unhelped self.' A look of pride, of wilful defiance, flashed in her eyes.

Oak looked up. 'Jinx isn't important, Moll. Not important like you . . .' He shook his head. 'Domino – my own son – he should've known better than to fall asleep on watch. Anything could've happened.'

'But – but I was saving Jinx from certain death over there!'

Oak shook his head. 'You disobeyed me, Moll. After everything you promised.'

Moll thought fast. 'Blame that blinking nightmare! Pulled me right over the river into the Deepwood this time.' Oak said nothing and Moll could tell he'd sensed her lie. She dodged his eyes. 'Well, at least I made the most of it – and I proved fair and square to Florence and the others that I'm no outsider.'

Oak put his hands on his thighs. 'You have to let that go, Moll. All that bad feeling – those comments – it was years ago and Florence has tried to be your friend since. They all have.'

A familiar hardness fastened inside Moll. 'They told me I didn't belong,' she muttered. 'Because of my eyes *and* the way I wasn't born in camp.' But deep down Moll felt that it was more than that, like there might be something else that set her apart from the others. And she was almost certain it had something to do with the whisperings of the Elders late at night around the campfire; she could have sworn she'd heard her name on their lips as she'd watched from the crack in her shutters. But when she'd questioned Oak and Mooshie they'd only shrugged her off and changed the subject.

30

Oak blew out through his lips. 'I'm not going to fight you on this tonight, Moll. It's late and we're both tired.' He paused. 'I thought I had your promise though. The nightmare's not strong enough to drag you over the river boundary; you went there of your own choosing.'

Moll ground her teeth but said nothing. She'd let Oak down, when it really mattered. Oak, who'd taught her how to climb trees, who'd sat up with her when the nightmares came, who'd built the wheels on her wagon especially thick so that it didn't topple over, no matter how much she crashed around inside it.

She had no family other than Oak and Mooshie Frogmore. Moll had been found in the forest, an abandoned stray, but the Frogmores had taken her in and given her a proper gypsy name. They'd stood up for her when the others in the camp had called her an outsider, and they were better than any parents she could have hoped for. Moll picked at her quilt.

But the drum, the rattle, the mask . . . There was a *reason* her nightmare kept coming for her, and Oak knew something about it – she could tell.

'I saw Skull. He wears a mask that looks like bone,' Moll mumbled through a storm of hair. 'And I heard his drum and rattle, like in my nightmare.' She met Oak's eyes. 'Only my nightmare isn't just a nightmare, is it?'

Oak said nothing but his body tensed. He tightened his neckerchief, then ran a hand over his dark brown hair.

'I've seen Skull before, haven't I? That's why I see him in

my dreams.' Moll struggled against a yawn, her voice thick with sleep. She was exhausted from the chase and from everything she'd seen, but there were questions – so many questions. 'Skull's gang are after me . . . They had a chant. Skull was calling me *and* Gryff to him . . .'

Still Oak said nothing but Moll could read his eyes. They were deep and brown and you could get lost if you looked at them too long, like peering into a dark wood. But Moll wasn't lost right now. Those eyes were keeping things from her and she knew it.

'The river . . .' Moll's voice hardened as she realised. 'It's only really a boundary for me, isn't it?'

Moonlight spilled in through a crack in her shutters and Moll could just make out one of the Sacred Oaks that formed a ring of ancient wood around the colourful wagons.

Oak stood up and closed the shutters tight. 'Some things are too dark for night, Moll.'

Moll's eyes narrowed, but, knowing she'd get no more from Oak tonight, she burrowed beneath her quilt until all that was left of her was a swamp of tangled hair.

Oak tucked the rest of Moll beneath the quilt. 'Tomorrow. We'll talk tomorrow.'

Moll heard her wagon door click shut and Oak's footsteps pad softly away. But, if she had managed to stay awake a while longer, she would have heard Oak knock quietly on four wagon doors. It was time to call the Elders together if Moll was to know the truth about her past.

Chapter 6
Keeping Secrets

The chickens woke her, like they always did. Mischievous, rowdy and named after legendary highwaymen, they squawked and screeched from sunrise until someone got up to scatter their grain. Moll opened her eyes a fraction; a ribbon of light seeped in through her shutters and her ears were filled with the sounds of morning: the sing-song of a cuckoo, the whistle of the kettle, Mooshie's impatient barks.

'Siddy, if you think for one minute it's fine to prod Rocky Jo with a twig, you'll feel my hand! He's a cockerel, not a highwayman!'

Children squealed and laughed. Everyone knew that Siddy had it in for the chickens and the cockerel, ever since Rocky Jo had eaten his pet earthworm, Porridge. Moll rubbed her eyes and sat up. She thought of Oak, of what he would have said if he was still in her wagon on a sunny morning like this: 'Best thing about this life is you wake up in the morning and you're free. You've only got one door and there's only one way to walk: outside.' She smiled and

33

then she checked herself as she remembered what had happened in the Deepwood. Skull's gang were after her and Gryff – and Oak knew something about it.

Moll splashed her face with water from the pail that Mooshie always left by her bedside, then she searched her wagon floor for the most purposeful dress she could find: the light blue summer frock with large pockets hanging from the sides. That would do. Wriggling it on, she pulled open a wardrobe door, hurling aside the jumpers, skirts, dresses and newly-ironed pinafores and stuffed her catapult and a handful of stones into her pockets. She paused for a moment; she wasn't overly keen on catapulting Oak, but if that's what it might take to get the truth then there wasn't a lot she could do about it.

She flung open the wagon door, her hair matted and wild, like a crow's nest plonked on top of her head, and marched out on to the steps.

'Still here then.' A hunched old woman was sitting on Moll's steps. She pulled a red shawl lined with fake gold pennies around her and the jewels on her crinkled fingers flashed in the sunlight. 'Well, that's something, isn't it?'

'Mmmmmn.'

Cinderella Bull was the camp's only fortune-teller – the Dukkerer, they all called her – and it was *she* who guarded The Chest of No Opening at Any Time or Your Life Won't Be Worth Living and the crystal ball. So, by and large, it was worth listening to her, even if you didn't agree with what she said.

Moll scanned the camp for Oak. Chickens darted across the clearing and barefoot children swarmed round the fire like puppies, their skin stained by smoke and dirt. Among them, women in brightly-coloured skirts and headscarves, some wrapped up like turbans, some knotted under chins, stoked the fire and separated strings of sausages for the spitting pans. Their faces were lined and pitted by years of open-air living, but their fingers and necks flashed with sparkling jewels: amber, jet, coral and gold. And set back from the fire, before a canvas tent, sat a cluster of men in flat caps and once-good overcoats, drinking tea from tin cups.

Cinderella Bull looked up at Moll with gargoyled features. 'If you're looking for Oak, you won't find him. He left early to chop logs for the feast tonight.'

'Chop logs!' Moll smouldered away on the wagon steps like an angry lump of coal, but there was no use arguing with a feast night and all its traditions. Moll knew that. And they'd been talking about this one for months. Wisdom, Mooshie and Oak's eldest son, was getting married to Ivy, and the Jumping of the Broomstick ceremony was tonight. Everyone would be there.

Moll's eyes ran over the ring of bowtop wagons: maroon ones with gold-leaf swirls and green ones, like her own, with bright yellow wisps and rearing cobs. Hanging from the front of each one were the camp's good luck omens: lemon peel, horseshoe nails, fragments of mirror, fox teeth … She looked around for Gryff, but she didn't expect to see him here. He always hung back from the clatter of the camp.

Thrusting a hand into her pocket, Moll seized her catapult and leapt off the steps. But, before she could dart off, Cinderella Bull clutched her by the arm.

The fortune-teller's hands were haggard like ancient bark and, as she ran a wrinkled finger over the lines that scored Moll's wrist, she whispered, 'The bracelets of life ... And your life's going to change now, Moll. You know that, don't you?'

Moll frowned past the sun into the fortune-teller's face, and whipped her hand away.

The week before Cinderella Bull had told Moll her Line of Life had a split at the end, meaning she was prone to outbursts of insanity, and that her short, square nails indicated that she had a fighting temper.

'I need to find Oak,' Moll said. 'There's important stuff he's not telling me.' She paused. 'I saw Skull last night in the Deepwood – and he was chanting for me and Gryff to come close.'

As Moll had half suspected, Cinderella Bull already knew. She nodded gravely, then rummaged in her pinafore pocket and drew out her talisman, a leather pouch of salt. She scattered it round Moll's feet. 'For protection,' she murmured. 'Skull's growing in strength now, mark my words. We'll need every charm we've got to keep you safe.'

Moll stormed out of the circle of salt, breathing hard. 'Someone needs to tell me what's going on!'

But Cinderella Bull only shook her head. 'It should be Oak who tells you, Moll. He's the head of the camp.'

'But Oak's out chopping logs!'

'He'll be back soon. He wanted a moment away from the clearing before he spoke to you – to think things through. But Mooshie's here. You could—'

Just at that moment there was a high-pitched shriek – like the screech of a desperate chicken – but Moll knew this was no chicken. She scoured the clearing. At the far end of the camp, beyond the fire, women clustered outside a tent, weaving hawthorn into ribbed baskets. And charging past them, sending pots of porridge and cups of tea flying, came Mooshie. Having noticed Moll, she was thundering towards her, bursting out of her clothes with fury, like some sort of overpacked suitcase with legs. Her skirt shook, her ruffled petticoats wavered, her headscarf flapped. Moll gulped.

Brandishing a tea towel, she marched towards Moll. 'MOLLY PECKSNIFF!' she roared. 'What the devil do you think you were doing last night?'

All thoughts about Skull's chant abandoned, Moll skirted behind Cinderella Bull and crawled beneath her wagon.

Mooshie's smoke-yellowed face glowered beneath her blue headscarf. She pushed past Cinderella Bull. 'When I get hold of you ...' She struck the side of the wagon with her tea towel. 'Oooooooh, you make me so cross, Molly!' Two lace-up boots stepped up right in front of Moll's nose. 'What in heaven's name were you doing last night? Come out of there AT ONCE!'

Moll curled up tight. It was one thing to cross Oak, but crossing Mooshie was another story ... 'I sleepwalked over the boundary,' she ventured. Moll's eyes widened as she realised the enormity of her lie and she swallowed, wriggling further away from Mooshie's boots.

'Jinx is back in the camp, safely tethered beside the cobs, and you expect me to believe you sleepwalked into Skull's camp to get her back?' Mooshie cried shrilly.

Moll ground her teeth together; it was too late to back down now. 'I've been doing lots of – um – astral-travelling recently.'

Silence.

Moll picked at her fingers, barely understanding what she was saying: 'Astral-travelling is when we dream and our souls break free at night and go on a journey. Cinderella Bull told me about it.'

Cinderella Bull cleared her throat. 'That's a lovely story, Moll; never let it tumble out of your mouth again.'

There was a thwack outside; Cinderella Bull had been got by the tea towel.

Moll tried to feel her way into her story. If Mooshie hadn't been on the loose with a tea towel, she might have almost enjoyed its twists and turns. 'Just last week I went to the northern wilderness on a donkey and last night—'

There was a yank to Moll's foot as Mooshie dragged her out from beneath the wagon. Moll wriggled into a tiny ball and winced. *Thwack, thwack, thwack* went the tea towel.

'I've got the breakfast to clear away, the chickens to feed and the laundry to wash and you think I have time to listen to your stories about donkeys in the wilderness?'

Moll looked up at the tanned grooves of Mooshie's face

and suddenly Mooshie's features softened and she knelt down by Moll, hugging her close. 'Oh, Moll! We could've lost you!'

And that was the way it was with Mooshie. You got used to it.

Moll leant back against her wagon wheel and Mooshie sat beside her, wiping her eyes with her pinafore.

'I'm sorry I snapped my promise,' Moll said. 'I know it was a big'un and not one for snapping. But—'

Mooshie straightened her headscarf and rearranged her numerous petticoats over her knees. 'You break promises, Moll, not snap them.'

Moll shrugged. 'Trouble is, the other children are happy just playing around the camp.'

She pointed across the clearing to where a handful of youngsters had gathered beneath a Sacred Oak tree. A boy of Moll's age, with sticking out ears and tufts of dark, curly hair poking out beneath a flat cap, was hoisting a girl with auburn ringlets up on to the rope swing. Moll sighed as she watched Florence shriek when Siddy jiggled her about. She'd never fit in like they all did. With Siddy, maybe, but Siddy was different. He had never called her an outsider. Not once. And he didn't care about getting drenched in mud and bruised by falling from trees. She watched as Florence and another girl swung back and forth. *They* would care about mud and stuff. Moll was sure of it. 'See, Moosh? They're all fine mucking about on rope swings and fishing for minnows in the stream. I need more ...'

Mooshie folded the tea towel on her lap. 'You'd like spending time with them all if you just tried.' She smoothed Moll's hair down, but Moll only scowled. 'Might be nice if you and Siddy showed the others your tree fort.'

Moll looked appalled. 'No. That would be horrible.' She huffed. 'I've got to see and do *everything*, Moosh. I've been running everywhere these past weeks just so I can fit all the stuff I want to do into one measle-puckered day. It's tiring but I can't stop. And when someone gets me angry – like Skull when he stole Jinx – then—'

Mooshie put a finger to her lips. 'Sometimes you've got to wait while your anger cools, Moll. Wait and then think and then – if you're really sure the anger's cooled and you're thinking straight – you can act. Bad decisions are made when we're angry.'

Moll plucked at the grass that had grown up over her wagon wheel. 'Most of my bad decisions happen when I'm hungry.'

'And I suppose you were just hungry last night when you crossed the boundary?'

Moll shuddered as she thought back to last night's supper of nettle soup. She'd barely eaten any of it. 'I was *starving*.'

'An imp, that's what you are, Miss Pecksniff.' Mooshie lifted a handkerchief from her pinafore, spat on it, then rubbed at the muddy mark on Moll's shin. 'Small and meddling, with a will of iron.'

Moll made a face. 'What's an imp then?'

'A sprite.'

'What's a sprite?'

Mooshie rolled her eyes and gave up.

Moll was silent for several seconds and then she said quietly, 'I know Oak will have told you what I saw last night . . .'

Mooshie stiffened but said nothing.

Moll went on. 'Skull's chant – it was sucking me and Gryff in. I could *feel* it when he crushed the wax figure. He's after me – us – isn't he?' She hugged her knees up to her chin. '*Why?*'

Mooshie ran her hand over the initials Moll and Siddy had carved into the wagon's side a few years before. 'Oh, Moll, you're too young for all this. Far too young.'

Moll unfurled her body and sprang forward. 'I'm not too young, Moosh! I'm old enough to have thieved Jinx back and escaped Skull's camp! You have to tell me what's going on. Last night I was just thieving back a cob, then suddenly I find out I'm wanted by Skull's gang!' Her cheeks were flushed and she was breathing fast. Mooshie tried to clasp her hands, but Moll shuffled backwards. 'I want to know the truth – straight and proper. Because you and Oak know things you're not telling me.' She narrowed cold green eyes. 'And, if no one tells me what's going on, I'm going to catapult the whole camp before breakfast.'

Mooshie took a deep breath and looked her straight in the eye. And, for some strange reason, Moll felt like Mooshie was seeing her for the very first time.

'Last night,' Mooshie bit her lip, 'you saw Skull performing a Dream Snatch.'

41

Moll shivered. 'What – what's a Dream Snatch?'

'It's a witch doctor's deadliest curse. When they—' she paused and fiddled with her rings, '—*want* someone, they form the victim's figure out of wax. They curse it, then crush it, then they mutter a chant – the Dream Snatch.'

Moll's eyes widened. 'And what happens to the victim?'

'The chant seeps into their mind and the more afeared they are, the stronger it grows. It feeds on fear. In your case, Skull's Dream Snatch steals into your sleep, turning your dreams to nightmares, making the fears you have in the daytime a hundred times worse in the darkness.' Mooshie's voice was low and guarded. 'He is trying to control you, Moll, trying to summon you from our camp.'

The colour drained from Moll's face. 'My sleepwalking – finding myself alone in the forest in the middle of the night . . .'

Mooshie nodded. 'Skull's been calling for you your whole life – only he's not just calling you to his camp. He's—' Mooshie looked out towards the fire in the middle of the clearing, '—he's calling for your death.' Moll's eyes widened and Mooshie leant in closer. 'Years ago Skull used his powers to such an extent that it left him weakened, but, now time has passed, his Dream Snatch is gathering strength and that's why the nightmare drags you closer and closer to the river boundary each time.' She paused. 'You say Gryff felt the chant in Skull's clearing too?' Moll nodded. 'Then the Dream Snatch is reaching its full strength. We feared this would come.'

'But Skull doesn't even know who I am,' Moll said. 'How can he be calling me?'

'Before last night, Skull didn't know who you are; he probably didn't even know you camped in the Ancientwood. But he'll know now his boy's seen Gryff, you can be sure of that … Because you and Gryff are part of something Skull wants to destroy and for his whole life he's been trying to find you. Dragging Jinx away from our camp might've been coincidence – another theft to force our camp from the forest …' Mooshie paused. 'Or it might've been Skull's Dream Snatch, spreading over everything you hold dear.'

Moll's stomach twisted into a knot. 'This Dream Snatch … I've *seen* it before. It's like I said last night to Oak. It isn't a nightmare, is it? It's a memory.'

Mooshie fiddled with the hem of her pinafore, avoiding Moll's eyes.

Moll stiffened. Something painful was happening inside her mind: a terrible memory, locked so deep inside her she thought she'd never find it, was sloping towards her.

It was a dark night, the forest muffled by snow, and she was hiding in the undergrowth by the river, not far from the drum and the rattle and the figures. Skull's mask was there, floating before her.

She gasped.

'I – I'm by the river and – and I'm not alone with the cloaked figures. There's more to my nightmare than what I've seen before! There are other people with me only I can't see their faces.'

43

Mooshie shifted on the grass but said nothing.

Moll felt the memory fading. 'What happened? What am I remembering?'

Mooshie shook her head. 'You've no idea who you are, Moll.'

'Who am I then?' Moll whispered. 'And what does Gryff have to do with it all?' Her voice crumbled into a shiver.

But this time Mooshie shook her head. 'Oak needs to tell you, Moll – he's the head of the camp.'

She tried to gather Moll into her arms, the way she did almost every time the nightmare came for her. But Moll scrambled away.

She stared straight ahead, a knot of fear fixing inside her. Things had been difficult before. But now they were a whole lot worse: she was more of an outsider than ever. And worse than that, somewhere not so far away, Skull was hatching a plan to kill her.

Chapter 7
Around the Campfire

'Wait by the fire, Moll, and I'll fetch Oak.' Mooshie's eyes had filled with tears again, but she brushed them away and stood up. 'It's time you two talked.'

Moll made her way towards the fire in the middle of the clearing where Patti was scraping the last of the porridge into a bowl. She and her husband had been members of Oak's camp for as long as anyone could remember and, while their daughter, Ivy, was easily the most alluring young woman in the clearing, the same could not be said about their son, Siddy, who combined a hopelessly misdirected enthusiasm with very little common sense. And there was a baby too, but she spent most of her time eating soil and sticking twigs in her ears. Excepting Ivy, Patti had it hard.

Today she was flaunting a purple waistcoat over a lilac blouse and a ruffled lavender skirt. Since the day she turned thirty, Patti had refused to wear anything other than purple. Most of the time she looked like a giant blue-bell, but she was the best hawker the camp had; rumour had it that she had so much charm she could sell a toad for a small fortune.

Moll perched on an upturned log, her thoughts whirling.

Patti pulled the kettle back from the fire and passed Moll a steaming cup of raspberry leaf tea. 'Here, drink this.' She smiled. 'And there's one bowl of porridge left.'

Moll poked a spoon into the porridge, but her mind was miles away. Why was Skull after her and Gryff? She scoured the trees beyond the clearing for the wildcat and thought she glimpsed a movement of grey-black stripes. For a second, things felt just a tiny bit better.

Moll ate a mouthful of porridge and looked across the fire. Folded into a threadbare armchair he'd taken three days to haul from his wagon, and a further three weeks to stitch with the saying 'Sometimes I sits and thinks; sometimes I just sits', was Hard-Times Bob, Oak's uncle and Cinderella Bull's brother. And he was doing what he did best in the mornings: taking a nap.

Moll finished her porridge, then looked back up at Patti. 'You Elders know about Skull's Dream Snatch, don't you? That's what you speak about late at night round the fire. I've heard you.'

Patti looked about to deny it, but when she saw Moll's glare she nodded.

'You all knew and I didn't!' Moll said.

'Only the Elders knew.' Patti reached for a broom and began sweeping up scraps of food. 'And that was because we needed to keep you safe. If we hadn't told you about the boundary, you'd have crossed into Skull's camp years ago. You and Siddy are always off exploring places.'

Moll knew Patti was probably right but she said nothing. There was only one person she felt like talking to now and, as she glanced up at the rope swing on the other side of the clearing, Patti seemed to read her thoughts. Hands on hips, Patti stood up. 'Oi! Siddy!' she shouted. 'Over here – now! And take that ridiculous scrap of paper out of your mouth! Your father might smoke his tobacco after breakfast, but you're only twelve and you look ridiculous!'

Siddy charged into the feeding chickens, sending them flying into a nearby wagon. He only wanted one thing in life: to be like his father. Jesse could tickle trout out of the river with his hands and he smoked hand-rolled cigarettes. So Siddy had to make do with catching minnows in jam jars and stuffing bits of paper into his mouth. He'd even admitted to Moll that it tasted disgusting, but had said, 'A man's got to do what a man's got to do.' Moll had no idea what a man had got to do, but she was pretty sure Siddy wasn't doing it.

Siddy made one more swing for Rocky Jo, then sidled back towards the fire. As he approached Moll, he dipped his flat cap, just like his father always did.

Patti sighed. 'Your shirt needs a wash, your hair's all over the place and your shorts are covered in mud. Have I taught you nothing?'

Siddy beamed, which made his ears stick out even further. 'You've taught me lots, Ma, but I haven't learnt anything.'

Patti clouted him round the head, but he only grinned harder. Then he looked Moll up and down, his paper cigarette still lodged between his lips. 'You OK?'

Moll didn't look up. She didn't need to – not with Sid. Ever since they were small, Moll and Siddy had gone around together. From an early age, it had been clear to everyone in the camp that Moll was going to be a terrible hawker. Her wire flowers were always slapdash (they looked more like wilting weeds than freshly-picked chrysanthemums) and during her first outing selling her goods in the village she had been so foul-tempered to customers who didn't want her flowers that Mooshie and Patti had vowed never to take her again. But, with Siddy, Moll could be herself. They shared a mutual love of *finding* stuff and *doing* stuff; searching for woodpecker nests and building dens had bound them far closer than wire flowers could have ever done.

Siddy looked from Moll to his ma. 'What've you gone and said to her? You been giving her grief over spying on Skull? I heard she was only trying to get Jinx back!'

'I think you'd better take a seat, Sid,' Patti said.

Siddy plonked himself down on to the log next to Moll while Patti busied herself with the dirty pans on the other side of the fire.

'It's Skull,' Moll mumbled from behind her hair. 'He – he's after me and Gryff.'

Siddy frowned. 'You and Gryff?'

Moll nodded. 'And now everything's dreadful.'

Siddy shook his head. 'I don't understand. Tell me what

you saw in the Deepwood, Moll.' He paused. 'Tell me every-thing.'

And Moll did. But she left out one thing. Gryff had touched her and that was a secret she wasn't ready to share.

Siddy blew out through his lips. 'So Skull's got a Dream Snatch and he's using it to summon you and Gryff?'

Moll sunk her head into her hands. 'Yes. And I don't even know why because Oak's out chopping logs so all I can do is sit here and eat porridge until he comes back.' She kicked the ground. 'And now Florence and the others will find out and call me an outsider all over again.'

Siddy lowered his voice. 'None of this changes anything, Moll. Oak's camp will always stand by you, no matter what you go around saying. You should know that by now.'

For a moment, the knot inside Moll loosened and then she thought of Skull squeezing the wax figure through his hands. 'But I'm different from the others. Proper different – not just my eyes and my beginning now.'

Siddy shrugged, pulling his pet earthworm, Porridge the Second, from his pocket. 'Different's good – you just can't see it yet.' He prodded his earthworm. 'Isn't that right?' Porridge the Second only ever wore one expression, a sort of long-suffering look of indifference, but it satisfied Siddy and he took an imaginary puff of his paper cigarette.

Moll shook her head. 'I shouldn't have let that boy in Skull's camp see me. Now Skull knows where I am.' Her shoulders drooped. 'Why do I always go and mess things up?'

Patti swept a pile of scraps round the fire towards them.

'It's what makes us real, Moll,' she said. 'There's a crack in everyone and everything, but that's how the light gets in.'

'Wish I didn't have so many cracks,' Moll muttered. 'I'm like a smashed-up eggshell, me.'

'What's this, Moll?' came a voice as rough as sandpaper from the other side of the fire. 'You planning another catapult attack on the chicken eggs with Siddy?'

'Not this time,' Moll said glumly.

Hard-Times Bob shot a glance at Patti, who just nodded, then he let out a low whistle. 'So you know about the Dream Snatch, eh?' He adjusted the snakeskin binding on his hand, Mooshie's latest (somewhat questionable) cure for his arthritis.

Moll and Siddy nodded.

Hard-Times Bob was an old man who had the posture of a tortoise, with skin as shrivelled, and stumps of black, decaying teeth, despite the hedgehog paw he carried which was meant to stave off toothache. But he could dislocate every bone in his body and fit through the rungs of a ladder – and that counted for more than shrivelled skin and stumpy teeth.

Hard-Times Bob yawned. 'Not like me to be napping through things like this.'

Patti raised her eyebrows. 'It's exactly like you, Bob.'

Hard-Times Bob looked at Moll. 'So Oak's told you all about the Bone—'

'That's enough, Bob!' Patti threw him a warning look.

'Oak's not back in the clearing yet; he's still to talk with Moll.'

Moll leapt up and rushed over to Hard-Times Bob. 'Tell me, Bob,' she urged, kneeling by his armchair. 'Why is Skull after me and Gryff?'

For a moment, Hard-Times Bob's face looked torn, then it shut like a cupboard door. He looked over at Florence and another girl peeling potatoes on the steps of a wagon. 'Why don't you and Siddy help the girls out with the feast preparations until Oak gets back?' Florence looked up from the potatoes and smiled, her auburn ringlets falling in perfect curls round her face. 'I bet they'd appreciate your help.'

Moll stood up, ready to storm from the fire. Then Hard-Times Bob winked. 'Would it help if I dislocated anything – just until you speak to Oak?'

Moll was in two minds but, when Siddy came bounding round the fire to see, she knew she didn't want to miss out. 'Maybe your elbow,' she mumbled.

Hard-Times Bob's arms disappeared into his waistcoat, his silver watch chain jiggled and, after several seconds of wriggling and wheezing, he held up a very floppy arm. And then his hiccups started; he'd had them for nearly thirty years now, but they were always worse after a dislocation.

Despite everything, Moll smiled.

Patti bustled round and patted him on the back. 'You're not remembering to cross your boots before bed, are you? Prevents cramps and hiccups. You should know that by now.'

Hard-Times Bob rolled his eyes. 'You think you've got it hard, Moll . . .'

But Moll was no longer listening. Oak was back in the clearing, laying down a pile of logs before the bender tent. His shirt was browned from the bark and his neckerchief flecked with wood chippings. Moll watched as Mooshie arranged the logs into a stack and Oak made his way towards the fire.

The camp clattered on – chickens screeched, a greyhound barked and children laughed – but those gathered round the fire were silent.

Oak stood before them, his hands in his pockets. 'Come on, Moll. Let's walk to the glade.'

Moll held his gaze. Oak had taught her the ways of the forest when she was little and he'd showed her how to carve catapults and animals from the trees, but, as she looked at him now, she felt that old, familiar world sliding away. She'd trusted Oak – and Mooshie – but they'd been keeping secrets from her, and she had a horrible feeling that the Dream Snatch was just the beginning.

Chapter 8
Forgotten Roles

Over the years the gypsies had worn a path through the trees towards the glade and, as Moll walked down it beside Oak, the leaves on the beech trees shimmered in the sunshine, brushed into flutters by the morning breeze. Moll thought of the Deepwood – so full of shadows and darkness compared to all this. She glanced around, past the sprigs of cow parsley shooting up among the ferns that lined the path, hoping that Gryff might be somewhere nearby. But he'd be resting in the hollow of a tree now, or curled up in the tangled undergrowth after his morning hunt, and she knew that no amount of whistling or calling would bring him close.

Oak ducked beneath a low-hanging branch and looked back at Moll. 'I'll need to start at the beginning for you to really understand,' he said, 'because you're part of something, Moll. Something that goes back a long, long time.'

Moll's heart quickened.

Oak waited until they were walking side by side again. 'Over three hundred years ago my ancestors, the Frogmores, came to Tanglefern Forest. They settled in the Ancient-wood, inside the Ring of Sacred Oaks, because they believed in the old magic said to be rooted here – the magic that stirred before the beginning of time, in the silence of the first dawn.' He looked around. 'It's been with us ever since, this magic. It's in the spirits of the wind and the trees, in the gurgling of the rivers and the grains of soil. You only have to lay your head against the earth to hear the old magic moving and turning. It's the goodness and the stillness at the heart of everything.'

Moll stooped to pick up a stick and tapped it impatiently against the trunks of the trees she passed. This part she knew; Oak's stories about his ancestors were campfire favourites.

Oak went on. 'Only most people move so fast they don't see the old magic any more. They're too busy worrying about other things that they forget what's really important. But, where ordinary folk see a feather fall, our people see the wind spirit fluttering between each fibre.'

'I know about the old magic,' Moll groaned. 'I've learnt about the tree spirits and the water spirits and the wind spirits AND the earth spirits! You talk about them all the time.'

Oak shook his head. 'Moll, there's a difference between knowing and *understanding*. You've only scratched the surface of the old magic. But it's stirring again now – deeper and more mysterious than anything you've ever known – and this time it's calling for our help.'

They walked further into the trees, past the very first beech

54

Oak had taught Moll to climb, and on past the silver birches the camp's cobs were tethered to. Moll smiled as she glimpsed Jinx, who looked up and whinnied as they walked on by.

Oak steered Moll's attention back to his words. 'Our roles – mine as head of the camp, Cinderella Bull's as Dukkerer, our fortune-teller, and Mooshie as the Keeper of Songs – they all fall to the Frogmore family, even though we've welcomed two other families into our camp, right?'

Moll scrunched up her nose. 'This is slippery talk, Oak; how's this anything to do with me?'

Oak ignored her. 'And those in camp over thirty years of age form the Council of Elders, whatever their family name.'

'Mmmmmn.'

'Well, there's another role in our camp – probably the most important one – and the only one I've never gone speaking about before. Not to you anyway.'

'What is it?'

Oak paused. 'The Guardian of the Oracle Bones.'

Moll stared at Oak blankly. *Oracle Bones?* She hadn't heard talk of those before.

The path widened into the glade. The spring bluebells had been and gone but the grass there was now long and lush. Moll noticed Oak's son, Domino, resting high up in the branch of a yew tree on the outskirts of the glade. So Oak had the Ancientwood guarded during the day now as well; Moll tensed as she remembered why.

Oak and Moll sat down beneath the oldest yew in the glade and, as Oak spoke, he turned the leather pouch containing his talisman over in his hands. 'The story goes that there used to be a silver stag that lived in Tanglefern Forest, with sixteen points on its mighty antlers. It was said it was the oldest and wisest beast in the land. On the day it died our ancestors found it and took its bones – and these sacred relics became the Oracle Bones. Our ancestors believed that the Guardian of the Oracle Bones, a gypsy chosen by the Council of Elders, could carve one question into the bones in his or her lifetime and it would be answered by the old magic. The very first Guardian was worried, even then, that folk were losing sight of the old magic so he carved the bones, asking them if the old ways were in danger. He tossed them into the fire and, on removing them, he interpreted the cracks.'

A ripple of excitement fluttered through Moll.

Oak's eyes were shining now, dark and deep. 'They revealed a message, a foretelling, called the Bone Murmur.'

'What did the Bone Murmur say?' Moll asked quietly.

Oak drew himself up and, when he answered, every word tingled down Moll's spine. 'The bones said this:

> There is a magic, old and true,
> That shadowed minds seek to undo.
> And storms will rise; trees will die,
> If they free their dark magic into the sky.
> But a beast will come from lands full wild,
> To fight this darkness with a gypsy child.
> And they must find the Amulets of Truth
> To stop dark souls doing deeds uncouth.'

Moll's heart was hammering inside her, thudding against her ribcage. 'I'm – I'm the child, aren't I?'

Oak leant forward and squeezed her hand, but deep inside Moll something stiffened.

'*Lands full wild* … You told me …' she murmured. 'You told me that wildcats don't go leaving the northern wilderness. But Gryff did because—'

'—because he knew he was part of something bigger than all that. He knew he had to come. A wildcat is the only animal that can't be tamed, but Gryff broke the rules. Somehow he knew you were the child from the Bone Murmur, even before we did.'

A coldness locked around Moll. She *was* different from the others and this was why. She shuffled further round the yew trunk, away from Oak, her shoulders bunched and closed. Oak stretched out an arm, but Moll was walled up, hardened against everything, against everyone.

Oak waited.

And then Moll's eyes met his and he gathered her back beneath his arm, to where it was safe and still. There she listened to his heartbeat: steady, strong, deep within his body.

'Do they know?' Moll mumbled. 'The others – Florence and everyone?'

Oak shook his head. 'Not even Siddy knows. Just the Elders.'

Moll watched the grass sway in the breeze. 'Why me? Why do I have to be the one fighting dark stuff and saving the old magic? Why can't it be someone else? Your Domino – he'd do. He's the fastest runner in the camp and I don't think he'd fall asleep on watch if it was something as important as this.'

Oak smiled, a large, soft smile that stayed in his eyes long after he had stopped smiling. 'You're brave and you've got spirit, Moll. Sometimes that's enough.'

'Enough for a cob chase maybe. Not for some sacred Bone Murmur.'

Oak squeezed Moll tighter. 'You're enough, Moll. You and Gryff. But now Skull knows who you are, you're in danger – the whole camp is – because he'll stop at nothing until he gets a hold of you. He wants to destroy what the Bone Murmur foretells because, if he can kill you and Gryff before you find the amulets, he can harness the power of the dark magic, a magic born in the blackest shadows. The Bone Murmur warns that, if Skull succeeds, he will unleash his dark magic into our skies and our lands will be torn apart by storms: trees will wither, mountains will crumble and seas will vanish as every last drop of the old magic is squeezed away.'

'And I'm meant to stop all that happening?' Moll spluttered.

Oak shook his head. 'You should be playing with catapults and fishing for minnows in the stream. Not – not . . .'

But Moll was looking at him with piercing eyes now. She was getting closer to something, to what Oak wasn't saying. 'Wait. There's something else, isn't there?' Oak skirted her look. 'Why hasn't our camp got a Guardian of the Oracle Bones then? We've got all the other traditional roles . . .'

Oak was suddenly very still and for a while he said nothing at all. Then he turned to face Moll.

'You've no idea how much you fit into this camp, Moll, and I've wanted to tell you for so long.' He paused. 'Our camp had two Guardians. And they weren't Frogmores at all: they were your parents.'

The words hung in the air and Moll's face paled.

'You come from a long line of Guardians, Moll.'

'But – but . . . that's impossible!' she stammered.

Oak hung his head. 'I've wanted to tell you so many times.'

Moll scrambled to her feet. 'My *parents*? But you said that my ma stumbled by the camp the night I was born.' She clenched her teeth. 'And you told me no one even knew about my pa!' Her voice toughened to steel. 'You *lied* to me.'

Oak was on his feet, beside her in a flash, but Moll was edging away.

'Where are they, Oak?' she cried. 'Where are my parents?'

Oak's eyes filled with tears. 'Oh, Moll, they're dead.'

Moll flinched. Her parents were *dead* – and yet there had never been any parents to remember before. Nothing had changed. So why did it feel like it had? She felt tears rushing up from somewhere deep inside her and though she tried to fight them they streamed down her cheeks. Oak and Mooshie had lied to her, when she'd trusted them and let them in. This changed things; this changed *everything.* She dug her nails into her palms, forcing back angry sobs.

Oak stood before her, his hands outstretched. 'I'm so sorry, Moll. Not a day's gone by when I haven't wanted to tell you, but we needed to keep you safe. If you'd known, you'd have gone to the Deepwood to find Skull.'

The storm inside Moll swelled and thickened. '*Skull* killed them?'

Oak looked down and then he nodded.

The tears fell faster and faster as Moll felt her past unravelling around her. She wanted to hear more – to find out why and how Skull had killed her parents – but a terrible knot of sadness and anger was rising inside her and the more she looked at Oak, the more the knot grew. She turned away.

'Moll, please!' Oak cried.

But Moll was already running. She tore through the grass to the far side of the glade where her and Siddy's fort balanced halfway up a yew tree. Blinded by tears, she scrambled up the tree and climbed into the fort. She could hear Oak calling from down in the glade, but she bolted the door fast and covered her ears.

Chapter 9
Answers in the Tree Fort

The fort didn't look much from the outside – just some slats of wood within the gnarled branches of a yew – but it was big enough to stand up and walk around in and it was notoriously hard to get to so Moll and Siddy could store any number of 'disgusting' and 'strange' things up there without being told off. Kept in old jam jars and labelled by Siddy with a series of misspelt words, these 'Forest Secrets' included: Funnie-lookin Mushhhrooms (hoppefullie poysonus), Odd Furns (mak u sikk if u eet em), Gyant Nettuls (the wuns Mooshie uzes in growse soop), Smooth Pebbuls (good fer catapultin annoyin peepul).

Siddy had hung wind chimes from the branch beneath the fort to ward off evil spirits and a week later Moll had added a dreamcatcher: *'The bright feathers might put the evil spirit in a better mood if it does chance on passing our way,'* she'd said.

Moll sat back against the slats, her eyes glassy with tears and her thoughts pushing down on her. Oak had left, reluctantly, when she'd shouted down that she didn't want to see him ever again. But that was hours ago; it was mid-afternoon now and still Moll hadn't moved. Oak's words were still ringing in her ears. She'd had parents – proper, real parents who had been the Guardians of the Oracle Bones. But somehow Skull had taken them from her. Her face darkened.

There was a knock on the door and Moll jumped. Perhaps it was Oak's son, Domino, come down from his watch to check on her. She rubbed her eyes and clenched her teeth.

'Who is it?' she growled.

'It's me. Siddy.'

If it had been anyone else, Moll wouldn't have moved. But it was Siddy so she shuffled forward and unlocked the door.

Siddy crawled inside the tree fort, lay Porridge the Second down on the floorboards and cleared a space for himself among the jam jars, opposite Moll. Rummaging in his pocket, he pulled out a handful of Moll's favourite treats: elderflower fritters. He held them out to her. 'I didn't dunk them in honey this time because Ma said she'd have to clean my pocket – and anyway it'd be a safety hazard for Porridge the Second as he spends a lot of time in there.'

But Moll's teeth were clamped shut and her eyes were slits. 'I had parents, Sid, only Oak and Mooshie never told me. And I never got to meet them.'

Siddy took off his flat cap and hung his head. 'I just spoke to Oak. He told me because he's worried sick about you and he knew you'd talk to me.' He paused. 'Mooshie's worried too, Moll. All the Elders are.'

'Good,' Moll muttered. Her eyes misted with tears again so she picked up an elderflower fritter and nibbled the end.

Siddy leant towards her. 'I know stuff, Moll. Oak wanted you to know, but he knew you wouldn't let him in here so he told me about—' Siddy lowered his voice to a murmur, '—about how your parents died.'

It was only a whisper, but Siddy words clamoured in Moll's ears. Siddy knew the truth.

'I'm going to tell you everything I know, Moll, and together we're going to – ' he searched for the right word, '*fix* all this.'

Moll fiddled with a jar of tadpoles. Then she nodded. 'What happened to them?'

'Before I tell you, Oak wanted you to know that your parents loved you more than any ma or pa could. He said you were everything to them.'

Moll swallowed. She *had* been wanted – wanted and loved. And yet knowing that had come too late.

Siddy took a deep breath. 'Ten years ago your parents went to Skull's camp and spoke out against his dark magic.'

Moll looked up. 'They went to Skull's camp, like I did?'

Siddy nodded. 'But Skull wouldn't listen and, every night after they visited his clearing, the Dream Snatch haunted them, just like it haunts you apparently. Oak told me Skull

63

wanted the Guardians of the Oracle Bones out of the way so that he had more chance of destroying the Bone Murmur.'

A lump was starting to form in Moll's throat again, as if all this unhappiness had been locked inside her and was suddenly struggling out.

'Apparently the Dream Snatch grew so strong it spread over everything your parents held dear, and then one winter's night it dragged them – and you – out of bed and down to the river. You were just a scrap then. Only two years old, I think.'

A chord within Moll wavered. Something about Siddy's words felt strangely familiar. 'They – they didn't come back from the river, did they?'

Siddy shook his head. 'The camp heard nothing – no cries, no cause for alarm. But, when your parents didn't show up the next morning, Oak went down to the river and saw them on the bank. There were no marks on their bodies but Oak could see they weren't breathing, that they were . . .' His voice trailed off.

Moll gulped. The faceless couple in her nightmare, the ones her mind refused to remember. She shivered. 'My nightmare – it's the memory of me watching my parents die, isn't it?'

Siddy shifted. 'I think it might be.'

Moll's eyes widened in horror. 'But didn't anyone go after Skull?'

Siddy shook his head. 'Oak couldn't prove Skull was behind it and it was too dangerous for the camp to stir up trouble without proof. Especially as Oak wanted to protect you.'

Moll stood up and paced to the end of the fort. 'But the Dream Snatch only *summons* the victims,' she stammered. 'Even if Skull summoned my parents close, he must've used something *else* to kill them. How could Skull do that without leaving any marks?'

Siddy shrugged. 'The stuff of dark magic – that's what Oak said. But he doesn't know any more than that. Even the Elders couldn't work it out.'

Moll frowned. 'You said I was with them … How did I wriggle my way out of dying? If Skull had the power to take my ma and pa away, why didn't he take me too?'

Sid paused. 'It was Gryff. He saved your life that night.'

'Gryff?' Moll felt her way back to the wildcat's touch: warm, strong, fearless. Ten years he'd been with her and he'd never allowed her to touch him. But now everything was changing.

Siddy nodded. 'The night Oak discovered your parents, he saw Gryff for the first time. Crouched among the undergrowth near the river, he was and he had you there with him – safe. He must've led you away, hidden you in the ferns.'

Moll sat down before Siddy, wide-eyed and speechless. Gryff had left the northern wilderness – for *her*. He must have raced over mountains and bounded through valleys just to get to her. But how had he known the moment she would need him? *Somehow* he'd known and he'd known exactly who she was. Moll listened to the wind chimes tinkling on the branch below the fort. Gryff had come from the wild and maybe some things about him would always stay wild.

Siddy shuffled awkwardly among the jam jars. He picked up Porridge the Second, who shot him a look of miserable indifference, then he turned to Moll. 'I'm sorry about everything, Moll. About the Dream Snatch and the Bone Murmur – and about your parents.'

But there was something more than just sadness and anger in Moll's face now. There was determination.

Out of the corner of his eye, Siddy glimpsed the penknife he kept on a shelf. He pocketed it quickly, unsure at this stage where Moll's determination would be directed. Hacking down the tree fort had probably crossed her mind by now.

'We need a plan, Sid,' Moll said. 'Skull's not going to get away with taking my parents from me.'

Siddy nodded, relieved the tree fort was to be spared demolition. 'The Bone Murmur talks about you and Gryff finding these Amulets of Truth – that's the only thing that can stop Skull. Now, at first when Oak told me about the Bone Murmur, I thought an amulet was a type of fish—'

Moll groaned. 'That's a *mullet*, Sid.'

He nodded. 'Right. So I asked Ma and she said amulets can be a number of things: coins, necklaces, statues, pendants . . .' He tuned his flat cap over in his hands. 'She said there are wild stories claiming the amulets are jewels from the ends of the earth and fragments from shooting stars.'

Moll's eyes glittered green. Even Porridge the Second had an unusually thoughtful look on his face.

'I'll help you find them, Moll. I'm good at finding things. Found a tawny owl's nest yesterday, I did.'

Moll thought of the things she'd found the night before: the dead owl and the rat, the gang circling the fire in cloaks, Skull squeezing the wax figure. She shivered. Somewhere in the Deepwood that night, Skull would be conjuring his Dream Snatch.

Siddy bit his lip. 'Pa said that past bone readings tell of the old magic locked inside the amulets and if the amulets are destroyed they're lost forever. The Bone Murmur breaks and Skull's dark magic grows.' He hung his head. 'This is going to take *ages*. Perhaps we should hide out in the tree fort until it's all over?'

Moll shook her head. 'We have to fight back – just like my parents did.'

Siddy nodded glumly, and then his eyes sparkled as he remembered something. 'Oak told me that your parents threw the Oracle Bones just days before they died. Your pa asked where the amulets were hidden, but, unlike many of the Guardians of the past, he got an answer to this question. Oak said he read out a riddle and, though they say it's near impossible to make sense of, we've got a lead – because they say the bones never lie.'

Moll's heart beat faster. 'What's the riddle? What did my pa's bone reading say?'

'I don't know. It's locked inside the Chest of No Opening

67

at Any Time or Your Life Won't Be Worth Living – in Cinderella's Bull's wagon with the bone readings of the past.'

'*That's* what's locked inside that chest?' Moll's face was aghast. They'd spent hours trying to guess what Cinderella Bull had hidden away in the chest she didn't allow anyone else to touch. But ancient bone readings? They hadn't thought of that.

Siddy nodded. 'And I always thought she kept a giant hedgehog in there.'

Moll put her head in her hands. 'How are we ever going to sneak it out?'

'Oak said he'd show it to you tomorrow morning, after Wisdom and Ivy's wedding feast is out of the way.'

Moll let Oak's name bounce right off her. He was a liar and she wouldn't be hanging around waiting for him to show her the bone reading. No, she'd get it herself if she had to – that night. She turned to Siddy. 'What did my ma go asking the bones?'

'Oak says no one knows what she asked because she destroyed the bones after reading them.'

An icy chill crawled down Moll's back. And in the furthest corner of her mind the Dream Snatch began to pulse. Moll's stomach tightened and her face drained of colour. She could hear the hiss of the rattle and the beat of the drum. She gripped her talisman hard. 'I – I can feel Skull chanting for me,' she whispered. 'He must be stronger now he knows who I am. He's reaching me while I'm awake!'

The forest around them fell silent until all that remained were Moll and Siddy's fluttering breaths.

Siddy clutched his talisman, a circular pebble with a hole in the middle which brought him more bad luck than good (he'd got his finger stuck in the hole when tree climbing a few days earlier and it'd snagged on a fence while he and Moll fled from the farmer the month before) but he'd grown attached to the thing and he gripped it until his fingers were white. Then he plunged his hand inside an old sack, brought out a handful of oats and scattered them over the floor. 'Keep us safe, tree spirits,' he whispered. 'Keep us safe.'

But the oats weren't strong enough to force Skull back and Moll felt his call, urging her to give up, to hand herself over to his gang. She turned to Siddy. 'Tell me something good, Sid, something that'll close my mind right off to Skull.'

Sid bit his lip and then he said, 'Olive. That was your ma's name. And your pa, he was called Ferry.'

And just like that something inside Moll stirred – something stronger and bigger than Skull's Dream Snatch. His curses dissolved into silence and Moll clenched her fists. She thought of her parents visiting Skull's clearing all those years ago. She thought of Gryff's touch, so warm and strong.

'I'll find out how Skull killed my parents,' she muttered. 'He may have owned their minds, but he's not owning me.' She paused. '*No one* owns me.'

Chapter 10
Jumping the Broomstick

That night a figure entered the forest and passed by Skull's camp unseen. On it crept, through the deadened glade and in between the sallow beeches, wearing the night like a cloak. It paused briefly by the river boundary, then lowered itself into the water and waded across. With silent stealth, it edged closer to Oak's camp.

Perched like a china ornament, an owl hooted from a branch. The figure stopped, brushing its long grey hair back from its face. There was music further ahead – a pan flute, a fiddle, an accordion. The camp were celebrating something. But this was no time for a party.

The figure continued on, creeping up to the first of the Sacred Oaks. It stretched out a blackened hand, the fingers burned to stumps, and placed a roll of leather into a hollow in the tree. The initials on the leather gleamed in the moonlight: MP. And then the figure slipped from the trees, back into the night.

*

The camp was buzzing with excitement: the Jumping of the Broomstick ceremony had arrived. The stars were out and Oak and Mooshie were sitting round the fire on stools carved from beech wood, drinking bog-myrtle beer and feeding titbits to the camp's two greyhounds. Beside them, wearing so much purple she was almost blue, Patti was sprinkling herbs into her husband's soup. 'It's lovage, Jesse,' she whispered. 'It'll increase your love for me – and ensure faithfulness at all times.' Jesse rolled his eyes, but drank the concoction nonetheless. To his right Cinderella Bull held a sparkling fortune-telling ball before Hard-Times Bob and the children gathered round the fire, sipping wood-sorrel fizzes – delicious, bubbly drinks Mooshie made from green-leafed plants that grew along the forest floor.

Moll watched from the edge of the clearing with Siddy.

'You sure you don't want to muck in for a bit?' Siddy said. 'You could stand by me when Ivy jumps the broomstick . . .'

Moll threw him a withering look so Siddy didn't push it further. It had been bad enough bumping into Oak and Mooshie on their way back to Moll's wagon earlier. When they'd tried to talk to Moll, she had been as uncommunicative as Porridge the Second and Siddy had found the whole thing so profoundly awkward his ears had burned red and began to twitch. And it was obvious the children in the camp had been told as they'd knocked several times on Moll's wagon door to see if she wanted to climb trees with them. But Moll hadn't answered; she was boarded up against them all.

Sparks from the fire crackled into the air and floated upwards, lost in the overhanging branches. Domino had come down from his watch and was playing the fiddle, slow and haunting, like a call to worship. Then came Mooshie's voice as Keeper of the Songs – gravelly like grain – lilting and drifting over the fire. The gypsies watched spellbound as Ivy, her hands covered in henna and her plaited hair scooped up over her head, took her place beside Wisdom, before the birch broomstick they had to jump over to bless their marriage.

And set back from the celebrations, from somewhere in the darkness of the Ancientwood, branches stirred.

'If you jump higher than Wisdom,' Patti shouted, 'you'll be the decision-maker of the family!' She tucked a coin under Ivy's arm. 'Seven years' good luck to the person who catches the coin when Ivy jumps!'

Beneath the branches of a Sacred Oak, Moll and Siddy looked on – half intrigued, half appalled. To them, Wisdom was a fist-fighter. Jumping the Broomstick seemed a bit of a let-down.

Patti glanced around the camp. 'Siddy!' she hollered. 'Wherever you've got to, you better come here now! Your sister's getting married and it's not the kind of thing you skulk off for!'

'I've got to go and join them, Moll,' Siddy said, tying Porridge the Second into a knot and popping him into his pocket. 'I'll bring you back a wood-sorrel fizz.'

But Moll was barely listening. 'I'm going to get my pa's bone reading from Cinderella Bull's wagon.'

72

'Can't you wait a while, then I can come with you?' Siddy hissed.

Moll shook her head. 'It can't wait, Sid. I need to—'

Siddy nudged her. 'I think someone wants a word with you, Moll.'

She followed his gaze. Tucked back from the Sacred Oaks, among the hawthorn bushes, two yellow-green eyes glinted and then Gryff stepped out, his footsteps softer than falling snow.

Moll felt a rush of warmth. 'Gryff.' She wanted to leap forward and wrap her arms round him. Somehow they were in this together – in a way that no one in the camp was, except perhaps Siddy. 'If Oak or Mooshie ask for me, Sid, say I'm sulking in my bed. Oak's boys aren't up on watch right now so Mooshie won't know I've slipped out.'

Siddy nodded, watching in awe as the wildcat slunk towards them. He'd seen Gryff many times with Moll, but there was always something unpredictable and wild about him and that kept the rest of the camp at a wary distance. 'Just stay here with Gryff; don't go to Cinderella Bull's wagon without me. OK?'

Siddy ran back towards the fire; Mooshie's lyrics were growing livelier and faster and before long Patti was clamouring on the spoons, Domino was spiralling out notes from his fiddle and Hard-Times Bob was making a series of squeezy noises from his accordion – in time with his hiccups.

And, nestled into the branches not so very far from Moll

and Gryff, a pair of eyes continued to watch, blinking every now and again and narrowing.

Moll smiled as Gryff stopped before her. 'Thank you, Gryff, for helping me last night.' She paused. 'And for watching out for me all those years ago.'

Gryff dipped his head and purred. His way of talking, of understanding.

'You left the northern wilderness – your home – for me. Didn't you?'

Again Gryff dipped his head. In the moonlight, his coat looked almost brown, just like the fur on his belly.

Moll knelt down slowly and, for some seconds, she just watched Gryff and he watched back. And then, so gently she felt like she might not be moving at all, Moll stretched out her hand. Gryff stayed where he was. Still. Watching. And then he took one step closer to Moll.

The movement was fluid, like liquid, and Moll watched in silence. Her hand was now just centimetres from the wildcat's head. His whiskers twitched and he craned his neck forward until his fur was touching the tips of Moll's fingers. She held her breath. Gryff moved closer, nestling his head deeper into her hand. A great warmth surged through Moll's body as she felt her fingers sink into his fur. She edged closer, stretching out her other hand. But Gryff didn't back away. He leant into Moll, curling his body into hers, burrowing his head into her neck and nuzzling into her chest.

Everything Moll had seen and heard – the Dream Snatch,

the Bone Murmur, her parents – fell away. All she could feel was Gryff. She didn't even realise she was crying. But Gryff did. And he nuzzled closer until all Moll could hear was his purr, rumbling deep within her own body.

And, like a stain in the darkness, the two eyes watched on, unseen. Minutes passed then the eyes moved. Closer. Towards a Sacred Oak, towards the one the figure had placed the roll of leather inside. A hand reached out towards the tree. Because, to the hand, it didn't matter whose initials the leather bore. The hand had come for Moll; the roll of leather was just a lucky find.

Back in the clearing the camp were dancing quick-stepping jigs round the fire as Wisdom and Ivy clasped each other's hands and leapt over the broomstick. Everyone roared and clapped before gathering round the fire for hotchi-witchi – baked hedgehog – a meal Moll strongly disagreed with since she'd struck up a friendship with an injured hedgehog a few years before.

Moll drew back from Gryff and together they watched the festivities unfold. Oak was laughing with Wisdom and Ivy while Mooshie fussed round them with food. Moll felt a pang of sadness as she thought of what could have been if her own parents were still alive. She leant in closer to Gryff and for several minutes they just watched. And then Gryff padded away from Moll, towards the trees.

'Go hunt,' Moll smiled. 'I'll wait for you here.'

Gryff melted into the forest but, within minutes of his leaving, a chill slithered over Moll's skin. Behind her, the camp was full of noise – music, cheers, shouts – but it was silence that fell upon Moll's ears. A silence loaded with danger. And then, almost so faintly it might not have been there at all, the Dream Snatch began to pulse inside her. Moll's heart quickened and the chanting pounded louder, feeding on her fear.

Something was shifting between the branches ahead. Not Gryff, Moll could tell. This was larger, darker, and it was gathering speed, coming straight towards her.

Moll drew breath to scream, but out of nowhere a hand clapped down over her mouth. The Dream Snatch screeched inside her. And the cloaked figure slid nearer still.

Chapter 11
Unwanted Visitors

Moll squirmed beneath the iron grip of the hand that trapped her mouth, but it held her fast, forcing her to look ahead. She recoiled in horror; the cloaked man who now stood before her seemed neither young nor old; he was barely even *human*.

One eye was stitched closed, the other half open and running. A vein throbbed in his forehead, amid strands of limp hair, and his skin was shrivelled, like a crumpled balloon. But it was the lump that frightened Moll the most. His back was hunched and it rose up in a deformed bulge as if the body of a shrunken child had been moulded to it.

Moll forced her body round, twisting her neck as far as it would go. The figure holding her had pale eyes and a mop of light hair: the boy with the cob called Raven. She tried to dig a hand into the pocket of her dress, but the larger man was too quick. He yanked out her catapult and hurled it into the undergrowth. Moll wanted to hiss and scream, but the boy's hold was firm and he muffled her cries. She struggled against him, slamming her legs into his, jabbing with her elbows, but he gripped her tight. Eyes wide, panting hard, Moll looked back towards the camp.

Shadows danced round the campfire and music flared. With all the celebrations, no one could hear her; no one was even looking her way.

The man with the shrivelled skin jerked his head towards the trees and the river. Moll knew where they were going to take her and she struggled harder.

'We'll gag her,' the man hissed. 'We haven't got time for this; Skull's waiting.' His voice was thick like glue and when he spoke his hunched back bulged.

Moll's heart hammered within her chest as the man tugged a cloth from his pocket and bound it over her mouth. She could feel his stale breath crawling up her nose and she retched – suffocated by the gag, choked by fear. The man drew out a rope and jerked it round Moll's ankles. She fell to the ground, writhing and twisting, as the man bound her wrists.

Where are you, Gryff? Where are you? Come back . . .

Towering above her, she saw Raven and, behind him, a mare. The man with the shrivelled skin turned towards the boy.

'Take Raven. I'll hoist the girl up to you,' he growled. 'Then make for camp – as fast as you can.'

The boy threw the man a defiant look. 'I know, Gobbler; I was there when Skull briefed us. Remember?'

Gobbler scoffed. 'You lost the palomino, Alfie.' He jerked his head towards Moll. '*And* you didn't get a hold of her first

78

time round. No wonder they don't respect you back at camp. Skull only feeds you and gives you shelter because he needs someone to tend the cobs and wash the dishes … Now get a move on! It's time you made up for losing the girl last time.'

Alfie flashed Gobbler a look, his eyes wild and fierce.

Moll trembled as she felt the blood race through her body and a sickening taste fix in her throat.

Gobbler seized Moll by the hair and yanked her up. She squirmed and wriggled, but she could feel the Dream Snatch within her already, making her fight weak. Alfie leapt on to Raven's back and Gobbler shoved Moll up to him. Gripping her hard, Alfie spurred Raven on through the trees.

Up until just the day before, a surge of curiosity had brewed inside Moll every time she thought of Skull's camp, but now that she was being dragged helplessly towards it, every fibre in her body wished it had never existed.

Eyes wide, Moll watched the Ancientwood flash by, scouring it for any signs of Gryff. Raven bounded over fallen branches and tore round gnarled trees, galloping faster and faster towards the Deepwood. Before long, the river was in front of them, shining silver beneath the moon. Moll yanked her body away, tearing herself back from the boundary, but Alfie rode Raven on, wading into the water. Gobbler charged in behind them, clattering over slippery pebbles.

Without warning, the reeds on the far side of the

riverbank burst open and Gryff was there, leaping towards the cobs, his claws splayed, his teeth bared. The cobs shied, rearing up in shock, hurling their riders into the river. Arms flailed and hands grappled, but Moll was wriggling her legs free. The cobs thrashed in the water, reins tangling Alfie's leg, a hoof clipping the back of Gobbler's head.

'They're—' water choked Alfie's words, 'they're getting away!'

Moll kicked and kicked, feeling the Dream Snatch weaken inside her now Gryff was near. She launched her bound arms into the current. Alfie tried to grab her feet, but the reins of his struggling cob were pulling him back; Moll booted him hard, then swam on, tearing at the ropes with her teeth. Water gushed into her mouth, but it was softening the ropes and she wriggled her hands free. Seconds later, Gryff was beside her and they were careering downstream in a tangle of limbs, round a bend – away from Gobbler and Alfie.

Moll yanked the gag from her mouth and her breath sawed through her. 'Keep us safe,' she panted to the water spirits.

The current quickened, carrying Moll and Gryff further and further downstream until Gobbler's and Alfie's yells were little more than faraway echoes. Gryff paddled beside Moll as they raced round rocks and bumped down rapids. Stones skinned Moll's knees, but she let the current take her until at last the water slowed and the river widened.

It was Gryff who started back-paddling first. The river was propelling them towards a lip where the water was black and shining. Moll's eyes widened in terror: she knew what came after.

The roar began, rumbling and fierce.

Moll turned against the current, clutching at rocks and weeds, grappling for overhanging branches. But the river beat on, dragging her and Gryff towards the waterfall. Moll closed her eyes.

She felt her belly shoot up as they tumbled off the edge, then they plummeted down, down, down, plunging into the foamy churn. Blood roared in Moll's ears as the fall sucked them deeper and deeper into its seething sway. Then they burst up into the misty spray while the torrent crashed down behind them. Kicking hard against the current, they swam towards the riverbank.

They hauled themselves up, coughing and spluttering, then flopped down into the reeds. The river rolled on beside them, smudging the silence of the forest.

'Thank you, Gryff,' Moll panted.

Gryff stood up and shook the water from his fur.

'I would've been mushed if you hadn't turned up.' Moll wrung her dress. 'I—'

Gryff's ears twitched and Moll fell silent.

Hooves – thundering through the trees towards them.

A bead of cold sweat trickled down Moll's forehead and Gryff's fur tightened in panic. But neither Gobbler nor Alfie burst out of the trees.

Moll's mouth dropped open. It was Siddy. And he was charging towards them on Jinx.

Moll rushed forward. 'Sid! How did you find us?'

Siddy slowed Jinx, then slipped from her back. 'When I saw you'd gone, I tracked Gryff,' he said simply. 'Pa's been teaching me animal prints and I've been getting good. I followed him to the river—'

'Skull's gang were trying to drag me across it!' Moll muttered. 'Did you see them back by the boundary?'

Siddy shook his head.

Gobbler's head wound, the cobs crazed with fear ...

'They'll have gone back to the Deepwood then,' Moll said. 'They won't be back tonight.'

Moll and Siddy sat on the banks of the river while Gryff tucked himself beneath the overhang where he could rest, hidden by the reeds and ferns.

'The banks by the boundary were scuffed by cob hooves,' Siddy said, 'so I knew there'd been a struggle. I figured you must have swum downstream, only,' he pointed to the waterfall, 'you didn't go over that, did you?'

Moll nodded. 'Didn't plan to though.'

Siddy straightened his flat cap. 'Well, it's a good job one of us has been planning.' He opened his fist and grinned. Because there, lying in the palm of his hand, were three small fragments of animal bone, their surfaces covered with tiny black markings, like the pictures of an ancient code.

Moll's eyes widened. 'My pa's bone reading. But how?' she stammered. 'You were at the feast!'

Siddy shook his head. 'I saw Gryff touch you! When I was standing by the fire ... He's wild, Moll, but somehow he trusts you. And, when I saw him actually nuzzling against you, I figured there were things to be done more important than drinking wood-sorrel fizz.' He paused. 'It all happened pretty fast actually. Cinderella Bull was reading Ma's fortune so I crept into her wagon. After that salt circle you said she did round you this morning, she must have gone back to the bone readings to get your pa's one ready for you. The key for the chest was out on her chest of drawers!' Siddy blushed. 'Didn't see it at first though so I might have turned the whole wagon upside down. But that's not the point; we can answer for that another time. I found a rusty tin inside the chest which said "Ferry" on it, and even I could work that bit out.' He tipped the bones into Moll's hands.

Moll grinned. 'Well done, Sid!'

The grooves had been carved by a knife, then filled with charcoal and there were dashes, circles with lines through, triangles upside down or drawn on top of squares and wispy markings like the veins of leaves. Moll held one fragment of bone up; the symbol on it looked like an eye resting on top of a three-pronged stick. She traced the bone script with her finger, then her heart sank.

'I should've listened more when Cinderella Bull taught us the alphabet. We were too busy burping it through while gargling river water. I can't read this.'

'Course you can't,' Siddy said. 'It's Oracle Bone script – I overheard Cinderella Bull talking about it to Hard-Times Bob at the feast. You have to practise for years to learn that stuff.' He flicked each fragment over in Moll's hands. 'Lucky for us, it looks like your pa carved a translation into the back of each bone.'

Moll gasped. The words were faded and cracked, but they were there, three of them, as if her pa had carved them just for her:

DEW HILL MAIDEN

Siddy plucked at the reeds. 'I mean, your pa could've translated the bone reading into something a *bit* easier. But still.'

Moll's shoulders hunched up. 'Dew Hill Maiden ... The stories Hard-Times Bob tells us round the campfire – about the maiden who lives out on the heath beyond the Deepwood! He says she munches the bones of children who wander her way, then boils their eyeballs for breakfast!' Moll's eyes widened. 'Do you think the bone reading's talking about *her*?'

'They were just stories, Moll. You know how much Hard-Times Bob likes a gory fireside tale.'

But Moll noticed Siddy's body had stiffened. She chewed her bottom lip. 'Or were his stories a warning because there really is a dangerous maiden out there?' She paused. 'But why would the bones send us straight into danger?'

'Hard-Times Bob always talks about a maiden on the heath,' Siddy said, 'and our bone reading talks about one on a hill. Might not be the same thing at all ...'

Moll's eyes lit up. 'There are hills on the farm – up where the cows graze. Maybe the maiden's a milkmaid from the dairy up there and she knows where the amulets are.' Moll flicked the hollow fists of her talisman open and slipped the bone fragments inside. 'At least it's the opposite direction to the Deepwood and the heath, away from Gobbler and Alfie – the devils who tried to kidnap me just now.'

'Oak's banned us from the farm though.'

She and Siddy had dropped by a few months ago as part of a two-day tempest of rule-breaking, a hobby both of them indulged in on a regular basis to mark their place in The Tribe, a secret club comprised of Moll, Siddy and when he was around, Gryff. Needless to say, the farmer hadn't appreciated their visit. It wasn't their fault he had interpreted their sun dance as a bewitching curse on the cows' milk. The farm folk could be so jittery.

'Which is why we can't go back to the camp tonight,' Moll replied. 'We'll go straight to the farm from here.' The darkness seemed to grow around them and Moll shifted among the reeds. 'At dawn though, when there's more light.'

'But Oak and Mooshie will realise we're gone soon. You could've died back there under the waterfall. Shouldn't we at least go back to camp and tell them about Gobbler and Alfie?'

Moll looked out over the river. 'I don't want to see Oak and Mooshie. Not yet.'

And Siddy knew that no amount of talking sense would change Moll's mind.

They talked and talked about the bone reading until their

eyelids were heavy with sleep. And the last thing Moll remembered before drifting off was Sid's round face sleeping in front of hers.

Not long afterwards, the nightmare came for Moll, stealing into her dreams, grappling for her mind. She felt herself falling under its power, sensed the desire to get up and follow Skull's drumbeats into the Deepwood. But then from somewhere deeper inside her came the memory of the Bone Murmur and her pa's clue. Hope stirred within her and the Dream Snatch faded to the swishing of the river and an owl hooting in the distance. She opened her eyes to the night.

Moll's belly tightened.

Staring back at her was a face. But it didn't belong to Siddy.

Chapter 12
A Face in the Darkness

'Time to get up, precious,' Gobbler snarled, his half-open eye red and running.

Hours must have passed; the sky above the trees was a purplish blue as dawn seeped in.

Moll made as if to leap away, but Alfie and Gobbler fell upon her. The gag came first, one jerk from Alfie, then Gobbler bound her hands and feet, his fingers cold and damp, like swollen worms. The wound to his head from his mare's hoof was still red and glistening and Moll could hear the terrified whines of the cobs as they yanked against the ropes that tied them to the trees.

Moll bucked her body and jabbed with her elbows, but their grip was a lock and they dragged her upright. Her blood pumped hard.

Jinx's tethering rope had been cut – she was nowhere to be seen – and there was Siddy, bound to a tree, his eyes wild with fear. He threw his head left and right, fighting against the gag, spluttering choked-up cries. Moll's throat closed. She should have listened to him and gone back to the camp like he'd said. She tried to break free, to rush over and untie him, but Alfie was already hauling her towards Raven.

Moll's mind whirred. How had all this happened? Why hadn't she heard a thing? The answer dropped like shattering glass: *Skull's Dream Snatch*. It had held her prisoner, blocked everything from her knowledge – all noise, all realisation of anything happening. She thought that she'd managed to defeat it, but it had attacked in a different way. Her glance slipped to the riverbank; she could just make out Gryff's body tucked behind the reeds. He was shaking and his eyes were closed. Perhaps he hadn't broken out of the Dream Snatch; she'd been the one back in Skull's camp who'd had to tear him from his trance. Moll wanted to scream out for him, to call him close, but what if Gobbler and Alfie seized him too?

She gulped down the lump in her throat and blinked hard at Gryff. *I'll find you again, Gryff, I promise. Stay safe.*

As Gobbler turned away to untie the cobs, Alfie threw Moll to the ground. Then he leant over her, a tangle of blond hair tumbling over his eyes, and ripped the boxing fist talisman from her neck. He grinned. 'I can sell that for a small fortune.'

Moll caught Siddy's eyes; they were filled with dread.

Alfie rubbed a grubby thumb over the initials, then his eyes widened in surprise. 'MP.' He said the letters slowly, savouring each syllable. He felt for something in his pocket and smiled. Out of the corner of her eye, Moll glimpsed a roll of leather, but Alfie tucked it quickly away. 'We're getting closer and closer to who you are, girl.'

But Moll wasn't thinking about that.

Don't open the boxing fists . . . Don't see the catch . . . Not my pa's bone reading, my only clue to the amulets . . .

Alfie glanced behind him to where Gobbler was trying to keep the cobs steady. Then he flicked the catch on Moll's talisman, pulled out the bone fragments and stuffed them into his pocket.

Siddy tore against the ropes, but they held him firm, and Moll's heart thundered within her.

Gobbler approached, riding his mare and yanking Raven behind him. Moll dug her heels into the ground, but Gobbler reached down and hauled her up behind him, and, before she could even turn back to Siddy, Gobbler had set off along the riverbank, racing further and further back upstream to where the crossing was shallower.

The wind picked up, screeching through the trees like the souls of dead witches. Its spirit was angry, Moll could tell. It buffeted against Gobbler and his mare, but they tore through its strength, surging on to where the river shallowed.

Again Moll found herself at the boundary as Gobbler's mare charged into the water, racing over the pebbles with Raven and scrambling up the banks of the Deepwood. Moll snatched a glance behind.

And there was Gryff, charging through the breaking dawn on the other side of the river. But he was too late.

The cobs were galloping into the Deepwood now and a strange darkness was growing, blocking the river and the Ancientwood from sight. Moll's head spun. It was as if the shadows had come alive: dark swirls of night that moved in ghostly swishes. Gryff was gone. All that was left was the sound of the shadows, moaning like wind trapped in a chimney.

Moll tried to break free, but Gobbler whirled round to face her. The vein in his forehead pulsed and his back bulged like some kind of overgrown wart. Moll could feel his sour breath on her cheek and see the scarlet veins glistening on his open eyeball. A smile festered in the corner of his mouth and he raised a hand – a clenched fist. Moll saw it coming, saw the knuckledusters glinting.

Then the darkness clattered down.

· Chapter 13 ·
Skull's Lair

Moll jerked awake, her head pounding.

Darkness. As far as she could see. So it was night again; she must have been out cold for a whole day. And where was Siddy? Still bound to a tree by the river? Her thoughts spun wildly, riddled through with guilt. If only she'd listened to him and gone back to the camp as he'd said. She bit down on her lip and hoped with everything inside her that Oak would find Siddy soon.

The air around Moll was still, frighteningly so. No birdsong, no rustling undergrowth, no whispering trees. The ground beneath her bare feet was hard, earthen and cool. She raised her hands, still bound, and they met with a wall. A few flakes of soil came away, slipping between her fingers like sand.

The cool, quiet stillness, the earth walls ... She was underground – trapped underground. In the heart of Skull's lair.

She thought of Oak and Mooshie, how they'd pleaded with her again and again to speak to them in the clearing, but she'd stormed off into her wagon and now she was alone.

Wincing, Moll pushed herself up. Her dress was torn, the rope burned into her wrists and her head throbbed. Shakily, she traced the wall with her hands. This was a pit and its sides rose up far beyond her reach. She felt for her catapult, and then remembered that it was gone. But they'd made their first mistake: they'd untied her feet – her fastest weapon – and she'd stop at nothing to escape.

Moll swallowed. She took a step forward, then another, feeling her way round the sides. The pit was bigger than she'd thought, possibly three metres wide and long, but any opening above her was masked by darkness.

Help me, earth spirits. Help me escape. But something told Moll that even the earth spirits didn't venture this far into the Deepwood.

Sweat settled in her palms. What *were* those shadows that had blocked Gryff from coming into the Deepwood? They couldn't have been real. A wave of dizziness flooded her. She needed to escape but her head was pounding. And as she crouched down, hugging herself into a ball, fear coursed through her.

Moll clenched her fists. Skull was out there and he wanted her dead.

And then the voices came from somewhere above.

'I need at least four, no less. And they should be here by now – they've had long enough.'

Moll shivered. The voice was metallic, cold, like a

92

splinter of ice. And she'd heard it before, when she'd stolen Jinx back. It belonged to Skull.

'Oh, they'll be here. The boys won't go messing up a thing like this,' Gobbler's voice came in reply – rasping, thick, like mud. There was a pause. 'They're not like Alfie.'

A fire crackled, but neither its light nor its warmth reached down to Moll.

'She's a Pecksniff all right.' Skull bit off his words like shards of glass. 'I could see it in her face – so like her mother, she is. And to think she was in Oak's camp all along.'

Moll's body tensed at the mention of her ma, then anger burned up inside her. Oh, she'd get out all right and then Skull would pay. For *everything*.

'But her talisman's got another letter too,' Gobbler snarled. 'M.'

Moll held her breath. The boy, Alfie, had given them her necklace. Her breath caught in her throat. Had he handed over the bone reading? That could lead them to the amulets ... *and if the amulets are destroyed they're lost forever.*

Skull's voice again, low and hungry. 'We need her full name to work the curse when the time comes. Without it, we can't do anything.' He paused. 'When she wakes, get it out of her.'

The voices drained away, swallowed by the distant clatter of wagon doors. Moll tried to think, but pain throbbed behind her eyes and her stomach churned.

From somewhere outside, a tree creaked. Moll covered

her ears. In the Ancientwood, the tree spirits whispered her to sleep. But here . . . She shivered.

'You'd better get used to it, shrimp.'

Moll spun round, fists raised. There was someone else in the pit.

'Who's there?' she whispered.

There was a shuffle in the darkness then the rasp of a match. The flame lit up a tangle of fair hair and two pale eyes. Alfie.

And, as the light filled the chamber, she saw that all around them, scattered on the ground, were bones.

Moll's chest tightened. *Just animal bones*, she told herself. *Nothing more . . .*

The pit wasn't round as she'd imagined. It was an oblong of sorts, a den of darkness that sank into shadows behind Alfie. Tree roots lined the walls and directly above her was an opening. Rough steps had been cut into the soil up to it, but the entrance was covered by a huge metal grate.

Moll's eyes darted back to Alfie. He was sitting against the wall of the pit, unarmed and still wearing his blue feather earring, but his lip was bleeding and his shirt was ripped. A torn rag and a plate of stale bread lay discarded by his feet and beside that was a flask of water and a small rusted tin in which he must have kept his matches. Moll raised her bound fists higher and scowled.

'Let's have you then, you mangled weasel,' she muttered.

Alfie kicked a bone by his foot. 'Don't cross me, runt.'

Moll narrowed her eyes but said nothing.

'Lost your voice?' Alfie sneered. 'A button-sized idiot, that's what you are. And one that dealt me the pit. You and your stupid pony.'

Moll remained silent, her eyes hot and dark. No one insulted Jinx.

The match faded. Alfie sprang up, lighting another against the box.

'Come on then,' Moll said evenly, tossing her hair over her shoulder. But her pulse was racing. Where was Gryff? And Oak? Would the camp even come for her after she'd shut them all out? She needed time to think, time to come up with a plan. 'I'll – I'll fight my way out, past you, past Skull – past the whole rotting lot of you.' She hissed.

Alfie raised his eyebrows. 'Oh, they won't kill you, if that's what you're frightened about.'

Moll spat. 'I'm not frightened.'

'They're waiting for the beast too, like the Bone Murmur says.' Alfie paused. 'So, when the wildcat comes for you and they find out your name, they'll kill you both. Got to be at the same time or the Bone Murmur jumps to another child, another beast. But, now Skull knows who you both are, this is his chance, and he won't let it jump.' He glanced down at the bones. 'See them? Animals that Skull's sacrifices for his Dream Snatch. The bones wind up here.'

Moll's gut twisted into a knot. 'Shut up.' And then she added, under her breath, 'You rotted polecat dipped in cow dung.'

Alfie leant forward but his fists weren't raised. 'I think

you're forgetting something.' The light from the match danced inside the pit. 'I've got the bone reading from inside your talisman.'

Moll's body stiffened. 'Why didn't you just give it to Skull?' Her voice was level but her heart was pounding. If Alfie had the bone reading, there was still a chance she could find the amulets before Skull killed her.

Alfie wiped his nose and straightened himself up. 'Because Skull isn't after the amulets – he's after you and your wildcat. But I've heard the gang talk about them. I know these amulets'll be worth something. A small fortune, I'll bet. And you're going to find them for me so I can sell them and get as far away from here as possible.'

Moll's heart skipped a beat.

Alfie pulled the bone fragments from his pocket and turned them over in his hands. DEW HILL MAIDEN. There was something else in his pocket, something Moll had glimpsed earlier. She'd bide her time on that though; she had to be sly.

She raised her eyebrows. 'And why would I help you?'

Alfie smiled, then he straightened his cap. 'Because I know what the bone reading means – and it's got nothing to do with the farm you and your pal were mumbling about back by the river.' He raised an eyebrow. 'I heard you when Gobbler was cutting your cob free.'

Moll's heart raced faster. He may have heard her and Siddy talking, but he hadn't seen Gryff. She reached out to grab the bones, but Alfie leapt back and the match faded.

'Who are you?' Moll said into the darkness.

'Never you mind. But I don't need Skull, or his wretched dark magic. I'm only interested in the amulets. And once I've sold them *everything* will be better.'

Moll squinted at him. 'You mean you'll have enough money to fend for yourself – without Skull?'

Alfie hesitated for a moment, fiddling with his feather earring. 'Yes.'

It was only a second's hesitation, but Moll knew in that moment that the amulets meant more to Alfie than food and shelter. He was after them for another reason, she was sure of it.

Alfie lit another match from his tin and looked Moll squarely in the eye. 'I know what the bone reading means. And I know how to escape Skull's camp. You need me if you're going to survive this.'

Moll looked around at the pit. 'You're burping out lies.'

'What if I'm not?'

Moll frowned. 'If you *know* all this, why do you need my help?'

'Because I found something last night and I think it's likely bound up with your bone reading and the amulets.' He looked away. 'Only I can't read well so I don't under-stand it all. I reckon you can help because you've been lettered up all fancy at your camp.'

Moll threw him a savage look. 'How do you know about that?'

'Because I've been in Skull's gang since I was a child and

from time to time I watched your camp from the trees. Picked up this and that – enough to get by.'

Moll stared at Alfie. *He* had been sneaking around Oak's camp unnoticed. To learn letters ... 'You're no gypsy, are you?'

Alfie met her bright, fierce eyes. He straightened himself up. 'I want to work with you to get the amulets. Once we find them, we sell them and we each take half the profit.'

Moll couldn't believe what she was hearing. She knew next to nothing about these amulets, but she felt one thing clear and true: they weren't things you could just sell. And splitting the money honestly? Alfie was bound to cut and run. But this was her only chance. She could go along with him, pretending to agree to sell the amulets while he helped her get away, then she'd try and somehow send a signal to Oak and her camp. She looked over at Alfie who was smiling slyly.

What if he was tricking her so that he could pass on information to Skull? But she'd seen the hatred in his eyes at the mention of the witch doctor. If Alfie was keeping secrets from her, Moll got the feeling it was about why he wanted those amulets so badly. She held out her hands and looked Alfie in the eye – the best thing to do when you're telling a lie. 'Deal,' she replied evenly.

Alfie shook her hand. 'Deal.'

Moll looked down at the rope which bound her. 'Untie me. Please.'

Alfie held out another lit match. 'Hold this.'

Moll flinched with annoyance that she'd have to co-operate with the very person who'd kidnapped her from the Ancientwood in the first place.

'Please,' Alfie mumbled.

Reluctantly, Moll took the match and Alfie drew a penknife from his rusted tin. Moll stiffened; so he was armed.

'I'm only untying you because we need to work together.' He sawed his knife through the rope, then glanced quickly at the grate covering the pit's opening. 'If they come down, grab the rope and wind it round your hands; I don't want any questions from them.'

Moll looked at his split lip and nodded. She reached over for the flask, took a big swig of water, then tore off a lump of stale bread and chewed it hard. The match faded but, when Alfie lit another, Moll saw that his eyes were shining and the pocket of his shorts no longer bulged. He was holding something – a roll of leather. A night breeze sifted in through the grate and Moll could almost hear it slipping inside the roll in tiny whispers. Her initials stared back at her in black. But they hadn't been written in ink; they'd been burned on.

Alfie held out the roll of leather in front of Moll. Her mouth widened and her heart fluttered as she traced the words with her finger:

FOR MP.
FROM THE MAIDEN

· Chapter 14 ·
A Dark Trade

Noises from above swallowed their whispers: the creaking of unoiled wheels; the crack of a whip; the grumble of voices. A cart was drawing near. Moll's heart leapt. Oak? Had he come for her?

Alfie snatched back the leather, put a finger to his lips and blew out the match. A crow's *caw-caw* scratched the surface of the night and then the cart pulled close, rumbling and snapping over twigs and leaves as it moved. A cob snorted, then there came a scrabbling of feet, a scratching of claws and a low growl. Chains clanked against the sides of the cart. Whatever was inside was trying to escape.

'Skull! Gobbler! We've got them!'

Moll's heart sank. Surely Oak and his camp could break past the shadows guarding Skull's camp. They were only shadows after all – and she'd managed to get through, though deep down Moll suspected that may have had something to do with the power of the Dream Snatch. A feeling began to gnaw at her mind and, however hard she tried to force it away, it crawled back. Perhaps there was a reason no one from the camp had come for her. Perhaps it was easier for them all if she was finally out of the way. She dug her nails into her palms.

'It's the boys come back from the village,' Alfie whispered.

From the far side of the clearing, wagon doors clattered open and footsteps hurried across.

Alfie tugged Moll beneath the opening.

'Listen and watch if your eyes can fight the dark,' he hissed. 'They've been talking about bringing something to the camp and we've got to find out what it is because no one's been telling me anything of late.'

'Why does it matter what Skull's bringing in?'

'Because I reckon we've got to get past whatever it is.'

Moll swallowed.

'Let's see them, boys,' Gobbler rasped.

'You're going to like what you see. We wouldn't even sit out back with them, they're that fierce.'

'That's Brunt,' Alfie's voice whispered in the dark.. 'Keep out of his way. He's worse than the other two. Almost as bad as Gobbler and Skull.'

There was a scuffling of feet from above. A cob brayed and stamped its feet, then a whip cracked down and the cob was still. But something was moving – and it was moving fast. Loud thuds hammered against the sides of the cart, followed once again by deep, rumbling growls. Whatever the boys had bought, there was more than one of them.

There was a laugh but it was brittle, as if it might have been made from glass. 'Very good,' Skull replied.

'The trader who sold them said they were made in hell!' It was Brunt's voice again, gruff and low.

Moll's lip was trembling. She bit it down. 'What've they got stuffed away in that cart?'

But Alfie didn't have time to hazard a guess because there were more footsteps now – and they were coming towards the pit. Alfie threw the rope to Moll who wrapped it round her wrists and huddled into the shadows.

A light approached, then a shrivelled hand holding a lantern, and a second later, Gobbler's face appeared above the grate. But he wasn't alone. He was joined by a white mask and it gleamed in the light of the lantern like porcelain.

Moll tensed. There were no eyebrows, no eyelashes, no lips showing beneath the wooden mask. It was as if Skull's features had been scraped from him and only the mask remained. And though the mask showed one expression – a grim smile shot through with jagged bones as teeth – Moll could sense a mouth beneath the surface, brooding with dark pleasure.

'Send Brunt in,' he muttered.

A line of cold sweat prickled down Moll's spine, but she looked the mask in the eyes and spat on to the ground. She couldn't let Skull know she was afraid.

'Oak'll come for me!' she hissed, but her voice was shaking. 'We aren't going to give in this easy.'

But the mask had already disappeared.

In its place was another face and it swamped Gobbler's in shadow: a bull neck with folds of gristly skin bunching at the back; a face spiderwebbed with scars, like a pane of shattered glass; a cruel, flattened nose between two mangled ears. Brunt rubbed his hands together; they were strong hands, the type that might bend iron. He looked at Alfie.

'Rip a piece off her dress, Alfie, then bring it up,' he snarled.

'And *then* will you let me out?'

Brunt cracked his knuckles and glowered down. 'Pass it up – and quick about it.'

Alfie was silent for a second, his eyes burning. Then he knelt close by Moll and tore her dress. He scrambled up the soil steps and passed the scrap through the grate.

Brunt shot his hand through the bars and seized Alfie by the collar. 'You better start being more sly with cobs and little girls, young man, or things aren't going to work out nice for you. No more mess-ups. Understand?'

Alfie mumbled something under his breath and Brunt flung him back down the steps.

'We need that wildcat of yours, girl,' Brunt grunted at Moll. 'And when the light's up you're going to show us where to find him.'

Moll sunk her body deeper into the pit, leaving only her voice behind. 'I won't ever give him up.'

Brunt raised a clenched fist. 'Oh, you'll give him up all right – along with your name. And if you don't talk we'll force it out of you. That's a promise. And I'm not one for breaking promises.'

The chains clanked against the cart again; Brunt and Gobbler sloped away.

'They'll track anyone I want?' Skull's voice twisted together with the snarls from the cart.

Brunt laughed. 'They're baying for blood; they'll trace anything. That girl down there isn't going nowhere, Skull.'

'Give them the scrap of her dress then,' Skull hissed. 'I want them to learn her scent so she never gets away.'

For a split second, there was silence. And then a cacophony of noise: pounding feet, desperate scratching, snarling bites. It sounded as though the animals were tearing the scrap of clothing to shreds. And then it came. It was low at first, low and braying, but then it rose – louder and more chilling – and suddenly the night air was filled with the blood-curdling howls of Skull's hounds.

Moll's body tingled with fear, but she shook herself and scowled in Alfie's direction. 'You gave him a scrap from my dress! How's that going to help us escape then?'

'Shut up and trust me,' Alfie growled back.

Moll seethed silently, her dark hair wild around her face like a lion's mane.

'Look, all I'm saying is that we have to use cunning to get us out of this. We have to go along with them – make them think we're helpless – then take a chance and run.'

But Moll wasn't listening. She was scrambling over the bones and feeling her way up the steps, craning her neck towards the opening. It wasn't just the hounds howling above them now. There were other noises too. Voices. And Moll would recognise those voices anywhere.

'It's Oak,' she whispered. 'He's come for me!'

Alfie leant back against the wall of the pit and shook his head.

Up above, the voices became words – so comforting and strong that Moll felt she could almost touch them. Oak sounded some way away, but he was shouting.

'Give her up, Skull! You've no right to take her!'

'I'm here, Oak! Here!' Moll yelled through the bars of the grate.

There were a few laughs and guffaws from directly above the entrance.

Oak was still shouting: 'I've got all my men here, Skull! We've come to take her back!'

Moll clapped a hand over her mouth as she thought of Skull's words: *We need her full name to work the curse when the time comes.* 'Oak, no! Don't say my name. Keep my name safe!' she cried.

'Up on to the cobs, boys. Then set the hounds on them,' Skull's voice spat from above. 'Let's see what they can do.'

Moll cowered beneath the bars as the chains clanked against the cart sides, then fell to the ground. The death-like cries of the hounds wailed through the Deepwood and she listened in horror as Gobbler, Skull and his boys' cobs rode out of the clearing with them. Moll pushed against the bars of the grate, shouldering into it and pummelling it with her feet. She could hear Oak, urging his men away. And then—

'Argh!' One of Oak's men was crying out in pain. Moll's mind raced. Was that Jesse, Siddy's pa?

The hooves faded into the distance until once again there was a wall of silence.

Anger rushed through Moll, burning up her veins, pounding in her head. She hurried down the steps and stood upright in the middle of the pit as tall as she could. And then she screamed. She screamed for Oak and Mooshie, for Siddy and Gryff, for her parents, for everyone she knew. She screamed and screamed until her eyes became saucers and she was blue in the face. The last of the scream wriggled out of her, bursting from her mouth, leaving her gasping for breath.

And then there was silence.

'Afeared now?' Alfie asked.

Moll spat. 'No. I had a scream stuck inside of me – practically bursting through my skin, it was – so I got it out.'

But Moll *was* scared. She was terrified. And her palms were tickling with sweat. Alfie lit another match and glared at Moll. She held his gaze, recognising the challenge, her face a mixture of intense concentration and absolute fury.

Alfie squinted at her. 'What you doing now?'

'Rummaging through my mind for a plan.'

Alfie scoffed, then turned away.

'What will happen to Oak and everyone?' Moll muttered. 'What will the hounds *do* to them?'

Alfie shrugged. 'Oak rides fast; I've seen him in the forest before.'

Moll blinked back fear. 'But those hounds – you heard them. They're monsters; no hounds shriek like that. They—'

Moll's words stopped short.

Something was scratching the soil away beside the grate.

Chapter 15
Vapours

Moll's spirits leapt as she made out the green eyes glinting in the darkness. 'You came for me,' she gasped, rushing up the steps.

She gripped the metals bars of the grate tight and Gryff brushed his head against her hands. Again his touch – so warm and strong. Alfie watched, wide-eyed, from the bottom of the pit.

Earth sprayed up behind the wildcat as his claws raked through the soil, burrowing closer and closer to Moll. He drew back, panting hard, his chest heaving. Alfie tensed. The animal was wild; it might slip into the pit and attack. He shuffled backwards. But Moll was smiling. There was a hole, and it was big enough for her to crawl through.

'You won't get past Skull's clearing,' Alfie muttered uneasily as he realised the hole wasn't big enough for him. 'Try me.'

Alfie held the roll of leather into the light of his match. 'Don't you want to find the amulets?'

Forces far bigger than Moll could understand tugged hard

inside her. She looked from the leather to Alfie and then up to Gryff. She lunged at Alfie, but he drew out his knife.

'Stay and I'll give you the roll of leather,' he growled. 'You won't escape Skull without my help.'

Moll's eyes grew dark, then she turned and scrambled up out of the hole.

Alfie watched in surprise. Who was this girl who charged headlong into danger, again and again and again? 'You'll be back,' he called. 'You've no idea what's out there!'

Moll found herself grabbing Gryff and clutching him tight, then they ran across the clearing and into the trees.

She hadn't gone more than a few steps before she felt them, squeezing out of the crippled trees like vapours of the night. Moll hadn't been imagining them when they'd crossed the river. These shadows were *real*. They floated towards Moll and Gryff, faceless and black, moaning like funnelled wind.

Moll closed her eyes and ran blindly on. But, as her fear swelled, the shadows grew, looming over her like bottomless caves. Moll clenched her fists. The shadows were slipping in between her and Gryff, forcing them apart. She reached out desperate arms, but the shadows grew larger between the two fugitives, driving them further away until Moll could no longer see Gryff and once more he'd vanished into the trees.

The shadows were all around Moll now and she skidded to a terrified halt. She felt the weight of their darkness pressing down on her chest. And she knew what they wanted. Cool fingers slipped down her throat, plucking at her trembling voice.

Your name, they moaned. *Give us your name.*

Moll doubled over, closing her mind to the shadows. But the darkness inside her was too much and she sank to her knees, alone again – and terrified.

Chapter 16
Unravelling the Clues

Moll glared across the cage at Alfie. It was the same one she and Gryff had spotted the night they'd rescued Jinx, only now it was strung up by rope, like some kind of giant metal claw, from the tallest tree in Skull's clearing – and she and Alfie were locked inside it.

It was dawn now and light trickled through the trees, shaping the branches into crooked silhouettes. Skull's boys and the hounds were still gone, and there was no sign of Gryff. But Skull and Gobbler were back, muttering together inside Skull's black wagon while a pan of sausages cooked over the fire in the middle of the clearing. Moll's mouth watered.

'First a pit then a cage,' Alfie spat. 'Were you this much trouble in your camp?'

Moll was, so she didn't bother answering.

The cage was huge and domed, large enough to stand up in and pace around, and the bones that had previously lined the floor had been hurled into the clearing below. Moll eyed the enormous padlock with disgust. Her throat was dry and, when she swallowed, it felt like the roof of her mouth had been rubbed raw.

'Did they get my name?' she mumbled. 'Did I give it up?'

Alfie shook his head. 'Somehow you held on to it – even though Skull and Gobbler turned back from the hounds and dragged us up here.'

Moll thought she could detect a trace of surprise, almost respect, in Alfie's voice, but he was glowering at her now so it was hard to be sure.

'What – what were those shadow *things*?'

'Vapours,' Alfie said. 'Skull conjures them when he wants to guard his clearing. He says they're made from the broken hearts of witches – and they feed on fear.'

'How do you ever get past them when you sneak over to our camp?'

'By being brave.'

'Oh.' Moll paused. 'And is that how we'll get past them then?'

Alfie nodded. 'That – and by you listening to me, Blip.'

Moll frowned. 'Who's Blip?'

'*You*. Means a small mistake – and that's what you are. It'll do while I don't know your name.' He let his head fall back against the bars. 'You mucked up, Blip.'

'I got us out of the pit,' Moll muttered.

'No. You got us *into* a cage. And I had a way out of the pit, only you didn't stick around long enough to learn it.' He looked away. 'Took me ages, but I tunnelled through the soil with my hands and penknife when Skull locked me down there before. I covered it up though – added the loose soil to the sides of the pit.'

Moll's eyes widened.

Alfie went on. 'The camp don't realise the pit's been changing shape. Not like they spend any time down there ... Looked just like ordinary soil – only the patch I dug was soft and, once you dragged out the loose stuff, you got to my tunnel.' He shot Moll a withering look. 'And it was big enough to crawl through.'

Moll bit her lip. 'Must've taken *ages*. How long were you down there?'

Alfie fiddled with his tattered waistcoat. 'Long enough. Not that it matters now.'

Moll wondered about mumbling an apology, then she remembered how much she hated Alfie and looked down at the clearing. Gobbler stalked towards the fire to collect the sausages, then he stole back inside Skull's wagon.

Alfie took the roll of leather from his pocket. 'Now the light's up we need to read this fast.'

Again Moll saw her initials burned into the outside of the leather, but what unnerved her most was the wording below: *From the Maiden*. Again. She turned cold inside. Why were her pa's bone reading *and* the leather roll so bent on sending her into the hands of someone who might well be a bone-grinding lunatic? She glanced at the seal on the leather; it was black, like an imprint of the night. Moll steeled herself. She wouldn't allow fear to snatch back her plan of finding the amulets and avenging her parents. She turned to Alfie, her eyes narrowed. 'Where d'you find this anyway?'

'Tucked inside one of the oaks I was hiding behind when Gobbler and me came for you at your camp. Didn't think much of it until I saw the bones inside your talisman.'

Alfie unrolled the leather while Moll scowled beside him. The inside was covered with black words and each one had been burned into the leather. Moll tensed. This was something that belonged to *her* and Alfie had no right to it. She swiped for it but Alfie held it close.

'Read it to me,' he said sternly.

Moll glared at him, then looked down at the burnt lettering. She was silent for a few seconds, and then, very quietly, she said, 'You can tell a lot about a person from their handwriting.'

'Load of old squiggles to me,' Alfie muttered.

Moll shook her head. 'Mooshie says writing's like a clue to what a person's like. Big bends in the g, f, j and q mean a person's greedy; small loops in the a, d, e and o mean a person's tight-fisted ...' She was fighting for time, trying her best to read the words in her head while blabbing away to Alfie.

Alfie shoved her in the back. 'Just get on and read it, will you?'

Moll arched her eyebrows. Just a little longer. 'Those wispy dashes across the t and f there mean this person's clever-thinking.'

'Look,' Alfie growled, 'we've got to read this and get out of here. We don't have time for this.'

114

Moll's mind was racing. Suppose this was a message only *she* was meant to see? But she *needed* Alfie; he was her only way out and for now she had to trust him. She took a deep breath. 'It's a poem,' she said slowly. Then she started to read aloud:

'MANY AND MANY A FOOTSTEP FROM YOU,
IN A HOVEL AMONG THE GORSE,
A WILD MAIDEN LIVES WHOM MOST ESCHEW,
BY MARSHLAND AND HEATHER GROWN COARSE.

THIS MAIDEN SHE WAITS FOR THE CHILD TO APPEAR,
TO MEET ON A HILL TURNED BLACK,
FOR DARKNESS IS SPREADING, STIRRING SO NEAR –
AND THE MURMUR IS STARTING TO CRACK.

FOLLOW THE PATH, PAST THE BOG-MYRTLE PONDS
WHERE THE NESTS OF THE WARBLERS LIE,
AND FURTHER ON, PAST DEWY BRACKEN FRONDS,
SEEK THE SHIVERING NIGHTJAR'S CRY.'

Moll scanned the words again. The dew, the hill, the maiden. It was all there, just as her pa's bone reading had said. And this maiden, whoever she was, was calling for 'the child to appear'. It had to be about her.

Alfie looked at Moll, wide-eyed. 'This maiden's living out in a hovel on the heath, among the heather and the gorse! And that child is you. She's waiting for *you*, isn't she? She left a poem that links with your bone reading so as you'd find it and seek her out!'

Moll's face paled. She had to tell Alfie. 'Hard-Times Bob, one of the Elders in our camp, used to tell us stories about a maiden out on the heath who gnawed on children's bones.'

Alfie smirked. 'And you believed him!'

Moll was silent for a second, then she waved her hand airily. 'Course not,' she scoffed. 'I kept telling my pal, Siddy, that there was no such person.' But shivers were crawling down Moll's back now. The poem and the bone reading were telling her to walk straight into the hands of the maiden she'd grown up fearing. Moll thought of Siddy and wished he was with her; he'd have said something to chase away the fear. She thought of him struggling against his ropes by the river. Surely the camp would have found him by now?

Alfie looked back at the roll of leather. 'You think this maiden knows where the amulets are hidden?' he asked.

Moll tried to pull herself together. 'Perhaps.' She paused. 'I've never been out to the heath. How far is it?'

'South from here for about two miles. It's just past the edge of the Deepwood.'

Moll squinted at the poem, then she blinked several times. She peered closer. She could have *sworn* that some of the letters looked different somehow – just for a second – as if perhaps there was another message hidden inside the poem. She frowned at the leather, but the poem stared blankly back, every letter just the same as before.

Alfie hadn't noticed and he turned to Moll. 'Who in their right mind would live in a hovel out on the heath?'

A bone-chewing psychopath, that's who, Moll thought. But she said nothing.

Alfie shrugged. 'I suppose it doesn't really matter who this maiden is. We've just got to trust the poem and follow it.'

Moll was silent for several seconds. 'What if it's a trap?'

'But there are the bones I found in your talisman: *Dew Hill Maiden*. Who read them? Because it's all there in your poem.'

Moll shifted her weight. 'My pa. He was the Guardian of the Oracle Bones.' Her jaw stiffened. 'Along with my ma before Skull killed them.'

Alfie gave a whistle. 'You're in this thick and fast then, aren't you?'

Moll nodded grimly.

A crow landed on the top of the cage and Moll was almost glad of its company, then it ruffled its feathers and took off into the pale sky. Moll's gaze fell on the feeble embers of the fire in the middle of the clearing. It was so different from the roaring flames in Oak's camp. She glanced at the grey trees craning over Skull's black wagon and thought of Gryff breaking through the vapours to find her, only to be torn away. Was he safe, she wondered? Would he even try coming back for her now he knew what lay in wait in the Deepwood?

Alfie looked at Moll. 'I didn't believe in the Bone Murmur for years – thought it was a load of old rubbish.' He paused. 'Then I saw your wildcat.'

Moll's stomach flipped.

'Something about the way he looked when he burst from the bank, like ... like he'd do anything to keep you safe. That's not normal. He's something, that wildcat.' Alfie turned his penknife in his hand, then his eyes sparkled. 'Maybe he'll help us find the amulets. Then we'll be rich and free.'

Moll could feel tears stinging the corners of her eyes.

'What's it like knowing a wild animal – one who hasn't been tamed by humans before?'

Moll swallowed. 'He's the closest thing I've got to family, aside from Oak and Mooshie.'

Alfie looked away. 'Wouldn't know. Haven't got a family.' He worked his knife over the ropes that bound Moll's wrists and they fell away. Then he knelt down before the padlock and, as the cage creaked and swayed, he looked up at Moll. 'Lucky for us, I might know a way to get out of this.'

Moll shoved the leather roll into the pocket of her dress and crouched before the lock. Then she jumped back from the bars. Dark shapes were crossing the clearing towards the cage. Could it be Oak and the others? Had they beaten their way past the hounds and come back for her after all? But as they grew closer, Moll realised the shadows weren't Oak and her friends; they weren't even people.

Far below Moll and Alfie, eyes burned into the early

morning light, wolfish and untamed, and jagged teeth shone, stained with blood. There were four of them and their muscles bulged out of their black coats as if they could barely contain their own strength. Chains still hung from their collars: even Skull's boys hadn't dared untie them. And they circled the cage, growling.

Brunt appeared through the watery sunlight, seizing the hounds by their chains, and Moll re-bound her wrists. He wrenched the catch on the rope that held the cage and it crashed down into the clearing. Moll was smashed against the side, her spine grating on the metal. Brunt thumped two bowls of lukewarm porridge through the bars.

Then the hounds stalked up close, their teeth like rows of broken glass, and Moll and Alfie cowered in the middle of the cage, their eyes glazed with fear.

Chapter 17
Dropping Secrets

'*I*gnore the hounds,' Alfie had said after they'd eaten the porridge Brunt had thrust in, '*and sleep as much as you can today; you'll need your strength to get past the vapours later.*'

But Alfie couldn't know what waited for Moll in the darkness of her dreams. The rattle and the drum prised their way in, beating inside her mind. And, when Moll awoke to the late afternoon sunshine searching for cracks through the withered trees, Skull was there, standing in the cage with them. His mask was absolutely still, his fingers laced beneath his chin. They hadn't heard or seen him unlock the cage; it was as if he'd slipped in like a shadow.

Moll shuffled backwards, pressing herself against the far end of the cage, next to Alfie. She could see Skull's pupils, and they were looking right at her. His feet were bare, cracked, beneath his dark robes and around his neck hung a fanged necklace. Moll knew the fangs, recognised their shape: adder fangs loaded with poison. She looked up at the grey eyes peering out from the sockets of the mask.

It's only a mask; it's only a mask . . . she said to herself.

'So *you're* the child from the Bone Murmur, the one who walks with the beast.' Skull's voice was a rasp, like a snake rattling deep within his throat. 'The one standing in my way.'

Moll clenched her teeth and leapt up, but Skull lunged forward and pinned her against the cage by her shoulders. Alfie shifted further away, his head bent low. Skull's eyes, lashless and pale, bored into Moll. She squirmed but the witch doctor only tightened his grasp.

'So *who* are you?' The eyes blinked once. 'You're a Pecksniff, your eyes say so – and we've got your talisman: MP.' He paused. 'What's your full name, child?'

Moll shook her head. 'My – my name's my own business, Sk-Skull.'

The mask hung before her, centimetres from her face. Then Skull seized her neck, holding it in an icy grip. 'Give up your name.'

Moll kept her lips tightly shut.

Raising his hand, Skull brought it down hard across Moll's cheek. Tears stung her eyes, but she didn't wince. He hit her again, harder this time, across the back of her head. And Alfie watched from the side of the cage, noticing that Moll didn't even move her hands to defend herself.

Skull stood back, a column of black. 'We're bringing you into the clearing soon because there's someone keen to see you – someone who's been searching the Deepwood for you just out of our reach.'

Moll's heart thumped.

A dark tongue flickered behind the bone teeth of Skull's mask. 'You'll call your wildcat close for us – Brunt'll see to that – and, once we've got you both, your pathetic Bone Murmur will be broken and a new power will emerge.'

Moll tucked Gryff's name into the deepest pocket of her mind, safe with her own. 'The wildcat isn't tame; he won't come when I call. It doesn't work like that.'

'Oh, he'll come when he sees what Brunt's got planned for you.'

Moll shook her head. 'Oak'll find the amulets before you lay a finger on me or my wildcat. You'll see.'

At the mention of the amulets, Skull's body stiffened. 'So you know about the amulets, do you?' His voice was sharp like a thorn's prick. And then he laughed. 'And Oak's got you thinking you're actually going to *find* them? Some tiny girl succeeding where all of your ancestors failed and your own pathetic parents couldn't see it through . . . ?'

Moll's fists were pumped with fury and she pushed forward. 'You leave my parents out of this! You don't know what you're talking about. And whatever you might've done to them I'll get you for it.'

But Skull's eyes had glassed over; he wasn't even listening. He was looking at Moll, carefully, quietly. He grabbed her chin in an iron claw and drew a deep breath in, as if he was drinking in Moll's fear. 'You know something – something about the amulets. I can feel it.'

122

'Only that we're going to find them before you get your hands on my wildcat!'

'You're lying to me; I can smell it.'

Skull slammed Moll's shoulder back against the cage. It clanged and she groaned as the impact shuddered through her. But now she knew that Skull cared about the amulets; they mattered to him as well.

'Wait.' Alfie stood up, his voice low and guarded, and Moll was suddenly glad that he was there. 'She's not telling the truth.'

Moll's breath caught in her throat. She looked at Alfie in disbelief and then a sinking feeling slid over her skin.

Skull released the pressure on Moll's shoulder and turned to Alfie. 'Well?'

Moll bit her lip. What was she *thinking* trusting a boy in Skull's gang? He'd probably been put in with her just to trick her into giving up information.

Alfie met Skull's glare with unreadable eyes. 'Her father left her a bone reading, a clue to the whereabouts of the amulets.'

Moll closed her eyes, willing Alfie's words to disappear. What had she done? She cursed under her breath and kicked the cage.

'Where is this bone reading?' Skull asked, clasping his hands.

Only then did Alfie look at Moll. 'In Oak's camp. He still has it. But she told me what it said. Stupid girl thought I was someone to be trusted – a way out of the Deepwood.'

Moll's heart was fluttering. What was he *doing*?

Alfie shrugged. 'I forced it out of her. Turns out I'm better at guarding little girls than you all thought.'

Skull blinked once, very slowly. 'What did the bone reading say?'

'SEEK VILLAGE BLACKSMITH. Might be nothing as she's the lying type, but she said it in her sleep too – like it was pressing on her mind.'

Moll couldn't believe what she was hearing. Alfie's face looked open and truthful and yet his lie was as thick as they come.

He picked at his nails. 'She isn't sure why the blacksmith's important, but it's a lead and one you'd best be knowing.'

Moll smirked inwardly. Clever Alfie. The village blacksmith lived in Tipplebury, which was north of the forest, and they needed to head south to get to the heath.

Brunt had appeared by the cage. On seeing him, Skull turned, unlocked the door and stepped out. His cloak twitched with excitement as he clicked the padlock shut.

'Hoist them up, Brunt; we've got a lead on the amulets. When night falls, Gobbler and I'll be off to the village.'

Brunt's enormous muscles worked the lever, lifting the cage back into the trees. 'Waiting for night,' he smirked. 'Sounds like you mean business.'

Skull's mask dipped, a smile perhaps, then he looked up at Alfie. 'I was thinking of letting you out, but you're doing well in there with *that*.' His eyes shifted inside the mask, drilling into Moll. 'Let's get one thing straight: Oak's given up on you; he isn't coming back.' And, with that, he stalked off.

'Why didn't you try to defend yourself when Skull hit you?' Alfie hissed.

Moll glanced at her wrists. 'Promised you I wouldn't let them see you'd cut the rope, didn't I?'

Alfie looked at her for a few seconds, then he shook his head. 'You're strange. Most people would've tried to shield themselves.'

Moll shrugged. 'Well, I'm not *most people*. And anyway it'd be a dull old world if everyone was the same.' She paused. 'Thanks. I mean, for the blacksmith stuff.'

Alfie half smiled and, to her surprise, Moll found herself smiling back. They watched Skull and Gobbler lead the hounds down into the pit, hurling slabs of meat inside to appease them.

Alfie turned to Moll. 'I think I can get us out of here, but you've got to trust me,' he whispered. 'I'm not going to cross you; I'm not going to give you away.'

And somehow Moll knew that was true. And she did trust him.

'And you,' she whispered, plucking at her dress, 'd'you trust me?'

'I'm not sure. You left me before . . .'

Moll looked him squarely in the eye; she had to show Alfie she trusted him if this was going to work.

'It's Moll,' she said quietly. 'My name's Moll.'

Alfie thought about it, then he nodded. 'As soon as Skull leaves, I'll get us out. He needs the darkness as much as we do.' He reached inside his pocket and drew out a long, thin bone. 'Rabbit bone – took it from the pit. And lucky for you there isn't a lock I can't pick.'

Moll grinned.

'The boys'll be drinking in the clearing tonight,' Alfie said. 'That's what they do when Skull goes off – that and the beatings, if they've drunk for too long . . .' He looked away. 'So this is our only chance. If we miss it, Skull will get you out into the clearing and—'

'—and make me call for Gryff?' she scoffed. 'Like he'd answer to a whistle or a call or something stupid like that.'

She froze. She'd let Gryff's name slip out into the open without a second thought.

Alfie sniffed. 'Gryff's a good name for a wildcat.'

Moll looked down at her feet, tears stinging at her eyes. 'I'm full of cracks,' she mumbled. 'None of them letting any light in – all of them dropping secrets out.' She kicked the cage.

'I won't go telling his name.' Alfie straightened himself up. 'But don't let it slip again. They've got ways – dark ways – of controlling people and animals when they know their names. You and Gryff need to keep your names safe.'

Moll nodded, shaking the ropes from her wrists.

But Alfie was looking at his feet, avoiding her eyes. 'If there's a chance anywhere in all of this – *if* we get out – I want to get Raven. He shouldn't be in with Skull's boys.'

Moll nodded. 'Can Raven really recognise himself in a mirror?'

Alfie nodded. 'And he knows good silver when he sees it.' He lifted up his hands; there were two spiked silver rings on his fingers. 'Raven's forever nibbling at my gypsy fighting rings.'

Except you're no gypsy, Moll thought to herself. But again she kept quiet. That could wait.

For now, they had to escape.

Chapter 18
Escape

Night fell fast. The flames of the campfire licked the sticks and the logs burned black like glowering eyes. After they'd eaten the watery gruel Brunt had thrust inside the cage, Moll and Alfie watched Skull and Gobbler, armed with pistols and knives, tear from the clearing. And before long, just as Alfie had said, Skull's boys began to drink around the fire.

Alfie nodded. 'Now's our chance.'

Reaching through the bars, he slotted the rabbit bone into the lock. He turned and twizzled it this way and that. Moll winced at its scratching, but Skull's boys wouldn't hear; they were drinking hard now, clattering mugs of beer together and trading dirty coins. Alfie fiddled on, twisting the bone at every angle, working the lock free.

Then just like that: *click*.

He pushed the door gently and it nudged open. Moll's heart leapt, but then she looked down. 'We'll never get past Brunt and the others – they'll see! And what about the vapours? I—'

All of a sudden there were shouts from the fire. Moll gripped Alfie's arm in horror.

'I can see it again!' Brunt was shouting. 'Over here, lads!' He leapt up from the fire and ran to the far end of the clearing, calling the other boys to him. They all peered into the trees.

Moll's heart hammered inside her. 'What are they looking for?'

But Alfie was grinning. 'I don't know, but it's going to give us a clear run. Go! Now!'

Moll twisted out of the cage, clinging to the bars then hauling herself up on to the roof. Her pulse raced in her throat as she scampered across the dome and leapt into the tree. Alfie followed. A magpie shuffled on a branch above them, staring down with beady eyes. Moll's heart rose; Mooshie had always said magpies brought good luck – and right now they needed it.

More commotion at the opposite side of the clearing: shouts, pointing, the boys edging further into the trees. Moll and Alfie were in with a fighting chance and they slipped from the tree down to the ground.

Alfie bit his lip. 'They've moved the cobs to the other side of the camp.'

'We're not going for Raven now,' Moll whispered. 'We'd risk everything. We'll come back after we find the amulets.' As soon as the words were out, she knew it was another promise she planned to snap.

Alfie nodded. 'Can you run?'

Moll shot him a scornful look. 'Can I run? I was born running.'

Like fleeting shadows, they sped between the trees, on and on, away from the clearing and towards the heath. And all around them the darkness grew as night deepened. Somewhere above the trees there might have been a moon, but the branches blocked the sky, warding off its light. Within seconds, vapours curled out of the shadows, a mist of faceless black. Moll's blood raced.

Alfie gripped her hand and yanked her on. 'Don't let them know you're scared!'

The vapours swam before them, whirling round their heads, moaning in their ears. Moll squeezed Alfie's hand as they swamped her face, plucking at her lips, snatching the air from her lungs. She closed her eyes and thought of Gryff and Siddy, of Mooshie and Oak.

And, when she opened her eyes, the vapours had shrunk back a little. They swelled together again, drawing close. But this time Moll thought of the Bone Murmur and her parents and, as she and Alfie bounded over fallen logs and stumps, the vapours faded once more.

'Keep going!' Alfie cried, letting Moll's hand go so that they could tear over the bracken and push past the low-hanging branches.

Moll dug deep inside herself. *Help us, wind spirits*, she pleaded.

Wind seemed to gust out of nowhere, drowning the moans of the vapours. Moll surged forward into its power, feeling her courage grow. The wind rushed round her, channelling through her hair, and, one by one, the vapours crumbled into trails of black thread. Moll and Alfie ran on, smiles spreading over their faces, until gradually the trees began to thin.

Alfie punched the air. 'We did it!'

Moll grinned and then, to her surprise, she found herself wishing her parents had been there to see her escape. She ran on. 'What's behind Skull's mask?' she panted. The question had lodged in her mind since she'd seen the witch doctor a few nights earlier. 'You ever seen his face?'

Alfie shook his head as he tore through a thicket of bracken. 'I don't think anyone has. Sometimes I think there's nothing behind it. Like there might've been something once, but it's rotted and died and now only the mask is left.'

Moll raced on, level with Alfie. 'There's something strange about him – something stranger than a witch doctor with a mask and an evil chant. Like he's not quite real, like he's a ghost almost.'

Alfie slowed down as he clambered over a fallen log and met her eyes. 'You're bright, brighter than I thought you'd be. There is something strange about Skull.' He shot Moll a glance. 'He hasn't got a shadow.'

Moll scrunched up her nose as she stopped to catch her breath. 'But everyone's got a shadow!'

'Skull hasn't. And don't ask me why. All I know is it isn't normal. It *means* something – only I'm not sure what.'

131

Almost without warning they stumbled out on to the open expanse of the heath. The landscape was bleak – a barren wasteland of heather, gorse and bracken – and it stretched out to the coast like a dark blanket under the night sky. Alfie drank it in, but Moll looked horrified.

She put a toe out into the heather and gasped. 'Where've all the trees gone? I'm not running out there in the open!'

'There aren't many trees on the heath,' Alfie panted. 'It's heather and gorse out here.'

Shoulders bunched up to her ears, Moll took a few steps forward. Her eyes widened. 'What's that great lump of water leading out to the edge of the world? Like the giantest puddle I've ever seen!'

'It's the sea!' exclaimed Alfie, looking at Moll as if she was mad.

The moon peeped out from behind a cloud and turned the surface of the sea to silver.

'The what?' she said.

Alfie rolled his eyes. 'You know – where boats and ships sail to other countries.'

Moll nodded. She had no idea what he was talking about, but she'd never have admitted it.

'And that's not the edge of the world either,' Alfie added.

'I know,' Moll replied. Then, under her breath, 'That definitely, absolutely is the edge of the world.' She opened the roll of leather. Moonlight shone on to it and she read aloud:

'MANY AND MANY A FOOTSTEP FROM YOU,
IN A HOVEL AMONG THE GORSE,
A WILD MAIDEN LIVES WHOM MOST ESCHEW,
BY MARSHLAND AND HEATHER GROWN COARSE...'

Moll's body tensed, partly because she knew the maiden might be close, partly because once again the letters in front of her seemed to quiver and swell. It was just certain ones, but before Moll could work out any sort of pattern the letters stilled and looked ordinary once more.

'The hovel will be further on,' Alfie said.

Moll nodded. '*Follow the path, past the bog-myrtle ponds ...*'

Alfie pointed to a sandy track just in front of them which led out over the heath. 'Let's take this path. It'll wind up at the marsh where the bog-myrtle ponds are.'

'Where we can start looking for—'

Something moved through the trees behind them. Something fast. Something strong.

'Run!'

Alfie yanked Moll on to the path and they hurtled down it. But the footsteps bounded closer, tearing up the sandy track behind them. Together they raced on, not daring to look back. And then Moll stopped dead and turned round.

'What are you doing?' Alfie yelled, spinning back to face her. But then he too stopped running.

A wildcat was standing right in front of them.

Chapter 19
A Hovel Among the Gorse

He'd come for her, even though she'd doubted him, and he was panting hard, his fur wet with sweat.

'Gryff,' she whispered.

Then came his greeting, low and soft. '*Brrrooooooo.*'

'You came for me,' Moll smiled.

The wildcat dipped his head but he kept his distance.

Moll looked back to the Deepwood. 'It – it was you who ran round the camp to distract Brunt and the others so we could escape, wasn't it?'

'*Noine, noine, noine.*' It was the sound Gryff made when he was content, like a purr but somehow wilder. His eyes flicked up to Alfie, then his hackles rose and he circled Moll.

'*Urrrrrrrrrrrrrrrrrr,*' Gryff growled, his eyes locked on to Alfie.

'He's all right, Gryff,' Moll whispered, crouching down. And then added quietly, 'We need him.'

Gryff tightened his circle and hissed.

'Your wildcat hates me,' Alfie mumbled, scuffing the track

with his boot, but he kept his eyes fixed on Gryff in case he pounced.

'Animals don't hate. Hate's what humans do. Gryff just isn't trusting you yet.'

Alfie took a deep breath and moved a step closer; the wildcat bared his teeth and growled.

Still huddled low, Moll locked eyes with Gryff. *Trust me. Alfie's all right. He won't charge us on his cob again.*

'Last thing a wildcat wants to do is touch you,' she said quietly to Alfie. 'So you don't need to worry.'

Gryff tucked his head under Moll's arm and nuzzled into her chest. Moll reddened. 'Well, Gryff is – he's – he's different somehow. He doesn't seem to mind touching as much as maybe some of the other ones might.'

Alfie looked back at the Deepwood. 'They'll let the hounds out when they see we've gone.'

Darkness hid the dips and rabbit holes puncturing the path, but they ran on despite them, Alfie keeping a safe distance ahead of Gryff and Moll. The heather petered out around them until only rushes, reeds and yellow gorse bushes lined their path.

'There,' Alfie panted. A huddle of wild ponies was drinking from a boggy marsh set back from the path. 'The bog-myrtle ponds – like the poem said!'

The ponies trotted away as Alfie, Moll and Gryff sped past. There were bogs all around the path now – black water surrounded by green bushes and rushes. Moll breathed in the herb-pine smell of the bog myrtle. They were getting close.

'Listen!' Moll gasped.

A bird call rattled out across the night sky, but Moll had traced the opening notes of its song and she stopped on the track, pointing to a thicket of reeds lining a bog to the left of the track. She bent down, pulled away the reeds, and sure enough, there was a bird's nest tucked inside.

'*Follow the path, past the bog-myrtle ponds where the nests of the warblers lie ...*' she whispered excitedly.

They took a few more steps. Bracken rose up between spiky gorse bushes on either side of them. Then the path began to narrow and the bracken rose higher still.

It was Gryff who started running first. They were almost there and he could feel it. Alfie and Moll followed, their ears filled with the rolling cries of the nightjars. Alfie grinned at Moll as they ran.

The path had almost disappeared, but still Gryff ran on. Bracken fronds swung back into Moll's face as Alfie charged ahead of her and gorse needles pricked at her bare feet. And, though nobody mentioned it, it was darker now. Much darker. Even the moon had been swallowed by the blackness.

And then suddenly Gryff stopped. He turned to face them, his eyes sparkling green against the night.

There was a reason for the impenetrable darkness and the absence of the moon. Rearing up in front of them, its base jungled by bracken and gorse, was a hill. It was blacker than the night itself and, behind it, bushes spread into trees which thickened into a small patch of woodland.

'*To meet on a hill turned back*,' Moll whispered. Her heart drummed as Hard-Times Bob's stories whirled inside her head. She stooped and picked up a stick lying by a gorse bush.

Alfie turned to her. 'What's that for?'

Moll shrugged. 'This and that.'

He grinned. 'It's for the maiden, isn't it?'

Moll scowled and they took a few steps closer to the hill.

'It's covered in black flowers ...' Alfie murmured.

Moll gripped her stick more tightly. She knew what black flowers meant.

Alfie glanced at her. 'What is it?'

Moll shifted her weight from one foot to the other. 'There aren't any black flowers in the Ancientwood, but Mooshie told me about them.' She paused. 'Black flowers mean trickery.' Her legs felt suddenly numb beneath her.

Alfie glanced at the forest, then back again at the hill. 'I'm not going up there if this is a trick.'

But Gryff had already set off.

Alfie stared at him. 'What's he *doing*?'

Moll was silent for a few seconds. 'Trampling all over trickery, I suppose.'

Alfie fiddled with his feather earring. 'And we're meant to follow?'

Moll summoned up a pretence of bravery. 'I don't like the sound of tricks out here on the heath, but my pa's bone reading matches the poem – and Gryff's never wrong.'

And, with that, Moll turned to follow the wildcat. She

gulped and then gave the darkness a crazed look of terror. It was all very well pretending to be brave, but her legs were shaking and her heart was thudding inside her frock. She made a few more demented grimaces into the darkness, then hurried on after the wildcat.

Black flowers covered the whole hill, crawling over it like a giant net spun from the night itself. And the closer they got to the summit, the more the flowers changed. They seemed to be getting bigger, taller, thicker, and they twisted into the night around them like crooked walking sticks. The flowers were taller than Moll now, with stems coated in fur. Pushing them aside, the three of them forced their way on. Gorse bushes unravelled in front of them and, together with the flowers, they almost completely obscured the run-down building that they were hiding. But Moll, Alfie and Gryff could see, huddled in darkness on the highest point of the heath, a small wooden hut: the maiden's hovel.

Its slats had been arranged any old how and the whole thing appeared to lean ever so slightly to the left. Black flowers and giant weeds crawled up its sides and across the windows like dead hair, barring the inside from view. The only sign that hinted of anything living inside the hovel was the light that crept out from beneath the door.

Alfie glanced down at the leather in Moll's hand, the words now visible in the gloomy light. His eyes widened and he clutched Moll's wrist.

'The – the letters – some of them look different!'

Moll looked down and then her face drained of colour.

Certain letters were quivering in the leather again, bolder, even darker than the rest. Only this time Moll could make out the word they so clearly spelt.

MANY AND MANY A FOOTSTEP FROM YOU,
IN A HOVEL AMONG THE GORSE,
A **W**ILD MAIDEN L**I**VES WHOM MOS**T** ESCHEW,
BY MARSHLAND AND HEATHER GROWN COARSE.

THIS MAIDEN SHE WAITS FOR THE **C**HILD TO APPEAR,
TO MEET ON A HILL TURNED BLACK,
FOR **D**ARKNESS IS SPREADING, STIRRING S**O** NEAR –
AND THE MURMUR IS STARTING TO **C**RACK.

FOLLOW THE PA**T**H, PAST THE BOG-MYRTLE PONDS
WHERE THE NESTS OF THE WARBLERS LIE,
AND FURTHER **O**N, PAST DEWY BRACKEN FRONDS,
SEEK THE SHIVERING NIGHTJAR'S C**R**Y.

Moll gasped: 'W-I-T-C-H-D-O-C-T-O-R! That's who this maiden is! But – but . . .' Her heart pounded faster. 'Why would my pa's clue lead us straight into the hands of a witch doctor?'

Gryff's ears swivelled towards the hovel.

Moll could taste her fear. Perhaps the witch doctor would have a spinning head with rolling eyes. Or a rolling head with spinning eyes. Or – or . . . She brandished her stick in front of her.

139

Gryff was prowling towards the door now. He turned to them and grunted.

Alfie looked at Moll. 'What's he saying?'

She thought of the camp, all safe in the clearing, of Mooshie cuddling her close. 'He says there are no such things as the amulets, there isn't anything in the hovel and we should head back to the Ancientwood right this minute.'

Gryff stalked towards Moll, his head held high. And then he nipped her on the hand. Moll winced.

Alfie looked at Gryff. 'He says we got to go in, right?'

Moll rubbed her hand. 'Perhaps.'

'You afeared?' he asked.

She beat back the image of a witch doctor who now had two bulging heads and eight eyes on the ends of rods. 'Nah. You?'

'Nah.'

But Moll's breaths were shaking and Alfie's eyes were wide.

Gryff was prowling by the door again, but Alfie hung back with Moll. 'We could send him in to meet the witch doctor first. They might get along all right . . .'

Gryff turned to Alfie, then he twitched his whiskers, his eyes narrow slits.

'He's – he's glaring at me,' Alfie stammered. 'He looks cross.'

Moll shook her head. 'He isn't cross,' she whispered. 'He's wild and wild things don't look cheery the whole time. Especially not when they're about to go breaking into a witch doctor's hovel.'

'You think there's *really* a witch doctor in there?' Alfie whispered. 'Looks more like an old sheep hut than a den of dark magic.'

Summoning all of her courage, her stick held high, Moll took a step up to the door. It was slightly ajar, like a mouth beginning to draw air, and there was absolute silence, save for the plop of a toad slipping into a bog somewhere below them. Palms sweating, Moll placed a hand on the door and pushed it open.

She wasn't expecting much: a few rusted pots, perhaps a weather-beaten table. But what met her eyes was altogether different. The hovel was bigger than she had expected and it was filled with a clutter of seemingly abandoned objects: a broken chair, dusty boxes, long-forgotten rags.

But among the chaos there was an eerie sense of order. Carefully arranged on to scooped-out pieces of bark that lined the collapsing shelves to the sides of the hovel were tiny animal bones, shimmering feathers, adder skins, owl pellets, spotted eggshells, unusual ferns and sharpened stones. It was as if the most intimate belongings of the heath and the forest had been stolen away and hidden inside the hovel.

On a rickety table beneath the window was a patch of reddish animal fur – a fox perhaps – and on it lay a rattle carved from walnut. Moll shivered. It had been decorated with black swirls of paint and the handle was tipped with bone.

Only then did Moll and Alfie pick up on Gryff's

movements. His tail was flat to the ground, his ears cocked and his eyes fixed ahead.

Alfie seized Moll by the arm and the hairs on her body froze. Hunched into a rocking chair in the far corner of the hut, almost completely obscured by rags, was a very old woman. Her skin was grey and crumpled and in many ways she looked just like another forgotten object in the hovel. But her eyes were open and shining blackly.

Chapter 20
The Others

The old woman stared at Moll, motionless and silent. She had a face of sagging skin, like the gnarled bark of an ancient tree, and long grey hair hung from her scalp in wiry strands.

Moll's stick trembled in her hand. 'Do – d'you think she's dead?'

Alfie shook his head. 'She's breathing – look.'

Sure enough there was a tremor of life inside the rags.

'She's sleeping with her eyes open?' Moll whispered, aghast.

'Maybe that's what witch doctors do.'

'You think *that's* a witch doctor?' Moll squinted at the old woman. 'The maiden who can tell us where the amulets are?' She didn't look like the monster from Hard-Times Bob's stories.

Still the old woman stared ahead: reptilian eyes, hooded by wrinkles, burning into empty space.

'But she hasn't got a mask,' Moll muttered. 'And she looks all bent and spindly to me. Like she's been beaten by winds too much – or – or drowned in a bog for longer than was good for her.'

Alfie gasped. 'She's got a black mark on her forehead – like a smudge of soot.' He took a step backwards. 'Looks like witch doctor stuff to me.'

Moll glanced up and down the shelves for boiled eyeballs or half-chewed bones, but there were none.

Gryff snarled. And then, all of a sudden, the reptilian eyes blinked. Moll clutched her dress.

'What do you want?' a prickly voice asked.

Alfie, Moll and Gryff stood rooted to the spot.

The words sounded rusty, as if they'd been locked inside the old woman for far too long. But her eyes never moved. Black flints, they bored into Moll.

Moll clenched her fists into balls, forcing back memories of Hard-Times Bob's stories. Then she took a step forward.

'Are – are you the maiden?' she stammered, her knuckles white as they gripped the stick. She rummaged in her pocket with her other hand and brought out the roll of leather. 'Was it you who left this poem for me back at Oak's camp?'

The old woman's eyes narrowed. 'Depends …' she muttered.

Moll's fists tightened even more. 'Depends on what?'

'Depends on *who* you are.'

Without warning, Gryff leapt forward. Hissing, he pounded his forelimbs on to the floorboards. Dust puffed upwards and, for the first time, the old woman dropped her gaze. Her eyes locked on to Gryff.

'It – it can't be,' she whispered. 'The beast *from lands full wild . . .*' Then she looked at Moll. *'You're* the child from the Bone Murmur?'

A wheeze rattled through her body, chasing away her voice. Gryff took a step backwards and circled Moll, growling. The old woman watched for several seconds, then hung her head and rocked it in her hands. They were black, claw-like hands with shrivelled fingers, as if her skin was made of scales. Within seconds, she was shaking out whimpered sobs.

Moll shot a confused glance at Alfie.

He scowled. 'You and Gryff have been in the hut for less than five minutes and you've gone and made the witch doctor cry.'

'How was Gryff supposed to know she'd be afeared of him?' Moll hissed. 'He's gentle enough.'

Gryff pounded the floorboards again, spitting and snarling. But, when the old woman raised her face, it told a different story. Her eyes were shining and her clawed hands twitched with excitement. She had been *laughing*, not crying.

'There's hope,' she whispered excitedly. 'There's hope left after all.'

She tried to get up, but her strength failed her and she slumped back into the rocking chair. Gryff paced back and forth in front of Moll and Alfie, his eyes narrowed cracks.

Moll nodded to Gryff. 'He wants to know if you're a witch doctor who's out to trick us – a crook like that maggot-breathing Skull. Because we're not trusting anybody unless we're sure of them. Isn't that right, Alfie?' She paused, waiting for Alfie to nod. He looked at Moll, lost for words. 'Alfie here would chop off your head with his penknife if you messed with us, wouldn't you, Alfie?'

Alfie fumbled for his blunt penknife, then shifted on his feet. 'I—'

'So.' Moll drew herself up. 'What we want to know is: how bad a witch doctor are you? Mostly bad or proper rotten to the core?'

The old woman smiled and the skin on her neck clung to her throat in a hollowed scoop. She looked Moll up and down. 'Funny the type of people called to do big things, isn't it, Molly?'

Moll stiffened. It was the first time she'd heard her name spoken by someone else since she'd left the Ancientwood. Even Alfie hadn't dared to use it. Gryff raised his hackles.

'Who *are* you?' Alfie said.

The old woman leant forward. 'Maybe I am a witch doctor,' she said quietly, her voice like the rustle of dead leaves, 'but I don't practise dark magic. All I've got are cures and remedies for those who pass my way.' She glanced at the shelves of berries, feathers, leaves, owl pellets and snakeskins. 'Bilberries to fight eye infections and cramps, dandelions to cure kidney disease, hawthorn for heart problems.' She licked her cracked lips. 'Maybe I do mix my cures up with spells, incantations – and magic.' Her eyes shone and Moll took a tiny step backwards. 'But that doesn't mean I'm rotten to the core.'

The witch doctor grappled for the arms of her rocking chair and managed to raise her bunched body upright. She leant forward, her bones groaning with the strain. Beneath her skirt, Moll could see her knobbly ankles, purple and spotted with age.

'I believe in the Bone Murmur, see – the one read years ago in the Oracle Bones. And I want to stand up against those bent on destroying it.'

Gryff was no longer growling. He had sidled up beside Moll – watching, waiting, guarding against the slightest danger.

'How do you know me?' Moll asked suspiciously.

'I knew your parents.'

Moll stiffened.

'I went to them just days before they . . . before they died. Because I knew things – things they needed to know.'

Alfie grunted. 'Didn't help them, did it?'

'They wouldn't listen,' the witch doctor said sadly. 'I told them I could help unravel what their bone reading meant if only they would let me see it. But, when your parents saw the mark on my forehead, they knew enough of Skull's dark magic to know it was a witch doctor's curse. And they assumed I was mixed up with Skull so they didn't want anything to do with me.'

Moll hardened her glare, but her heart was thudding. Hard-Times Bob had invented the stories about a maiden on a hill because he'd seen her pa's bone reading and then been warned by her parents not to trust the witch doctor out on the heath. And yet here Moll was, miles from Oak's clearing, in the witch doctor's hut, because, unlike her parents and all of the Elders, she'd followed the bone reading and trusted the poem.

The old woman took a step closer to Moll. 'But I swore to myself that I'd look out for you as I knew one day you would become the Guardian of the Oracle Bones.'

Moll scoffed. 'I'm able to look out for myself. I've had to. I'm nippy and meddling. No one as old as you could look out for me.'

The witch doctor smiled. 'I wrote you that poem calling you out to the heath.' She paused. 'Sometimes it's the people we don't expect who wind up looking out for us.' She shook her head. 'I knew Skull once – I knew them all. But, when I found out what they planned to do, I—'

Alfie frowned. 'You knew Gobbler – and Brunt and the boys?'

The witch doctor looked surprised. 'No. I knew *the others*.'

An icy finger slid its way down Moll's spine. No one said anything.

The witch doctor's eyes widened. 'You don't know, do you?'

Alfie and Moll remained silent. Gryff's ears flattened to his head.

The witch doctor gasped. 'You think it's just Skull who's after you and your wildcat?'

Alfie and Moll stared at her blankly.

A look of horror washed over the old woman's face. 'I

thought you *knew* ...' She shook her head for several seconds, then she hobbled still closer to them and said in a low voice, 'Listen, child, and listen well. There are seven powerful witch doctors in our country – known for their powers to cure people with leaves, ferns, flowers. Once that was all they did. Then, ten years ago, in the dead of winter, they gathered in Tanglefern Forest.'

Moll listened in silence. Ten years ago. The year her parents had died.

'And you,' Alfie said slowly. 'Were you there? Are you one of the seven powerful witch doctors?'

The old woman nodded. 'I'd lived in Tanglefern Forest all my life, not far from your Sacred Oaks, and it was inside my hut that the witch doctors gathered. At first, it was nothing – just talk of the ancient magic they'd heard had settled here in the beginning of time.' She looked down. 'And then things started to change. The talk became darker, deeper – and I backed away. I told them I didn't want to be a part of it. But it was as if something had got hold of them and all that mattered was destroying the Bone Murmur and setting the dark magic free.'

A rattling wheeze frothed up inside the witch doctor and she coughed.

'The others turned on me. They said I knew too much, that I'd stand in their way.' She tucked her clawed hands beneath her rags. 'And then they – they burned my hands ...'

Moll recoiled in horror. 'Why your hands?'

149

'A witch doctor's hands are their tools. We can shape spells with them and twist incantations between the tips of our fingers.'

Moll shivered as she remembered Skull crushing the wax figure between his fingers.

The witch doctor looked round her hut. 'They burned my hut and all my belongings, then they outlawed me to the heath and told me they'd kill me if I ever returned to the forest.'

'Only you *did* return,' Alfie added. 'To speak to her parents?' he asked, nodding at Moll.

'Yes, but it didn't help. Their curse was too strong and it blinded your parents to the truth – that I was only trying to help them unravel the bone reading so they could find the amulets.'

Moll's stomach was a churning pit. 'Why didn't you tell my parents about the other witch doctors? Maybe it could've saved them if they'd known!'

The old woman shook her head. 'Oh, I tried. But, when a witch doctor curses you, that curse follows you wherever you go, undoing any goodness you might try to do.'

Alfie gasped. 'Is that why the letters of your poem spelt out *witch doctor*? Because Skull's curse is following you?'

The old woman nodded grimly. 'It must've seeped into my words. And, if I give up all the witch doctors' names, the curse will kill me – it'll eat me alive.' She raised her eyebrows. 'You don't know who you're dealing with.'

'They killed my parents, didn't they?' Moll said, avoiding

the old woman's eye. 'It wasn't just Skull; he was with the five others.' She thought back to her nightmare. It was starting to make sense now. The masked figures weren't Skull's gang – his boys didn't wear masks – they were the *other* witch doctors. Moll looked up. 'You know what happened to my parents, don't you?'

'You're just a child. I can't tell a child about magic this dark.'

'But—'

'I won't do it. Nothing would make me.'

Alfie took a step towards her. 'Tell us the names of the others. You could burn them into the leather, like you did with your poem.'

The witch doctor was silent for several seconds. 'You've got courage, young man – and you're going to need it.' She tore a scrap from her rags. 'I can't tell you their names because I won't give myself up to their curse. But I can tell you one thing and, if you're wise enough later, it might help you. Pass me the ink and quill.'

Moll watched as the witch doctor's shrivelled hand wrapped itself round the quill. A single word was taking shape. Seconds later, it was complete:

SHADOWMASKS

The old woman underlined the first six letters. 'SHADOW: six letters, six witch doctors, six masks. They became the Shadowmasks after I left them ten years ago.'

Moll's eyes widened and she turned to Alfie. 'Skull hasn't got a shadow.'

The old woman was silent, her eyes darting to the window then the door, as if she was afraid of being overheard. 'When the six gathered in Tanglefern Forest ten years ago, they performed a hex full of darkness and evil.' She paused. 'They tore away their shadows.'

Moll's eyes were wide. 'What! How's that *possible*? And – and why?'

The witch doctor shook her head. 'I've said too much. And you'll learn soon enough.' Then she picked up the rag and added, 'Keep this safe. You'll need it to understand things later because, although it's only Skull now, they will all come and you're the only one who can stop them, Molly. You and your wildcat.'

'And Alfie,' Moll added, looking at the boy.

The witch doctor looked a little surprised and then nodded. 'Perhaps.'

Chapter 21
Spells and Incantations

'Both my parents threw the Oracle Bones before they died,' Moll said slowly. 'No one knows what my ma saw, but my pa read out a message, a clue.' She willed her words on. Even though her parents hadn't trusted the witch doctor, somehow Moll did. 'If we show you, can you help us make sense of it?'

The old woman blinked, hooded eyes closing over purple shadows. 'We'll see.' She looked Moll up and down. 'But you'll have to put that stick down.'

'It was Alfie's idea,' Moll mumbled as she propped it against the wall of the hut.

Alfie glowered at Moll, then reached into his pocket and held out the bone fragments:

DEW HILL MAIDEN

The witch doctor said nothing, but Moll could almost feel her thoughts whirring in tight circles. The clue had meant something to the old woman; that much was sure.

'So can you help us?' Moll asked. 'Because we haven't got much time.'

The witch doctor shook her head, 'Neither have I . . .'

She looked up, as if waking from a heavy thought, and then she smiled, the sad smile of someone who has seen too much of the world and is ready to depart it. She took the bones from Alfie in her withered, shaking hand then, for a moment, her eyes danced.

'There's another message within this.'

Moll glanced at Alfie who grinned. Then Gryff padded over to the door. At the threshold, he turned back and met Moll's eyes.

'He's going to keep guard outside the hut,' Moll said. 'He'll warn us if anything's coming.' She followed him to the door. 'Stay close,' she whispered and Gryff dipped his head before slinking into the darkness.

'The pestle and mortar by the fox fur, Alfie,' the witch doctor wheezed, pointing the blackened stump of a finger towards the table. 'Pass them to me.'

Then she hobbled to the shelves at the side of the hut. Her clawed hands, more wrinkled than raisins, fumbled with the contents of a scooped-out piece of bark. She came back to the table with a fistful of yellow and pink flowers.

'Gorse and heather,' she muttered and lifted a jar down from the shelves; it was filled with hollowed-out eggs: green and speckled. She took one out, crushed the shell in her palm and let the pieces patter into the mortar.

'Warbler's egg,' she muttered. She took a brown feather

from a jam jar and used her knuckles to strip the vanes from the shaft. 'Belonged to a nightjar once.'

Moll raised her eyebrows. 'How's all this going to help?'

'Never underestimate the power of a bird, Molly. In a bird, we see our soul set free.'

Moll thought of Rocky Jo, the murderous highwayman cockerel back in Oak's camp. She felt certain her soul hadn't been set free inside him. She pictured Siddy taking a swing at the cockerel and hoped harder than ever that Oak had rescued her friend from the river.

The witch doctor hobbled closer. 'In my mind, the Bone Murmur's about freedom. Freedom from *the others*. And I'm looking to these birds for help.' She ground everything together with the pestle. 'Now the phial – on the second shelf, Molly.'

The phial was filled with black liquid. It felt cold in Moll's hands and she was glad to hand it over. When the old woman shook it, black petals swayed inside the glass.

'Mellanthas – soaked in bog water.'

Moll turned up her nose.

The witch doctor smiled. 'You want the truth?'

Moll nodded. She wanted it more than anything; it would be one step closer to avenging her parents.

The witch doctor poured the black liquid into the mortar. 'Well, the truth isn't always pretty.'

'The flowers inside the liquid ...' Alfie murmured. 'They're the ones leading up to your house, aren't they?'

The witch doctor nodded. 'Mellanthas are rare flowers. Not always pretty and known by most as standing for trickery. But they're loyal, always flowering at the same time every year.' She looked at Moll. 'You knew the flowers stood for trickery, didn't you?'

Moll nodded.

'Yet you still came, though your parents and your camp didn't believe me. That's something – trusting and hoping, despite what other people say. It's a good sign, Molly.'

'Mmmmmmn,' Moll mumbled. She wanted to tell the witch doctor that it had been Gryff who'd led them up to the hovel while she had been thinking about spinning heads and rolling eyes.

The old woman looked at the black flowers settling on the surface of the liquid. 'Some say a name chooses you,' she whispered. 'And I came to be known after these black flowers. Mellantha.'

Moll wasn't sure how to respond to this so she clicked her tongue and focused on the mortar.

Mellantha reached towards a row of jars on the shelf. 'No, not bat spleens . . .' she muttered to herself. 'And not toad tongues this time.' She lifted a jar of jellied eyeballs up. 'Hmmmmmn . . . Perhaps not eels' eyes . . .' She picked up another jar. 'Of course, of course . . .'

Moll grimaced at the contents of the jar: a small, dead reptile floating in liquid.

Mellantha passed it to Alfie who winced but unscrewed the lid nonetheless.

'We need the tail of a newt,' she said, 'because newts are special creatures.'

'Why?' Alfie asked.

'If they lose a limb, they can grow another. One of nature's miracles.' Mellantha sliced off the tail with a knife. 'And we need a miracle right now.'

'Don't believe in miracles,' Alfie mumbled.

'Yet you believe in magic,' Mellantha said quietly.

'And what I've seen of that isn't pretty.'

'How can you live in a forest and not believe in the glittering magic of it all?' Mellantha whispered.

Alfie looked to Moll for support. But she only shrugged. 'Haven't you heard the tree spirits whisper? And the wind – it helped us escape the vapours! That's proper magic. The drums and chants and pits in the ground that Skull calls magic is just a rotten copy of the real stuff.'

She peered into the bowl. The liquid was a swirl of black, purple and yellow, like marbled dyes mixing together, and the ground-up egg and feather floated on the surface.

'We're nearly there,' Mellantha said.

She picked up the bones from the table and placed them in the bowl. They bobbed on the surface of the multi-coloured mixture, the words staring blankly up at them. Alfie and Moll watched for several seconds.

'Nothing's happening,' Alfie mumbled as Moll glowered at the bones.

'Wait,' said Mellantha.

She picked up a rattle and closed her eyes. And then, into

the silence, she shook the rattle again and again. Each thrust sounded like a gust of wind rushing through the trees. Moll's breath caught in her throat. The last rattle she'd heard had been from Skull's Dream Snatch. She swallowed. This was different, she told herself. It *had* to be ...

And then, very quietly, Mellantha began to whisper strange words under her breath: they seemed to start from the very back of her throat, deep and guttural, and then finish in soft swishing sounds. Moll had never heard anything like it before. It wasn't like the Dream Snatch. It was different somehow and she wasn't afraid.

Then something extraordinary happened. The bones started to judder, as if brushed by an invisible wind, and, almost so slowly that it seemed as if it wasn't happening at all, they started to break.

'Look!' Moll whispered, clasping her mouth.

As they watched, the bones broke into tiny pieces, each carrying a single letter from the original words. The letters bobbed on the surface of the mixture until the bones no longer spelt *Dew Hill Maiden*, but were a jumble of meaningless letters.

Mellantha struggled across to the window and nudged it open. She pushed her clawed hands through, bending them, twisting them, curling them into the night. Moll remembered her words: *a witch doctor's hands are their tools.* And suddenly Mellantha's didn't look ugly any more – they were almost beautiful as they shaped the incantation. A silken breeze floated through the window and it seemed to come in a whisper of sparkling black dust, as if Mellantha had called the very essence of night itself into her hovel.

And, before their eyes, the letters in the bowl began to move. They clicked against each other, almost dancing on the surface of coloured swirls. Moll's eyes widened as she watched the letters rearrange themselves into four recognisable words:

I AM WELL HIDDEN

No one said anything and then Alfie shook his head. 'But – but that's not any clearer. It's another riddle!' He kicked the leg of the table. 'We're still no closer to the amulets!'

Mellantha had closed her eyes and was whispering under her breath. 'Keep waiting,' she said quietly. 'It's not over yet.'

She shook the rattle one more time, then the moon peeped out from the clouds, falling like a spotlight on one of the words:

WELL

The letters jiggled before them.

And then Alfie gasped. 'It *is* a riddle; the Oracle Bones are playing with the words! I am *well* hidden … Are the amulets hidden *inside* a well? Is there a well in Tanglefern Forest?'

Moll looked blank but Mellantha nodded. 'In the heart of the forest—'

Gryff burst into the hovel, his ears flattened to his head. '*Urrrrrrrrrrrr.*'

Moll hurried to the door and peered out. 'There's nothing there.'

Gryff began to growl and hiss and stamp.

'What is it, Gr—' Moll started.

A blood-curdling howl split her words. A few seconds went by and then another howl followed, its call swelling in the marrow of their bones.

The hounds were coming for them.

Chapter 22
Snapping at Heels

'They'll find you if you stay here! They know where I live!' Mellantha wheezed, hobbling over to the door and bolting it fast.

Moll looked down at the bowl and noticed that the bone fragments were now nowhere to be seen.

'Pull back the crates on the far wall. The slats of wood behind are broken and you can crawl out through the gorse bushes and trees behind the hut! They'll hide you until you reach the bottom of the hill.' Mellantha gripped Moll's hand. 'And then run – run like the wind! You're the only person who can stop the madness of the Shadowmasks!'

The howls were louder now, slicing the night to slivers. Moll could feel her body shaking as she and Alfie grappled with the wood, tearing it back to reveal a hole.

Mellantha seized another tiny phial of black liquid from a shelf. 'T-take this,' she stammered, thrusting it into Moll's hands. 'You'll need it when they're fighting for your mind. There's still so much you should know.' She pointed to the rag she'd given Moll earlier. 'But there's no time now. Think about the letters, the word. It's all there.' Her eyes were half crazed with fear. 'Go – go!' she cried, pushing Moll towards the hole.

There was a pummelling at the door as the hounds drummed against it with ominous thuds.

'But you – aren't you—' Moll began.

Mellantha shook her head. 'It was written in the Oracle Bones; I knew when I saw your pa's bone reading. In my dreams, I see a place where one day I'll rest from all this pain. The place is on a hill, Molly – only it's bigger, taller and safer than my one here and it's not covered in darkness; it's covered in glittering dew. DEW HILL MAIDEN: the Oracle Bones have come to take me home.'

'No!' Moll cried. 'We didn't know!'

More thuds crashed against the hovel door.

'It's time, Molly, and I've outlived their curse at least.' Mellantha smiled sadly. 'Hounds, you say? I can bear that pain more than being haunted by the dark magic of the others.'

Alfie seized Moll's arm and dragged her towards the hole. 'Come on!'

But it was Gryff who finally tore her away, wrenching at her dress with his teeth. They pushed through the hole, into the undergrowth, a tangle of mellanthas, brambles and overgrown gorse. The sun was rising above the horizon on the sea and a wind had gathered, rushing across the heath below them like a tormented breath. Above them clouds loomed, swelling across the unsettled sky. Heads down, the two

162

children raced through the undergrowth, blind to the gorse bushes tearing at their skin.

There was a loud thud behind them and then the hovel was a frenzy of noise: crashing objects, gnashing teeth and Mellantha's whimpered cries. The wind moaned with Mellantha in desolate gusts, but soon her cries were drowned and once again the hounds wailed.

And then suddenly their cries subsided and a voice pierced the groaning wind. 'There's a hole at the back,' came Gobbler's unmistakable snarl.

As if in response, the hounds growled together, then pounding feet thundered into the undergrowth behind Moll, Gryff and Alfie.

'They're getting closer!' Moll cried, her eyes wide with terror.

The wind raged on, whipping their hair from their faces and gusting through the gorse. At last, the undergrowth and trees pulled back to reveal a ragged track across the heath. Boggy marshes swamped the track, but the three of them charged on through, water spraying their faces. Moll could feel the wind spirit's strength, urging them on, away from the hounds.

Alfie seized Moll's wrist. 'Faster! We can make the forest, we can make it!'

The wind grew wilder, catching their heels and whirling them on. They could see the trees now, green giants rearing up before them. Gryff pounded on beside Moll, never breaking from her for an instant.

Another voice came from behind, calling into the darkness – cold and hollow. 'Keep the hounds on her scent, Gobbler!'

Skull.

Moll threw a glance over her shoulder and what met her eyes chilled her. Some way behind them on the track, four huge hounds were craning their necks towards them, their yellow eyes glowing, their mouths foaming. And behind them were Skull, Gobbler and the boys, mounted on cobs. Moll turned back and fled on towards the forest.

Suddenly, from the shadows of the forest, a line of cobs burst out on to the heath. Moll's eyes widened. Her heart thundered.

'Oak!' she screamed. 'Oak!'

'Don't cry out!' Alfie panted.

Moll screamed again, unable to stop herself. 'Oak!'

Gryff tugged at her dress with his teeth. *No, Moll, no*, he seemed to say.

The cobs rushed forward: Oak, his sons and Siddy's father, Jesse. They'd come for her – despite what Skull had made her think – because *'Oak's camp never leave a man behind'*.

Moll sped along the path between Gryff and Alfie, her heart surging. 'Oak!'

And then Oak answered. 'Keep running!' His shout was loud, louder than the wailing wind, and Moll rushed towards it.

She turned her head. Behind them, the hounds edged closer. And yet there was something strange about them.

Their necks weren't craned towards her; their eyes weren't even fixed on her. They were hunting someone else entirely.

She glanced to her side. Alfie. They were hunting Alfie.

'Oak!' Moll cried again as the hounds shrieked behind her.

'Moll!' Oak roared.

His cry lingered in a gust of wind. And from behind them came Skull's terrible laugh, twisting above the pounding hooves of his cob.

Moll raced on, blotting out the sounds from behind her as she realised something with sickening dread. Alfie had tried to warn her. Gryff had tried to warn her. But still she'd called out. And Oak would have always answered.

They'd handed Skull the last piece of the Dream Snatch. Her name.

Moments later, Oak was among them, yanking Moll up from the ground on to the back of his cob and spurring them both away. Moll leant into Oak's body for a second, glimpsed Gryff racing along beside them, but, when she searched for Alfie, he was nowhere to be seen.

She craned her neck back and there, some metres behind them now, Alfie was cowering among the knotted gorse to the side of the track, his face white, his eyes wide. The hounds were prowling close to him, their ears flattened to their heads, saliva hanging from their fangs in drooling chains. Moll watched him, her breath caught in her throat, as Oak's cob carried her further and further away. Alfie had given Skull the scrap from her dress, so why had the hounds tracked *him*? She glanced down at her dress and felt

165

suddenly weak. There was no scrap missing; her frock was untorn.

She leant into Oak. 'We need to go back for Alfie! He – he . . .' What was she saying? She didn't need him any more. She knew where the amulets were and she had only needed him to help her escape. Why did she feel responsible for him?

Oak hauled his cob to a halt.

'Keep going!' roared Wisdom. 'Or the hounds'll attack like before!'

Only then did Moll notice Wisdom's hand was bandaged up tight and Jesse's ankle was bound. So Skull's hounds *had* caught them that night.

Oak urged his cob further down the track, away from Alfie and the hounds.

'But . . .' Moll started. Her lips quivered as she watched a hound scratch back the undergrowth where Alfie crouched.

Gobbler hurried closer and grabbed Alfie by the collar, spitting into his face. Alfie's eyes were fierce, but Moll could see his body trembling.

Oak started back towards them, but Skull reached into his robes and drew out a pistol.

'Ride!' Oak roared. 'Ride!'

There was a loud crack. Oak's cob stumbled slightly as blood ran down its piebald leg, then it galloped on towards the forest, speeding Oak and Moll with it.

And, with her stomach churning, Moll kept her head turned and watched Alfie's body disappear as the hounds closed in.

Chapter 23
Raven

There was a smile behind the mask and it curdled with pleasure.

'Moll.'

The word rolled over Skull's tongue, then buried itself deep inside his mouth.

It was the dead of night and it was raining heavily. Leafless trees craned over the clearing where Skull and his gang squatted and lichens trailed from the branches like burnt hair – long, tangled and grey. The only light came from a lantern set down in the centre of the gang's circle.

Rain smeared down Skull's mask. 'Moll. Moll Pecksniff . . . We've got her good and tight now we know her name. She won't get away from the Dream Snatch this time.' The mask tilted towards Gobbler. 'Polish the ceremonial table. Bring out the drums. It won't be long before she's back.'

Gobbler's hunched back swelled with anticipation. 'The time's come, hasn't it, Skull? For what we've all been waiting for.'

Skull's mask dipped. The boys stiffened.

'It's time to summon the Master of the Soul Splinter,' Skull growled.

One of the boys moved the lantern closer.

Brunt shoved him. 'You'd better toughen up all right.'

Gobbler curled his tongue over his teeth, sucking in the rain. 'This is how the Shadowmasks'll kill Moll Pecksniff and her wildcat after the Dream Snatch brings them in.' He jabbed a sharpened stick into the ground, centimetres from the boy's hand, and then he smiled. 'An untraceable kill ...'

'What about the amulets? Do they have a chance of finding them in time?' Brunt asked.

Skull's voice gnawed at the inside of his mask. 'We need to know why they went to Mellantha. Did the traitorous hag know something about the amulets after all?'

Brunt sat forward. 'With Mellantha dead, can't we ask our little friend Alfie?'

Gobbler's running eye blinked several times, then he sniggered. 'The hounds took a liking to him – a *strong* liking. He's not in a state to talk yet.'

Skull spat. 'I told you to hold the hounds back. We need to get the boy to speak.'

Gobbler lowered his voice. 'He won't be speaking for some time, Skull ...'

Skull's lifeless eyes blinked once. The lantern the boy was cradling shivered and went out.

'I don't care what state he's in. Until we have the girl, Alfie's the only one who has the answers we need,' Skull replied.

'But he's a stubborn one – with a will of iron,' one of the boys ventured.

The rain slid down Skull's mask in snaking lines. 'Then beat his cob. Beat it in front of him. That'll get him to speak.'

All around them the night was a black abyss, filled with the sounds of rain.

At the other end of the clearing, set back within the trees, there was a choked whimper. Breath ripped out of Alfie's body, dragging him back into consciousness. Shooting pains burned through his legs, pounding upwards into his body. He tugged against the ropes that bound him to the tree, but they held him fast. Alfie winced. Even his hands, now throbbing at the wrists, had been bound behind his back.

What had happened? Mellantha, the bone reading, Moll, and then the hounds . . . They had been pounding through the undergrowth towards them – a terror of teeth and claws. Then Moll had disappeared. Oak had come for her and she had escaped and left him for dead.

He flinched as he straightened himself up. The tree he had been tied to jutted into his back, grating on his spine. Again shooting pains coursed through his body. His shorts had been shredded around the knees and his skin torn by cuts and scratches. Grimacing, he rolled his ankle over. Two rows of teeth marks were gouged into his flesh, rupturing his leg into a mangled wound.

A spasm gripped his body and Alfie retched. Fighting

back the tears, he bit down on his lip. A gust of wind rustled the dead leaves and tugged his ripped shirt open. Bloodied scratches marred his chest. Still the rain beat on. Alfie wanted to cry out into it, but the pain swallowed his strength.

From the trees nearby, Alfie heard Raven whinny. And this time the boy couldn't fight the tears. They fell from his eyes freely until sobs shook his body. Raven stepped forward, as far as his tethering rope would allow. He craned his neck towards Alfie, breathing gently through his nostrils. But, however far he stretched, he couldn't reach the boy.

And that's when it came to Alfie: a small tatter of hope. He looked at Raven through misted eyes.

'You're after my rings,' he said to his cob in a cracked voice. 'My – my rings . . .'

Each word wrung his body with pain. But now he had a plan. Though it might take hours, there was a chance he could cut his way free of the rope with the spikes on his gypsy fighting rings. He looked at the clearing with desperate eyes. *Where would they go? And on a night like this?* He shook the thought from his mind. That could wait; the most important thing was escaping Skull's clutches once and for all.

Hours drifted by and still the boys remained with Skull and Gobbler in the clearing. Their voices twisted through the rain to Alfie – strange words loaded with terror: they were planning to summon something. He strained to hear what they were saying – something about a Soul Splinter to

170

use on Moll and her wildcat. Alfie stiffened; the word was somehow familiar, as if he'd heard it many years before. He shook his head, turning back to the ropes. Facing his past was a task for another night. Now he needed to focus on getting free.

Alfie's rings cut into the rope, bit by bit, a soft scuffing amid the rain-filled night.

'It isn't working, Raven,' Alfie groaned, his voice cracked with pain.

But just at that moment, when he felt the last of his strength seep from his body, the rope fell away and Alfie slumped forward. He twisted his neck towards Raven who neighed softly and pawed the ground.

'Shhhhh, boy.'

Alfie made to get up, but his legs buckled beneath him and he collapsed. Raven turned his back to Alfie.

Alfie winced. 'Don't – don't turn away, boy,' he whispered. 'I'm sorry. It's just – I don't have the strength . . .'

Raven yanked his neck to one side and then there was a crack as the tethering rope, which had been fastened from a ground peg to his halter, snapped off. Raven stepped gingerly towards Alfie, then lowered his neck and nuzzled the boy's head. His warmth surged through Alfie and he lifted a shaking hand to his cob's mane.

'My boy,' he whispered, closing his eyes. 'My boy.'

He sank his head into Raven's mane and then watched, his mouth wide in disbelief, as Raven lowered himself to his knees.

Alfie shot a look at the clearing, but Skull and his gang were still deep in conversation. Summoning all his strength, Alfie clung to Raven's mane. 'That's it, boy, that's it! There's a chance now . . .'

Flinching in pain with every movement, Alfie hauled himself up on to Raven's back. His own leg was bloodied and limp, but he felt the power of Raven's legs as the cob thrust his body upwards to a standing position.

Alfie was silent for a few seconds, then he let his head fall down on Raven's mane. 'I don't know, Raven. I don't know where to go.'

Rain poured down on to Alfie's face making his teeth chatter, but Raven didn't hang around. He picked his way away from the clearing into the heart of the Deepwood. As soon as the camp was out of earshot, Raven quickened his pace. Trotting. Through the deadened glade. Then faster. Cantering. Through the crowd of beech trees. Until, at last, they were racing away from Skull, through the sodden forest.

Alfie clung on. 'Don't let me fall, Raven. I can't go back to Skull. Don't let me fall . . .'

His body slumped on Raven's back and waves of pain washed over him, dragging him back into unconsciousness. The trees around him fell away, and with it the raw aching in his leg. Still the black cob raced on.

Alfie's eyes fluttered open as they slowed by the river. But the pain was rolling over him again and, lulled by the pattering of the rain, he felt himself falling away once more into nothingness. He was numb to everything around him: numb to the splash of water as he fell from Raven into the river; numb even to the strong, firm hands that hauled him to the bank.

Chapter 24
A New Arrival

Moll sat on the end of her box bed. It had been raining for days and this morning it clobbered down on her wagon roof like thousands of marbles dropping on to a tin tray. Gryff was nestled within the folds of crumpled clothes on Moll's floor. Before Moll's kidnap by Gobbler and Alfie, the closest the wildcat had been to the camp was when he'd occasionally crept beneath her wagon at night to sleep. But since their escape on the heath he hadn't left Moll's side, not even to hunt, and Oak's boys brought him rabbits, voles and mice. During the day he followed her like a reflection and at night he watched over her, a friend amid the forces of the Dream Snatch.

Moll looked at the figure in her bed. 'Should I poke him?'

Gryff opened one yellow-green eye and growled.

'Stop staring,' Moll hissed. 'You're meant to be sleeping.'

Gryff made a short *pppttt* noise through his teeth, then closed his eye.

'Maybe a little poke,' Siddy whispered, 'to check he's still alive.'

Moll and Siddy had got their poking fingers ready when the wagon door creaked open and Mooshie stuck a bedraggled head in.

'You two – OFF!' she hissed. Raindrops dripped off her dimpled chin and her headscarf was soaked through. Behind her, children whispered in anxious, excited voices. Mooshie shooed them away. 'I'm sure Moll will tell you everything soon.' She closed the door. 'Won't you, Moll?'

'Mmmmmmn.'

Siddy gave Moll a thwack. 'Come on, admit you missed everyone when you were in Skull's clearing.'

Moll sighed. 'There was a lot going on, Sid. Not much time for missing people, I'm afraid.' But she had missed them. Not just Siddy, whom Jinx had led Oak to after Moll's kidnap, but even Florence, and that was worrying on a whole new level. Moll stared across at the body in her bed.

'If you carry on staring at him like that,' Mooshie said curtly, 'he might never wake up. I know I wouldn't bother coming round if the first thing I had to look at was your scowling mug.' She unhooked a copper pan and turned to the stove. Lighting it, she boiled down the pig fat she'd brought in, then reached inside her pinafore. 'Blossom gathered in a thunderstorm – carries extra healing properties.' She scattered the petals into the simmering pot, then strained the mixture. 'For his bruises – and I've lavender oil and woundwort to soothe the wound.' She brought out a small tin. 'It's mixed with mashed potato, see – the best dressing you'll find.'

Moll made a silent decision never to have another cut or bruise.

Mooshie shooed Moll and Siddy off the bed. 'Can't you busy yourselves elsewhere?'

Siddy threw his hands into the air. 'We've been busying ourselves for ages!' He pointed to the mounds of moss, birds' eggs and feathers he'd collected with Moll. 'Any more busying around and we'll have half the blinking forest in here!'

Moll nodded. 'He had all of yesterday and the day before to come round. And we've got so much to do: understand why the Shadowmasks have no shadows; figure out how they killed my parents; find the well with the amulets inside … And he needs to help, instead of lying there covered in mashed potato!'

Mooshie shook her head. 'You saw those hounds, Moll. You saw what they managed to do to Wisdom and Jesse – and they were on cobs.'

Moll looked down. Even after Mooshie had held her close and tucked her into bed the night of their escape, she couldn't untangle herself from what she'd seen. Every time she closed her eyes, she saw the hounds. They chased her into her nightmare that night and it was only when the familiar click of her wagon latch sounded that she had been rescued from their snarling jaws. Oak was carrying a small body in his arms. That had been two days ago and still Alfie hadn't sat up or spoken a word.

He lay before her, breathing shakily. His eyes, swollen and

bruised, were closed, and the scratches on his face were still raw and red.

Moll sat forward. 'Alfie?' she whispered. 'Alfie, Alfie, Alfie, Alfie, Alfie, Alfie, Alfie, Alfie—'

Gryff buried his head under Moll's discarded clothes and Mooshie glowered at her, picking up two mud-stained skirts from the floor and folding them over her plump arms. 'Hush, Moll, you're being a pest. Leave the boy to sleep, will you?'

Then, quite unexpectedly, Alfie's eyelids fluttered and one eye opened.

Moll beamed at Mooshie. 'Ha!'

'Stay with him, both of you,' Mooshie said, 'and I'll get Oak.' But her eyes were sparkling and as she left the wagon there was a spring in her step.

Alfie's other eye opened and his gaze fell upon Moll. He looked at her for several seconds, his face completely blank, then his eyes travelled over her wagon and its belongings. Seconds later, he looked back at Moll with empty blue eyes.

She stuck out her leg and nudged Gryff with her foot.

Gryff yawned, his whiskers twitching either side of his nose. He dipped his head towards Alfie. '*Brrrooooooo*.'

'That's his greeting call,' Moll said.

Alfie didn't respond, but he tensed as he took in Siddy.

'That's Siddy,' Moll explained. 'He pinched the bone reading from Cinderella Bull's wagon – and he races earthworms in his spare time.'

Siddy lifted his flat cap, then beamed. 'You're Alfie, aren't you?'

'You know he's Alfie,' Moll hissed.

Siddy grinned. 'I had a pet worm called Alfie once. Before Porridge.' He lifted the earthworm from his pocket. 'Now I've got Porridge the Second and I'm training him up to be a racing worm.'

Porridge the Second shot Alfie a look of resigned boredom, then sank back into Siddy's pocket.

Alfie swallowed and looked at Moll. 'Is this your wagon?' His voice was scratched, like a broken instrument.

Moll nodded. 'Yup.' She drew herself up nice and tall. 'We've been looking after you, even though you thieved me from Oak's camp—'

'You catapulted me in the head! And you – you left me for dead on the heath!'

Moll blew through her teeth as she tried to remember Mooshie's advice again. Think then get angry. Or was it get angry then think? Or maybe it was don't get angry and don't think. She tried that: 'I wanted to come back for you; I tried to make them. But Skull – he . . .' She trailed off. 'Anyway, you can borrow the wagon for a while if you want.'

Alfie raised his eyebrows. Moll scowled back. So here she was, making peace with the enemy again. And yet Alfie had tricked Skull with the blacksmith note and he'd got them out of the cage. And there was her dress. Somehow she didn't want to snap a promise to him any more. It felt like the right thing to do.

'Is Raven safe?' Alfie asked, biting his lip.

Siddy nodded. 'Tied up with our cobs just beyond the clearing. Oak's boys have been looking after him.'

Alfie breathed a sigh of relief. Pushing the quilt back, he eased himself up so that he was sitting against the wagon wall. Moll pretended not to notice the way he winced every time he moved.

'What – what happened to me?' he asked. 'And why do I have mashed potato on my ankle?'

Moll sat cross-legged, planning her words as carefully as possible.

Sensing the disaster Moll was capable of being in situations like this, Siddy intervened. 'See those raw marks on your fingers? Oak thinks you used your rings to cut through the rope Skull tied you up with.'

Alfie held up his hands and then his mouth fell open. 'I – I remember,' he stammered. 'It was Raven who helped me. He broke free from his tether and knelt down so as I could mount him. Then—' Alfie struggled on, '—then I don't remember. Last thing I knew I was riding through the Deepwood.'

'Oak found you,' Moll said.

'Oak?' Alfie mumbled. 'But – but I stole you from his camp. Oak must *hate* me.'

Moll waved her hand in the air. 'Course he doesn't. Not after I told him you didn't have a rotten brain like Skull's – that you were against all of his gang's dark magic. Isn't that right, Gryff?'

Gryff leapt up on to the bed and settled himself between

Moll's legs. Siddy's eyes widened as he glimpsed Gryff's claws, but the wildcat just stared across at Alfie for several seconds, unblinking. Then he dipped his head.

Alfie looked from Gryff to Moll. 'You've got the same eyes as Gryff, Moll.'

Gryff curled his tail round Moll's toes. Alfie had used her real name for the very first time. He'd kept it safe until they'd reached the Ancientwood, just like he promised he would. She squinted at him. Even if he was lying about who he really was, he'd kept her name safe. And somehow that counted for more than losing it to Skull.

Alfie shook himself. 'I've got to fly from here – your camp aren't going to want me.'

Siddy raised his eyebrows. 'Where to?'

Alfie was silent.

'Raven brought you to the river,' Moll said, 'and Oak carried you to our camp. You're here for a reason, Alfie. Oak and the others aren't going to give you up. They're not like that.'

Siddy nodded. 'Moll does terrible stuff the whole time and they've never chucked her out.'

Alfie looked down. 'But Oak doesn't know who I am ... Not properly.'

'Who are you then?' Moll asked.

Alfie sighed.

Moll shrugged. 'Well, you're against Skull and his dark magic; that's enough for Oak. Didn't Mellantha say something about help coming from unsuspecting people? Or maybe it was about us all being birds and not really human at all. Can't remember. Point is: Oak will look out for you while you're here.' She leant in closer; there was something she wanted to ask. 'It was *your* scent the hounds had, only I could've sworn it was *my* dress you ripped a bit off.'

A rumble of thunder filled the wagon and the ground beneath them seemed to shake. Moll ran a hand over Gryff's back.

Alfie considered. 'May've looked like I was giving away a scrap of your dress, but when I was up close to you I ripped a corner off my shirt and gave that to Brunt instead – same colour as your dress, see.'

Gryff lifted his head from beneath Moll's arm.

'I figured we had one chance to get out of the Deepwood alive and if the hounds had my scent we'd get further since I can outrun you. Only it didn't work out that way as I never expected Oak to show up like he did.'

Moll held his eyes for a moment, then looked away. 'You're strange.'

Alfie shrugged. 'It'd be a dull old world if everyone was the same.'

The corners of Moll's mouth rose as she recognised the echo of her own words.

Gryff prowled over the bed sheets until he was centimetres away from Alfie. The boy held his breath, but Gryff just looked at him for several seconds and then he dipped his head down low.

And, although no one said anything, Alfie understood.

Thank you.

The wildcat slunk off the bed and stalked to the other end of the wagon, where he tucked himself beneath a chair and closed his eyes.

Alfie looked down at his leg and flinched. And, in a moment of rare forward thinking, Moll got up and poured a glass of water from the jug Mooshie had left. She handed it to Alfie and he drank it down.

'We still need to find the amulets,' he said. 'The well Mellantha talked about, we have to find it before Skull gets a hold of you and Gryff.'

'Mellantha said the well was *in the heart of the forest*,' Moll said. 'Oak and the Council of Elders have been meeting to try and work out what that means. The Rings of Sacred Oaks around our camp is the heart of the forest as far as we know it, and there isn't a well here, that's for sure.'

Siddy nodded. 'Cinderella Bull – that's Oak's mother – she thinks the heart of the forest might mean trees so deep into the forest that no one's been under them. Once we figure it out, we're going to find the well.' He paused. 'You should come.'

Alfie fiddled with the quilt, then he looked Moll square in the eye. 'I was going to cut and run with the amulets when we found them.'

Moll held his gaze. 'Well, I was planning to steal them off *you*. And I had a pretty nasty plan too. Was going to involve a very big spade.'

They all grinned, but Moll knew she'd been right about

Alfie. He wanted those amulets for a reason of his own – and it had nothing to do with money.

'Why do you want the amulets so badly?'

Alfie ran a hand over the pine wall, then looked at Moll for several seconds, saying nothing. Eventually he shook his head. 'It was an idea I had – to – to fix something that happened a long time ago.' He looked down. 'But it was a stupid idea. It would never have worked. And, besides, I've discovered a better reason for finding the amulets now.'

Moll smiled. 'You've started believing in the old magic in the Bone Murmur, haven't you?'

Alfie blew out through his lips, then he smiled. 'Why else d'you think I gave Brunt the scrap from my shirt?'

Moll looked from Alfie to Gryff to Siddy and at last she remembered Mellantha's exact words: *Sometimes it's the people we don't expect who wind up looking out for us.*

Chapter 25
Shadows

The wagon door swung open. Gryff's head shot up but, seeing Oak stride in, he turned away and settled back to sleep. Oak hung a dripping hat on the door hook and smiled at Alfie. 'How're you feeling?'

Out of the corner of her eye, Moll could see that Alfie's body was tensed. 'Bit better,' he said stiffly. He looked down at his chafed hands, then mumbled, 'Thank you.'

Oak smiled. 'It's that cob of yours you've got to thank.'

'You'll want me gone from here. I understand—'

'We'd like you to stay with us, Alfie – until you're better. After that, you can go as you choose.' Oak nodded towards the window. 'You'll be safe in the camp and there's food and water for you here which you'll be hard pushed to get any place else without money.'

Alfie reddened. 'But you're never going to trust me. None of your camp are.'

Oak shook his head. 'Your past with Skull isn't important. It's the present that counts and what you decide to do with it. And, from what Moll tells me,

184

you can run, you can ride, you can pick locks – and you can be trusted.'

Alfie shifted under the covers. 'But I'm not even a real gypsy ...' He fiddled with his jay feather earring and Moll and Siddy listened with bated breath. 'Skull told me no one knew who my father was, but my mother worked up at Tipplebury Farm, looking after the cobs: feeding and watering them, grooming them, breaking them in ...' He looked towards the window. 'Apparently she died giving birth to me and Skull said that, when he was passing the farm to buy supplies not long afterwards, he offered to take me in and raise me if I looked after his cobs when I was older.' Alfie sighed. 'I suppose the farm didn't want to waste time raising an orphan like me so they just agreed.'

Oak shook his head. 'I don't believe the farm would have handed over a baby to someone like Skull.'

Alfie shrugged. 'That's what he said happened.'

Moll looked at Alfie for several seconds but, when he caught her eye, she looked away. She didn't know Alfie well, but she knew him enough to know that what he'd just said was a pack of lies. Even if Skull had told Alfie that's what had happened all those years ago, it was obvious Alfie didn't believe a word of it. And, what was more, Moll was almost certain now that the reason Alfie wanted the amulets so much in the first place had something to do with him finding out the truth behind his beginning.

Oak shook his head. 'Whatever happened back then, you're in our camp now, Alfie, and we'll look after you.' He

185

leant forward, rubbing his hands together. 'But, until we work out where this well is, we need to keep you safe. Skull's planning a raid – my boys've seen his gang lurking by the river, working out the layout of our camp.'

Alfie took a deep breath. 'They'll bring the hounds.'

Siddy nodded. 'But Cinderella Bull's been working on something for those beasts.'

It was true. Moll and Siddy had seen her late the night before, kneeling by the fire before a pot of bubbling liquid. And, although they had only watched from their wagon steps, they'd seen Cinderella Bull turn her head up to the trees and whisper to their spirits.

'They're planning more than a raid,' Alfie said quietly. 'I heard them before I escaped. They'll perform the Dream Snatch again only it'll be stronger now they know Moll's name.'

'We're ready for that,' Oak said. 'We'll never give Moll up.'

'But it won't be like before. It's not just the chants and the drums and all that stuff she shouts about in her nightmares.' Moll looked at Alfie questioningly. 'I heard you back in the pit,' he explained. Moll blushed. 'All that isn't anything compared to what's coming. Skull's summoning something – something I think he's used before ... on Moll's parents.'

Gryff opened one eye and his fur prickled. Oak, Moll and Siddy stiffened.

'I heard them talking about something called a Soul Splinter.'

'Why d'you think they used that on my parents?' Moll asked.

Alfie swallowed. 'Because they've been saying it's a weapon that kills without a trace. Skull's calling it from somewhere – from its master, he said.'

Siddy shifted. 'You think the Master of the Soul Splinter is one of those Shadowmasks Mellantha talked to you about?'

Oak nodded. 'The Soul Splinter ... Things are making more sense now. You said that Mellantha told you that the witch doctors performed a hex that tore away all their shadows?'

Alfie and Moll nodded.

Oak rubbed his jaw, deep in thought. 'Gypsies, travellers, wandering people, we believe our souls are part of our natural surroundings – wild and free. That when we walk through the forest, the heath, the fields or the moors our souls walk beside us, as a shadow.'

'So souls and shadows are sort of the same thing if you think like that,' Alfie said.

Siddy gasped. 'So the Shadowmasks – when they tore away their shadows – they—'

'—tore away their souls,' Oak finished for him. 'And this Soul Splinter, perhaps that's what tears away the souls of living people?'

Gryff growled.

There was another peal of thunder and into its roar Moll whispered, 'If the Soul Splinter killed my parents, I'm going to rip it apart.' She clenched her fists. 'Then I'm going to do the same to Skull.'

As if the rain was waiting for a reply, the pattering on the wagon roof stopped for a second.

Oak looked at Alfie, Moll and Siddy. 'We're stronger than the Soul Splinter and we'll find the amulets before Skull and his Shadowmasks get anywhere near us.'

And, as quickly as it had stopped, the rain burst into life again, swallowing their voices and hammering on to the roof in thundering thrusts.

Chapter 26
Darkness Lurking

Moll sat inside a tent in the clearing, beside Mooshie and Patti as they sang a ballad about lovers lost at sea and prepared the hawking goods with a handful of girls. Moll loathed songs that favoured lovers over highwaymen and looting, so she tried to listen to the rain pattering on to the canvas roof instead. Gryff crouched in the far corner of the tent, away from the clatter, and, although Florence and Ivy tried to get on with shaping wire into flowers, their eyes kept glancing nervously towards him.

Siddy walked across the clearing with an armful of firewood, past his father and Oak who were sitting on Oak's wagon steps, sharpening knives in case Skull's gang came close. On seeing Moll with the girls, Siddy gave her a surprised thumbs up. Moll shifted her stool away from Florence and Ivy (and their beautifully ironed dresses and brushed hair) and scowled back at him. Most days Moll would have been entranced by the simmering pots of melted wax and vanilla essence and she would have watched, wide-eyed, as the wax hardened round the wire flowers. But not today.

She rocked back and forth on her stool. 'I need to get Alfie up. It's already midday!'

'Get him up?' Mooshie spat as she twisted a wire flower in the pot.

Moll nodded. 'How are we going to beat Skull if I'm sitting here helping you make wax flowers?'

Patti scowled, rubbing the wax from her finger on to her purple skirt. 'You're not sitting here helping us make wax flowers. You're sitting here being a pest.'

Moll grabbed a flower and dunked it furiously into the melted wax. It splashed up on to her hand and she jumped backwards. 'No one ever, ever, ever understands me,' she hissed. 'We need to be up and looking for this well. It's in the forest somewhere – and finding it is our only chance against Skull. And how are we going to do that when I'm stuck in here and Alfie's in my wagon with Rocky Jo?'

Mooshie's eyes narrowed. 'Why've you left Alfie with a cockerel?'

'He's not a cockerel, he's a legendary highwayman – of the *worst* kind,' Moll said. 'And I thought Alfie might want the company.' She sighed. 'But he's probably bored stiff of Rocky Jo by now. Unless you know the highwayman well, conversation can be a bit tricky.'

Mooshie rolled her eyes, then adjusted the pinafore string around her waist. 'You're not taking Alfie to look for the well until he's better, and until Cinderella Bull has read her crystal ball again for clues as to where the thing might actually be. We can't take any chances now, Moll.'

But Moll wasn't listening. Alfie had appeared on the steps of her wagon across the clearing.

Florence gasped. 'That's him? The boy who helped you escape?'

Moll nodded and, quite by accident, she found herself replying, 'He can pick locks *and* whisper to cobs.'

Florence's eyes widened.

Patti wiped her hands on her lilac pinafore, then turned to Mooshie. 'We could get Moll to show Alfie what's what around the clearing – they'd be safe in here.'

Ivy sat forward. 'And Moll could take Siddy too. Wisdom caught him slipping minnows down our chimney earlier. He said it was a wedding present ...'

Mooshie fiddled with her rings, then she stuck a hand out of the tent. 'I suppose the rain is clearing and Oak's boys are all up in the trees on watch.' She drew herself up in front of Moll and pointed to a wheelbarrow full of logs that Siddy was now lugging. 'You can wheel Alfie once or twice round the clearing so that he can see what's what, but mind his ankle and, if you so much as step into those trees, your life won't be worth living. Remember, Moll – the whole camp's watching out for you now. STAY INSIDE THE CLEARING.'

As Moll sprang up from her stool, Florence added, 'Perhaps we could do some hawking together once all this is over?'

Moll considered and Mooshie and Patti braced themselves for something vile. But it wasn't too disastrous. 'Or we could watch Gryff hunt for things; he's great at killing voles. Really gets his claws stuck in.'

Florence gave a shaky smile. It was a start.

Gryff skirted round the edge of the tent towards Moll, then they sploshed across the puddles, mud splattering all over Moll's newly-ironed skirt. She grabbed the wheelbarrow from Siddy, emptied it of logs and pointed to Alfie. 'We're putting him in it.' She glanced at the bandages wrapped round Alfie's ankle and, for a second, she wondered whether the wheelbarrow was in fact an entirely appropriate means of transport.

Alfie followed her gaze. 'It'll heal,' he mumbled. 'They always do.'

Moll bundled two pillows out of her wagon while Siddy helped Alfie into the wheelbarrow. The rain had stopped now and shards of sunlight filtered through the trees. Bracken glimmered after their drenching and the undergrowth looked greener than it had in months.

Several metres away, Mooshie stood with a hand on her hips. In the other hand she brandished a wire flower like some sort of fencing sword. 'Remember my warning, Molly Pecksniff.'

'Who's that?' Alfie whispered. 'I recognise her face. Did she help me – in your wagon?'

Siddy nodded. 'She put the bandages on you and the mashed potato.'

'*Really?* That's where that came from?'

Moll nodded. 'Her name's Mooshie; she's Oak's wife and she's good news when she's not tempered up with her tea towel.'

Moll grabbed the wooden bowl of chanterelle mushrooms Mooshie had left for them on the wagon steps. She and Siddy chomped a handful down and even Alfie managed a few mouthfuls.

'They're good,' Alfie said. 'Better than anything I tasted in Skull's camp.'

'Mooshie's a good cook,' Siddy said.

Moll nodded. 'Except when she makes nettle soup.' She placed the last of the mushrooms on to the ground before Gryff.

He circled them once, sniffed the plate, then gobbled them down before settling himself on Moll's wagon steps as she and Siddy pushed Alfie forward into the heart of the camp.

The clearing was filling up with people now the rain had stopped, but the carefree atmosphere that usually hung in the air had gone; everyone knew Skull and his gang were lurking close. Instead of charging round the fire, children were gathered close, carving catapults in case of an attack, and, although Mooshie insisted the girls help her with the hawking, the men were still sharpening knives and polishing saddles.

Some miles away, beyond the forest, church bells pealed out. Moll sometimes forgot that life in Tipplebury village muddled along beyond the fringes of the trees. She and Siddy wiggled round the children, then jerked the wheelbarrow to a stop by the old armchair set back from the fire.

'*This* is Hard-Times Bob!' Moll cried. 'He's great at dislocating his limbs.'

Hard-Times Bob, who had been enjoying an afternoon snooze, jumped out of his seat like a jack-in-the-box, then wheezed out a series of rickety hiccups.

'Who? What?' he snuffled.

'This is Alfie,' Moll said. 'We were just showing you to him.'

'*Showing* me to him . . .' he muttered, but he adjusted his spotted bow tie all the same and threw them a smile with two rows of yellowed teeth. He glanced at Alfie. 'Ah, so this is the famous Alfie. Moll tells me you see things others don't – like ways to escape cages and means to trick Skull's boys.' Alfie blushed. Hard-Times Bob thumped his fist on the arm of his chair excitedly. 'Just like me, you are, because I see things others don't – like whiplash snakes. I saw one just last week in Punchbowl Copse. Moving in cartwheels, it was . . .'

From the armchair beside him, Cinderella Bull cast a withering look. 'You haven't left the clearing for two weeks, Bob; you haven't seen no whiplash snake.'

Moll leant closer to Alfie. 'He's going to be famous one day – people will pay hundreds and hundreds to see Hard-Times Bob the Limb Dislocater. I know they will.'

Siddy shrugged. 'I think I might be famous one day.'

Moll scowled. 'What for?'

'Fitting eleven chestnuts into my mouth at once. That or racing earthworms.'

Moll rolled her eyes. 'Let's keep going.'

Siddy pointed up to one of the Sacred Oaks. 'See that bloke with the ponytail up in the tree?' Alfie nodded. 'That's Wisdom – Oak and Mooshie's eldest son. He's won the Fighting Crown for three years running. I reckon that's why my sister married him because it can't have been for his ponytail.'

Moll nodded. 'Oak's got two more sons. There's Noah, who always wears a red neckerchief and can throw a knife on to a bullseye with his eyes shut, and then there's Domino, the smallest one. But don't be fooled by his size. Domino's the fastest gypsy in the camp! He'll be up in an alder near the river so, if Skull's gang come close, he'll be here in a flash to warn us.'

Alfie gulped. 'Can I see Raven?'

Moll and Siddy steered him away to the edge of the clearing watched by Mooshie and Patti. Gryff sprang down from Moll's wagon steps. The children in the camp stopped carving their catapults and stared, wide-eyed, as Gryff prowled towards Moll – alert now, his eyes flicking between the trees.

Alfie leant forward when he saw the cobs tethered to the trees just behind the oaks. He put his fingers to his mouth and whistled, and, within seconds, Raven had picked his way between the sun-dappled trunks until his rope was taut. Alfie hauled himself out of the wheelbarrow and stood before his cob. Raven placed his head into Alfie's palm and Alfie leant into his mane.

'My boy,' he whispered. 'Thank you.'

Jinx walked nimbly through the trees towards Moll. 'Hi, Jinx.'

Siddy looked down at Porridge who had poked his head out of his pocket. 'I need an upgrade,' he muttered.

Moll tickled the special spot behind Jinx's ears, then she looked around her and listened. The forest was coming alive again after the rain: animals scavenged for berries and nuts and unseen birds called to one another from towering branches.

She turned to Alfie and Siddy. 'The forest—' And then she stopped. A feeling – one of unsettling coldness – had scuttled under her skin. Her eyes darted over the trees, deeper into the forest. Nothing. And yet there was something nearby. She could *feel* it. Moll blinked. Was there something dark moving among the furthest trees? She shook herself.

'What is it?' Alfie asked.

'I'm not sure,' Moll replied. 'Only I felt something – like there was someone nearby. Not the camp, not Gryff. Someone else . . . Out there in the trees.'

Siddy took a step backwards, further into the clearing. 'Even though Oak's boys are up on guard, perhaps we should be staying close to the fire.'

Moll looked across at Gryff. He was just a few metres away, only he wasn't looking at her. He had his neck craned towards the trees in the distance and his whiskers were twitching. He had seen something.

'Let's get back to the fire,' Siddy said.

Moll nodded, stooping to pick a handful of strawberries growing among the undergrowth. 'Could've been a deer,' she said as she scoffed the berries down.

Alfie climbed into the wheelbarrow and they pushed him back towards the centre of the clearing.

Moll stopped. A strange dizziness was clouding her head, throbbing inside her temples. She clutched on to the wheelbarrow and then a burning sensation ripped through her mouth and her throat tightened, forcing her breath into gasps.

She collapsed to the ground, aware of shouting in the clearing, of Gryff charging towards her. But second by second the sounds and sights faded and, as the fever shot through her body, only one image remained clear: a long face made of grey slate, with a jutting mouth and gaping eyeholes, darting between the furthest trees.

Another mask had come for her. Just as Mellantha had warned.

Chapter 27
Fighting Back

'What's happening to her?' Siddy cried. 'Someone help her! Make it stop!'

Moll's face drained of colour as the fever raged through her, forcing her body into spasms. As she writhed and twisted on the ground, Mooshie dabbed her face with a wet cloth. But still the sweat poured from her forehead.

Oak bent down, trying to hold Moll's body still. 'What happened, boys?'

'I – I don't know,' Alfie said. 'One second we were talking and then – and then ...' His eyes widened as he watched Moll's head thrash back and forth. 'She saw something in the forest. Only she couldn't work out what it was.'

Spit frothed up between Moll's teeth and the muscles in her throat tensed and knotted. She began to cough and splutter. Oak propped her head up and something choked out of her mouth: a clump of half-chewed berries.

Mooshie looked at Oak. 'She's been poisoned, hasn't she?'

The whole camp had gathered round now. Cinderella

Bull knelt down beside Moll. She placed a hand on her forehead, but Moll's eyes were wild, glowing with a savage brightness.

'It's poison all right, but these berries are strawberries; there's nothing poisonous about them.'

And then, all of a sudden, Moll groaned. 'There's another Shadowmask,' she gasped. The camp strained towards her words. 'With – with a long grey mask of slate – and with clumps of dead flowers for hair and – and,' her body started to shudder again, but she forced the words out, 'rotted berries for ears – red and rotten, like blood. I saw it running through the trees; it's come for me, hasn't it?'

Oak knelt close to Moll. 'There's no mask here, Moll! It's just us. Just us.'

And then Mooshie cried out. Moll's body wasn't shuddering or shaking now; it was growing still, frighteningly still, and her face was pale. There was a growl as Gryff wove in between the bodies and nuzzled against her.

'Get her water!' Mooshie told Siddy. 'Quick!'

As Siddy ran off for a bucket, Moll spoke, her voice tight and rasping, like someone was squeezing it out of her. She looked up into Gryff's eyes, as if only he could hear. 'Skull's chanting for me back in his camp. I can hear the drum and rattle again, it's like he's only calling me this time – but he's stronger now he knows my name,' she whispered. 'And it – it's like my mind's closing down – like it doesn't belong to me any more.' For a second, she looked almost peaceful. 'Like there isn't any point in fighting it . . .'

'You've got to fight it, Moll!' Oak said. 'Fight back against the Dream Snatch.'

'If I give up, the Shadowmasks'll leave you alone. It's only me they're after ...'

'Don't listen to it, Moll!' Alfie cried.

Moll was silent for a few seconds as the Dream Snatch crowded in. And then she gasped. 'I – I can see my nightmare inside my mind – clearer than I've ever seen it before ...' She choked on her words and, when she coughed, blood stained the cloth Mooshie held to her face. 'I can see the Shadowmasks. But there's only five of them, and – and – my parents are there too!' Moll closed her eyes; she was sobbing now. Her body contorted and then her jaw shuddered as she fought the Dream Snatch, trying to use its power but not let it take her completely.

Gryff pawed at Moll's skirt and looked deep into her eyes.

'Do something, Oak!' Mooshie shouted. 'A child isn't meant to go through this – to see what she'll see. We need to help her!'

Cinderella Bull put a hand on her shoulder. 'Moll will see how the Shadowmasks kill ... If she can handle the Dream Snatch.'

'It's not right!' Mooshie cried.

Oak took Mooshie's hands. 'Moosh, we've never known the truth about how the Shadowmasks kill. If we know what happened to Moll's parents then we've got a chance of stopping them.'

Moll tore her hair against the pulsing rhythms of the

Dream Snatch, sweat glistening on her chest. She looked into Gryff's eyes, begging him to rescue her. But she had to stay inside the nightmare – she knew that – because she had to unlock the last part of her memory. She closed her eyes.

Her mother was there, lying on the bank of the river, her green eyes wide with fear as one Shadowmask pinned her down by her arms and another clutched her long black hair in a fist to hold her still. Nearby was a tall, strong man – her father – and he was fighting against the other three Shadowmasks. But they had surrounded him now and were forcing him to his knees. They bound his hands and held him to the ground. And then the Shadowmasks' chant began:

'Tonight we summon you to finish our chant,
Master of the Soul Splinter, do what we can't.
Come from the shadows, the gloom most dim,
Use curses of power, deadly and grim.

Guardians of the Bones before you lie.
Fill them with darkness, so much that they die!
Pour out our shadows into each soul,
Kill all that is living, turn it blacker than coal!'

And from the shadows came a figure, with wild black hair surrounding a mask of charcoaled wood, like burnt skin. It prowled forward, drawing in the enormous leathery wings that jutted from its back and trailed along the ground. In its long, thin fingers, the figure held a splinter of black ice that didn't seem to melt. It stole closer to Moll's parents, its mask raised high, and then it towered over Moll's mother, lifting the Soul Splinter above her mouth. Moll's mother screamed, but the Shadowmasks held her fast and, as she panted into the night, the Soul Splinter began to melt and droplets of black dripped into her mouth. Her eyes widened, drowning in horror, then she lay still.

Her father recoiled as the Soul Splinter came towards him, but he was powerless against the Shadowmasks and, like droplets of death, the ice fell into his mouth. Moll watched as a blanket of darkness enfolded the scene.

And then she screamed.

'This isn't my nightmare any more! It's gone – gone! It's just the Dream Snatch now and I can't escape it!' She ripped at her ears, thrashing her head from side to side. 'I can hear Skull's chanting and muttering! I can hear the wax squelching through his fingers! And I can hear another voice – it's the Shadowmask with the face of slate I've just seen! He's saying my name, like he's come for me!'

Moll struggled to get up, but Oak pinned her down.

'He's saying it over and over again: *Hemlock's come for you, Moll. Give yourself up to the Dream Snatch!*'

Moll's body began to shake uncontrollably. 'Help me, Gryff! Help me!'

Gryff wrapped his body round Moll's, but she continued to shudder, wrestling beneath his weight.

'Fight it, Moll!' Oak cried. 'You can beat it!'

Cinderella Bull bent closer over the strawberries Moll had spat out. And then she gasped. 'These berries aren't what they seem. See here – these white seeds . . . I'd know them anywhere. They're *hemlock* seeds – *poisonous* seeds. And they've been growing inside our berries!'

Oak's face was grave. 'The second Shadowmask's come for Moll in the very form of his name.'

And then it dawned on Alfie, clear as day. He limped away from the gathering and up the steps to Moll's wagon. Moments later, he returned with a small phial of black liquid. Mooshie looked at him guardedly. Beneath her, Moll was crying out against the Dream Snatch, tossing from side to side.

'Mellantha gave it to us,' Alfie explained as he unscrewed the lid. 'She said Moll'd need it: *You'll need it when they're fighting for your mind,* she said. Maybe – maybe it's a cure for the hemlock berries!'

Cinderella Bull blinked. 'An antidote to the poison?'

Alfie nodded.

No one moved. Alfie could feel their distrust. But it was Gryff who acknowledged him first. He stepped back from Moll and stood before Alfie with shining eyes. Moll's eyes. And then he dipped his head.

'Go on,' Mooshie said quietly. 'We trust you.'

Alfie bent over Moll and tipped the black liquid into her mouth. For several seconds, Moll continued to shudder and shout but, as the antidote felt its way into her body, the fever withdrew and she lay on the ground, panting but free.

The Shadowmasks had come for her, but she'd broken their Dream Snatch.

And beyond the river, in their darkened lair, Skull and Hemlock knew it.

Chapter 28
The Soul Splinter

I t was night but no one slept. Even the youngest members of the camp lay awake in their wagons, wide-eyed with fear. Gryff sat just back from the campfire, facing out towards the trees, his ears swivelling at the slightest noise. And around the fire, sitting on tree stumps, were the Elders, together with Moll, Alfie and Siddy.

Hard-Times Bob puffed on his pipe. 'You did well, Moll – fighting back against the Dream Snatch like that.'

Moll pulled the rug tighter around her. 'I don't understand why the Dream Snatch opened up the last bits of my nightmare. Why do the Shadowmasks want me to know about the Soul Splinter?'

Cinderella Bull stoked the fire and her gold-penny shawl jangled. 'They don't. The Shadowmasks wanted you to give yourself up to Hemlock's poison and their Dream Snatch. They thought, now they know your name, they'd be strong enough to destroy your mind, but you fought back before they could work their curse in full. And, in fighting back so hard, you uncovered the memory they wanted you to forget.'

Gryff crept towards the fire and burrowed beneath Moll's rug, away from the eyes of the camp. Then he leant against Moll's legs.

Alfie frowned. 'But the hemlock inside the berries, how did they get it in there? You've got your people guarding the camp from the trees the whole time.'

Oak shook his head. 'Hemlock didn't need to touch those berries – or even come close to the camp. He must've worked his curse from a distance, and that's when Moll saw him between the trees.'

Siddy shifted on his stool, cuddling his earthworm close. 'And to think poor Porridge the Second could've eaten those berries.'

Patti threw him a scathing look.

Alfie turned to Cinderella Bull. 'This Soul Splinter – the shard of black ice that one of the Shadowmasks dripped into Moll's parents' mouths. How can something like that *kill* people?'

Cinderella Bull was silent for several seconds, then she looked at Moll. 'You know, don't you, child?'

Moll looked down at her toes and nodded.

'How do you know?' Siddy asked.

Moll looked up. 'Because I *felt* it – the horror and the darkness all seeping into my bones at once – and I heard their chant, the one worse than the Dream Snatch . . .' She took a deep breath and beneath her rug Gryff wound his tail round her ankle. 'The Soul Splinter is filled with the darkest curses.'

206

Cinderella Bull nodded. 'There'll be curses in there darker than the deepest night, more rotten than decaying fungus.'

Moll shrank further inside her rug. 'The Shadowmasks tore away their shadows – their *souls* – for a reason.' She paused. 'They've locked them inside the Soul Splinter and that's how they kill: they drip their cursed souls into the mouths of their victims and the darkness that grows in them is too much for any living soul.'

The fire crackled on into the inky darkness, but no one spoke.

Then Alfie rummaged in his pocket and drew out the tattered rag Mellantha had given them on which was written:

SHADOWMASKS

Limping, he pulled his stool nearer Moll's. 'The letters,' he said quietly. 'S for Skull ... H for Hemlock ...'

Moll's eyes widened. 'Just like Mellantha said: *Think about the letters, the word. It's all there.* It's a pattern, isn't it?'

Cinderella Bull peered at the rag, then nodded grimly. 'And you've got to see it through.'

Siddy pointed to the letters. 'If Skull came with the Dream Snatch and Hemlock with the poison, maybe every Shadowmask has a different curse.' He paused. 'Who does the Soul Splinter belong to?'

Moll shuddered. 'The Master – that's what the others called him.' She looked up at Oak. 'But I saw something else. Something I know you saw too, when you found my parents. Something which none of us will know how to explain.'

Oak hung his head. Mooshie raised a hand to her mouth.

'The Shadowmasks had shaved my parents' heads.'

And to that not even Cinderella Bull had an answer.

As they made their way to their wagons, Cinderella Bull stopped in her tracks. She was clasping her obsidian fortune-telling ball and her eyes were closed.

'Oak,' she said gravely.

Oak hurried over and Moll followed with Gryff.

'I can see them coming – as clear as if I'm looking at a picture.' Her voice sounded distant, like an echo. 'Skull and all of his gang, with the hounds at their feet, straining forward on their leashes. They know Moll broke their Dream Snatch. They'll come from the Deepwood – and they'll come tonight.'

Her voice stopped suddenly, like a tap being turned off, and her eyes opened. They flitted over Moll's and Gryff's faces and then rested upon Oak.

'We haven't got much time.'

Chapter 29
Waiting For the Ambush

Night deepened. Oak's camp was silent and still, as if holding its breath. Tucked up in the branches of the Sacred Oaks, they waited.

Mist slunk into the clearing below them, settling on the branches of the trees like an unwanted guest. All of the wagons had been bolted and the cobs and greyhounds tethered to trees hidden deep within the Ancientwood. Even the chickens and, on Siddy's insistence, Porridge the Second had been caged up and concealed.

The embers of a fire glowed in the middle of the clearing, turning the hanging mist to amber, and, far above this, Moll, Gryff and Alfie crouched inside the biggest of the Sacred Oaks. Siddy had been prised away into another tree to take care of his baby sister, but, on the branch below Moll, Cinderella Bull, Mooshie, Oak and their sons huddled.

Gryff leant into Moll and she ran a hand along his back. He'd keep her safe. She'd seen him leap from the tallest branches of a beech tree and land on his feet unscathed. She tucked her knees under her chin; so long as Gryff was with her, she'd be all right.

'It must be past midnight now,' Moll whispered. 'Perhaps they're not going to come after all.'

Alfie shifted beside her and the leaves on the branch trembled – as if they too knew what was coming. 'Skull will come,' he said. 'He always does.'

'And you think Cinderella Bull's plan is really going to work?'

A branch creaked beneath them. 'It'll work, Moll.' It was Mooshie's voice, but Moll noticed that even she couldn't mask the fear that had settled itself over the camp like a hard frost.

Seconds later, it came.

At first, it was the pounding of hooves they heard; then came the feverish shrieks of the hounds. Whips cracked, shattering the stillness, and the hounds bayed louder. But there were no voices. Skull's gang were approaching the camp in a terrifying wave of silence.

Moll's palms were hot and her heart was thudding inside her. But no one moved or uttered a word within the trees, exactly as they'd planned.

The beating of hooves was louder now – and closer. Then, bursting through the mist, Moll saw the dark shapes of Skull and his gang, urging on their cobs. Six hooded shapes thundered towards them: Skull, Gobbler, Brunt, the other two boys and . . .

Moll's heart raced. The second Shadowmask.

The hounds rampaged through the forest and stormed into the clearing, tearing at their leashes, their teeth bleached against the night. And then suddenly they were still.

One of the riders threw back his hood; Skull's white mask hung in the mist.

'The cowards are locked inside their wagons.' His voice was brittle, like dried-out clay.

Gobbler's hunched back was a shadowy bulge in the darkness, and beside him was a man with a mask of slate, a jutting mouth and gaping eyeholes. Clumps of dead flowers for hair and poisonous berries rotting away where ears should have been ...

Hemlock. And he was muttering under his breath.

Almost at once Moll felt his curse, crawling through the night to her soul, feeding on her fear. *Come to us, Moll Pecksniff. You're ours now. You're not one of them. You never will be. And, so long as you stay here, you put them all in danger. Come away now; give yourself up to our curse.*

Moll's mind raced. She was safe, tucked up inside the highest oak, but every fibre in her body wanted to climb down and give herself up. As if he sensed this, Gryff put two legs in front of her. His claws dug into the bark, but it would only be a matter of time before Hemlock's curse sought him out too.

Moll wanted to shake Gryff, to make him understand. What chance did any of them have against the Shadowmasks and their curses, against the Soul Splinter?

211

And then Gryff began to shudder as Hemlock's curse hunted him down.

'We've come for Moll Pecksniff and her wildcat, Oak!' Skull shouted. 'If you give them up now, we'll leave you and your camp in peace.'

Moll could feel Gryff's heart thumping with her own.

And then Hemlock spoke, his words slithering over his tongue like venom. 'If you refuse to hand over the girl and the beast, every wagon in this clearing will be savaged by the hounds.'

Moll thought of her box bed, of the catapults Oak had carved for her and the mounds of feathers and fir cones she'd collected over the years. And then she thought of Mooshie's wagon: her finest china, her precious lace and the bobble-fringed curtains. She wanted to leap down through the branches and hug Mooshie tight. Cinderella Bull's plan had to work, it *had* to.

'You give us no choice, Oak!' Skull shouted. 'Drop the leashes, boys!'

Moll held her breath. A second later, the night was filled with a terrible baying. Skull and Hemlock laughed – a clash of shrill, hideous laughter – as four blackened shapes raced up the wagon steps.

Moll covered her eyes; she couldn't bear to watch.

The hounds stopped baying suddenly and into the silence of the clearing came the sound of jaws working – greedily, furiously – at the slabs of meat left on the steps of every wagon.

Moll's heart leapt. The riders shifted on their cobs.

Moll could hear Cinderella Bull whispering to Oak. 'It should work: a wisp of mist; the sliver of a moonbeam; a spoonful of midnight dew; a drop of sap from each of the Sacred Oaks; a pail of crystal-clear river water. I brewed the Lull just as our ancestors taught us ...'

At that second, the hounds' jaws stopped grinding, and there were four loud thuds.

'No!' Skull roared. 'Get over to them, boys!'

Brunt edged towards Mooshie's wagon where a hound lay sprawled on the steps. Its eyes were closed, its body rising and falling gently as if it was asleep, and beside it was a half-chewed lump of meat.

Brunt nudged the hound but it didn't move. 'They've – they've left meat coated in something, Skull!'

Gobbler raced up the steps of Moll's wagon: another sleeping hound lay before the remains of a chunk of meat. 'It's that Dukkerer of theirs. She's laced the meat and it's sent them to sleep!'

'Into the wagons!' Skull muttered. 'Smash them up hard.'

A cold sweat clung to Moll's skin.

Doors were wrenched off and thudded to the ground and the night was filled with pandemonium: furniture crashed to the floor, windows shattered, objects clattered against walls and china was smashed to smithereens.

And then there was silence.

'Oak!' Skull roared.

But it was Wisdom who answered. 'Skull,' he replied, his voice gravelly and tough.

Moll could see Skull's mask searching through the mist.

'Oak's taken Moll,' Wisdom said. 'They left as night fell.'

Wisdom lowered himself down several branches and finally, as he crouched upon an outstretched branch, Skull and his gang rested their eyes on him. But he was above their grasp and there were no hounds to leap for him now.

'Leave,' Wisdom growled. 'You've destroyed our homes and we've nothing here you want.'

Hemlock nudged his cob closer to the tree. A deep burning sensation throbbed inside Moll; it felt as if Hemlock was looking right at her. 'The girl and her wildcat could be up in the trees with you,' Hemlock crooned, 'and we *want* them very much.'

Moll buried her face in her knees.

Wisdom threw a dagger down from the branches and it landed centimetres from Hemlock's cob. 'That's a warning.' He spat through the leaves, then sprang up on the branch so that he was standing. 'They've gone after the amulets – and they're going to find them before you can break the Bone Murmur. You'll see.' He was silent for several seconds. 'Leave. You've no business here.'

There was a murmur of voices from Skull's gang and then Hemlock started muttering. Moll could feel her body weakening – doubt, fear and guilt flooding her thoughts. Beside her, Gryff was shivering.

And then Wisdom did something no member of Oak's camp had done in Moll's lifetime: he fired a gunshot into the air. Its harsh crack burst out and silenced Hemlock's curses.

Moll flinched. Below her, Skull's gang shuffled backwards on their cobs. But Hemlock and Skull remained rooted to the spot, unflinching.

'Stay away, Skull,' Wisdom muttered.

Moll strained her ears; she could just make out Skull's voice – a scornful hiss. 'Guns and knives,' he mocked. 'You're not going to get rid of the Shadowmasks like that.' And then even quieter to Hemlock: 'We need to prepare the clearing. Moll and the wildcat will be there soon enough.' He turned to Brunt and the boys. 'Haul the hounds up on to your cobs. They'll wake later.' He jabbed a heel into his horse, then turned his head up towards Wisdom. 'If I find out you've lied, I'll burn your camp to the ground!'

With a crack of whips, Skull, Hemlock and their gang charged off into the trees with the sleeping hounds. And, as if they had been holding their breath all this time, Oak's camp finally breathed from the trees. Below Moll, Mooshie was sobbing.

'Everyone down from the trees,' Oak called. 'Stoke up the fire and keep the children away from the wagons.' But he stayed where he was for several seconds, cradling Mooshie close.

Moll twisted her body down between the branches with Gryff, an uncomfortable lump forming in her throat. Mooshie's wagon had meant the world to her. Now it lay in shreds below them. And it was all *her* fault.

The mist had lifted and the camp huddled round the fire. Oak's boys hurled on more and more logs until the flames towered high above them and the clearing was once more filled with light. Even Alfie, with his bandaged leg, was throwing wood on to the fire with Siddy.

A heaviness hung inside Moll and she shuffled over towards Mooshie and Oak who were staring at the crackling flames in silence. She picked up a log and tossed it on to the fire.

'It's all because of me,' she mumbled. 'It's not fair that Skull smashed up the wagons.'

'None of it's fair, Moll. It's not fair Skull destroyed our homes. It's not fair you're part of something you never asked to be. But life isn't fair – never is.' Oak paused and then looked Moll full in the face. 'You've got to be brave. You've got to keep going no matter how unfair it gets.'

'But all that work you and the camp put into making our wagons. You might as well not have bothered,' Moll sniffed.

Mooshie shook her head. 'If you think like that then you'll never build anything in your life, Moll. You build knowing things might go wrong. And sometimes it's when things get broken or lost or damaged that you realise all you've got to fight for.'

Moll twisted her hair into an angry knot and watched Gryff as he padded round the broken steps of her smashed-up wagon, his head hung low. 'But it's causing so many problems you hiding us away – us trying to fight back. Gryff and I would be all right out there. Might get into a few scrapes, but we can hunt and stuff.'

Oak smiled. 'Did you expect it would be easy fighting

back against the Shadowmasks?' He rubbed Moll's back. 'None of this is going to be easy or fair, but we've got to do it – because the Bone Murmur is something worth fighting for. It's the old magic and all its goodness is at stake and, no matter how scared you are or how guilty you feel, you keep going and you don't give up. Because there's a chance – however small – for all of us in this and, when you've got a chance, you fight on, however ugly things get.'

Mooshie smoothed down her pinafore. 'Tomorrow we'll rebuild our wagons. They'll always be our homes and, years from now, there'll be people who will say, "Mooshie Frogmore's wagon – now *that* was one to remember".'

Moll tried to smile. She wished she would stop feeling like she might burst into tears every time anyone spoke.

Wisdom approached with a bundle of quilts, blankets and cushions. 'It's a warm night and Skull won't be back. We'll be all right sleeping round the fire.'

Hours passed and Moll waited until everyone in the camp had gone to sleep, until the night belonged to only her and Gryff.

'We're going to find the amulets, Gryff,' she whispered. 'We have to because I won't let any more bad things happen to this camp – and I won't let my parents' deaths be for nothing.'

But across the river, in the darkness of the Deepwood, Skull and Hemlock were muttering a deadly incantation. And somewhere far, far away, the Master of the Soul Splinter was awakening.

Chapter 30
An Unexpected Discovery

'It's time to go, Moll.'

Moll squinted into the sunrise, her ears filling with the taps of a nearby woodpecker. Oak was kneeling before her, a knife and pistol tucked into his waistcoat, and a mug of dandelion tea in his outstretched hand.

The camp were curled inwards towards the fire even though it was now just a rubble of glowing embers. Children nestled close to their mothers, scooped into their chests like newborn puppies, and fully-grown men stretched arms and legs round their families. Moll felt a pang of loneliness until Gryff nuzzled her cheek before arching his back down to the ground in a stretch.

Moll nudged Alfie awake.

'Get some clean clothes on, both of you,' Oak said. 'Mooshie's laid them out just beyond the fire, together with fresh bandages for Alfie's ankle. Then meet me under the Sacred Oak behind your wagon, Moll.'

Moll's shoulders dropped as she looked across at her wagon. The door was hanging from one hinge and the window had been smashed right out. She glanced back towards the fire where Siddy was sleeping by his pa. 'And Sid?'

Oak shook his head. 'Not this time, Moll. The more people we are, the more likely it is we'll be seen.' Moll was about to protest when Oak said, 'You'll need to wear the belts I've laid out for you. No questions; we need to get going.'

Minutes later, Moll and Alfie stood beneath the tree and Oak approached, carrying two sheathed daggers.

He held one out to Moll and her eyes widened. It stretched from her wrist to her elbow and the sheath had been made from dark leather. It was scratched and scuffed and the initials FP had been stitched on with lighter thread.

'Ferry Pecksniff,' Oak said. 'That was your pa's dagger, Moll – a light knife but a deadly blade.' He looked down. 'Was my plan to give it to you when you were older, but it's best you carry it now; you might need it on this trip. After that, I want it back until you're grown.'

Alfie smirked. 'Grown? She'll be button-sized forever.'

But Moll didn't hear him. She drew the dagger from its sheath; the handle was made out of bone and just before the blade it was bound with string. She held it tight, as if she was holding her pa's hand.

'Careful,' Oak said. 'The blade's so sharp it'd slice a man's wrist clean off.'

Moll gulped and even Gryff took a step back.

Oak smiled. 'Your parents were honest, kind people, Moll. Your pa was big and strong and he knew this forest better than anyone. He could track an animal by its prints for miles and he could kill a rabbit stone dead with his catapult – and that's not to mention what he could do with this knife. As gypsies come, he was one of the bravest and most loyal any of us've known.'

'And my ma?' Moll asked.

Oak ruffled her hair. 'Sometimes I think I'm looking at her when I look at you. She was small, so small, with hair and eyes just like yours.' He laughed. 'And she was kind and funny – and mischievous like her daughter ...'

Moll held the words tight while Oak gave the second dagger to Alfie. 'So you won't need to use your rings to cut. It was my father's – an ancient iron dagger – but it's the best blade you'll find.'

Alfie drew back the sheath and the blade sparkled in the morning sun. 'It's shining, this is. Doesn't look like ancient iron to me.'

Oak smiled. 'That's because it's made with moon silver.'

'Moon silver?'

'You've never heard of moon silver?' Moll said. *That's because you're no gypsy. But your story's not as Skull told it either*, she thought, but she held her tongue because finding the amulets was more important than the lies Skull might have told Alfie. For now.

'When the moon's full, we take our iron and copper out under it,' Oak said. 'And, when we hammer it into coins, jewellery and daggers, the moonbeams sink into the metal and turn it to shining silver. It's real silver to us, moon silver is.'

Alfie let his dagger glide through the air. Its blade was so sharp that it seemed to slice the sunlight to slivers.

As Moll tucked hers back inside its sheath, she noticed something else. Three feathers: one red, one blue, one brown. 'Robin, jay, wren . . .' she murmured.

Oak nodded. 'Red for luck, blue for protection and brown for friendship. I put them inside each of our sheaths.'

Out of the corner of her eye, Moll watched Alfie turn the brown feather over in his hands and grip it tight.

Oak reached into his pocket and tossed them two chunks of bread. 'Breakfast. We haven't got time for more.' Gryff wrinkled up his nose at the bread but, when no voles or mice appeared from Oak's pocket, he ate it. 'And there's something we need to do first, before we look for the amulets,' Oak said.

They stood round the Sacred Oak, Gryff's whiskers twitching at near-silent sounds: a deer stepping among the undergrowth, a hedgehog shuffling in the leaves. Dreamcatchers hung from the lower branches, their beads and feathers fluttering in the breeze. Oak pulled out his dagger and, bending beneath the dreamcatchers, he began cutting into the trunk of the tree.

'What are you doing?' Moll asked, her mouth full of bread.

Oak had chipped out several small chunks of bark,

leaving an arrow shape within the trunk, pointing towards the clearing. 'I'm leaving a patteran.'

'A patteran?' said Alfie.

'Gypsy traveller's sign – sort of like a trademark that gypsies leave to show they've been here and settled. You carve your initials next to the arrow – and the number of years you've been here.'

Oak began to carve his initials.

Moll beamed, delighted at the prospect of using her pa's dagger so quickly.

But Alfie wore a very different expression. 'You don't think we'll be coming back, do you, Oak?' he said quietly.

Moll stiffened. But Oak continued to carve. 'I want to believe we'll be coming back, but gypsy traditions die hard and I want to leave my mark. Just in case.'

Alfie stepped forward and raised his dagger to the bark, but Moll pushed him back.

'No.'

Alfie reddened. 'Suppose I haven't got a right to carve your trees.'

Moll shook her head. 'It's not that.' She looked at Oak and then back at Alfie. 'I don't want you to carve the tree and I won't be carving it either because we're coming back – all three of us.' She looked at Oak's initials and scowled. 'Even if Oak has gone and carved his stupid pattern.'

'Patter*an*,' Oak corrected.

Moll glowered at him. 'The Ancientwood belongs to us and—'

222

Gryff was growling. He leapt in front of Moll, baring his fangs as he scanned between the trees. And then he turned back to the clearing, his head cocked to one side. Charging towards them, like a miniature bull, was Siddy.

'Moll! Moll! You won't believe what I've seen! I've found it! I know where the heart of the forest is!'

Mooshie was storming across the clearing behind him, waving her tea towel like a war flag. 'Siddy! You come back here right now! What would your ma say?'

Siddy ducked beneath the dreamcatchers. 'You've got to believe me, Moll! It's true! I found it!'

Oak stepped forward. 'Siddy, you've got to stay with the camp this time. We'll get caught if there are too many of us.'

Mooshie and her tea towel were getting closer.

Siddy shook his head. 'I *was* staying in the camp. Then I lost Porridge the Second and I went to search for him—'

Mooshie stooped beneath the dreamcatchers and took a swipe at Siddy.

Siddy sidestepped. '—and, when I was looking for Porridge the Second, I found it – the heart of the forest. I'm *sure* of it!'

Mooshie put her hands on her hips and Moll shook her head. 'You can't have done, Sid. Even the Elders don't know where it is.'

Siddy's face began to crumple and then it hardened with anger. 'Just because I'm not an Elder and quick-thinking like some of them back in camp – with their fancy letters and

223

long words – doesn't mean I haven't got just as much chance of finding things as they have!'

There was an awkward silence and Moll thought about doing a quick burp to break the tension.

But it was Alfie who spoke. Avoiding their eyes, his hands in his pockets, he said, 'Maybe we should listen to what Sid's got to say. You all listened to me back when Moll got sick.'

Mooshie tucked her tea towel into her apron pocket. 'This had better not be involving those highwaymen chickens, Siddy.'

They followed Siddy across the clearing to the oldest and biggest of the Sacred Oaks, the one Moll and Alfie had hidden in the night before. It was so huge and ancient it looked like the type of tree that might have existed even before time dawned or the earth began to breathe.

Siddy pointed to the stump that jutted out near the bottom of the trunk. Coins had been slotted into knife slits made by Oak's camp.

'See those coins? The ones we stick in to ward off evil spirits?'

Everyone nodded.

'Well, after I found Porridge the Second, I was just slotting in a coin to help frighten off the Shadowmasks and—'

Moll was good and ready to thump Siddy in the head. Did he honestly think that a coin could ward off Skull and Hemlock?

'And I know you won't believe me,' Siddy added, 'but,

when I slotted the coin into the stump here, the tree groaned.'

He paused, waiting for a reaction. No one said anything. In fact the silence was so profoundly awkward that Moll began to hum to distract everyone.

'It groaned – proper groaned – as if its spirit was alive!' Siddy exclaimed. 'And I think it's something to do with the heart of the forest – what you've all been searching for!'

Oak glanced at Mooshie. 'It can't be ... We need to get on, Moosh.'

Mooshie eyed her tea towel.

Gryff stepped closer to the stump. He looked back at Moll, who held his gaze, then he looked at Siddy.

Moll thought about it for a moment. Then she said, 'I believe you, Sid.'

Alfie threw up his hands. 'I was all for trusting Siddy, but you really think the tree's been talking?'

Moll nodded. 'It's got a spirit – all the trees have.' She paused and then under her breath, she said, 'And I suppose, if they've got spirits, there isn't any reason why they shouldn't talk.' She turned back to Siddy. 'Put your coin back into the slot, Sid.'

He fumbled in his pocket, accidentally bringing out Porridge the Second. Blushing, he pushed the bewildered earthworm back and drew out the coin. Siddy manoeuvred it into the slot he'd carved. Nothing happened. Alfie rolled his eyes and Oak looked anxious to press on.

And then it came. From somewhere deep, deep inside the

bark, a low, tired yawn, like a heavy door opening for the first time in a thousand years.

Siddy withdrew the coin and the yawn crumbled into silence again. They looked at one another, speechless, and then Alfie gasped.

'I – I can see a face,' he said slowly. Then, more confidently, 'Yes! A face shaped into the bark. Two eyes – there!' He pointed to two circular knobs protruding from the trunk, lines like wrinkles surrounding each one. 'And a nose!' He pointed to the long ridge of raised bark beneath the knob-like eyes. 'And a huge great mouth – see!' A large domed marking jutted out from the trunk and spilled down to the ground where the roots started.

Siddy's eyes shone. 'Only the mouth isn't just a mouth, I don't think. Looks like it might be a door!'

Mooshie frowned. 'Why's that?'

Siddy pointed to the stump with the coins slotted into it. 'Because I reckon that there's the handle . . .'

Moll gasped. 'Why haven't we seen this before?'

Oak shook his head in disbelief. 'Things that are important are mostly invisible to the naked eye until you need them. It's the ways of the old magic.'

'Here, take the coin, Moll,' Siddy suggested. 'The tree just groans when I try.'

Moll had slotted coins into the bark before, but nothing had ever happened. And so, not expecting much, she took Siddy's coin and slipped it into the tree.

Once again the tree groaned, its rumble seeming to wake

the very roots buried deep within the ground. And then suddenly the bark stirred. The domed shape of the mouth quivered and then it wriggled and very slowly it creaked out towards them.

Moll grinned. The old magic was fighting back now they needed it. The door into the heart of the forest had been unlocked.

Chapter 31
The Heart of the Forest

It was dark inside, dark and cool. And, as Moll had almost expected, the entire tree was hollow. The grey-brown bark twisted upwards into dizzying heights, but in the very centre of the oak was what Mellantha had promised them.

A well.

Mooshie looked at Oak, her mouth twitching with excitement. 'I'll go back and tell the others. You'll want the whole clearing guarded, Oak.'

He nodded. 'Make sure everyone's armed – men and women. We can't let Skull in now we're this close.'

Mooshie hurried away, leaving the domed door a fraction ajar. Shavings of light slipped in, illuminating Siddy's dancing shadow.

'I found it! I found it!' he whispered.

Oak nodded. 'You did good, Sid. You did good.'

The well rose up tall in the middle of the oak and it was different from most wells: instead of stones or bricks, knobbly tree roots wrapped themselves round one another to form the sides.

'Who put it here?' Moll asked.

Oak was silent for a few seconds. 'I don't think anyone did.' He paused. 'I think it's always been here, since the beginning of time.'

'Like the Bone Murmur,' Alfie said.

Gryff sprang up on to the well's edge, his whiskers twitching as he looked inside. Holding their breath, the others peered in after him.

The well had only about thirty centimetres of water inside, but somehow this water looked different, strange. It was glowing turquoise, like a shimmer of fallen stars.

'I can see the roots at the bottom,' Alfie whispered. 'There's nothing in there except strange shiny water . . .'

Gryff was prowling round the top of the well, peering inside.

Moll watched him, trying to understand. 'I – I think the amulets are inside,' she said.

'But we can't see them,' Alfie said. 'We can't see anything in there.'

Siddy frowned. 'But we couldn't see the heart of the forest either.'

Wincing, Alfie hoisted himself on to the well, but Oak held him back. 'No, Alfie – not with your ankle.'

'I've got nothing to lose.' And before anyone could stop him Alfie had lowered his body into the well. The glowing water swished round his legs. 'Feels different this water – softer or something.'

'Careful,' Moll whispered.

Alfie gasped. 'My – my ankle!'

Moll clapped a hand over her mouth. The bandage was unravelling in the water and beneath it, where the wound from the hounds' teeth had been, Alfie's skin was now unbroken. His wound had completely healed.

'It's – it's *better*,' Alfie said in disbelief.

'That's the stuff of the old magic, sure enough,' Oak whispered. 'It's what the bone readings of the past talked of. A magic that brings healing to wounds ...'

Alfie balanced his feet on the twisted roots either side of the well, then he reached into his belt for his dagger. Thrusting it into the bottom of the well, he heaved it through the roots until eventually water began to slip between the gaps.

In minutes, he had cut a circle nearly as wide as the well itself. More water gushed through the slits. He punched the circle with his foot and it swung away. There was a sudden rush as the rest of the water drained from the well, plunging down somewhere far below Alfie's feet. He looked up and grinned, then he slipped through the hole and was lost in the shadows for several seconds.

When he emerged, he looked back up at them, wide-eyed. 'You're not going to believe this.'

Moll lowered herself into the well, manoeuvring her body through the hole. She couldn't see a thing, but she could feel roots jutting out beneath her feet in downward step-like formations. And following her every move she could feel Gryff's near-silent steps.

Behind her, Oak struck a match.

Goosebumps bristled on Moll's arms. 'It's – it's not possible . . .'

They were standing halfway down a staircase made entirely from twisted roots which led down into a very large chamber. The room's ceiling arched above them, so big it sprawled out beyond the light of the match, fading away into shadows.

The group edged down the stairs, deeper into the heart of the forest. Oak's match went out and they were smothered by the dark. Water that dripped from the well echoed through the chamber like a leaking bath tap.

Oak fumbled in his pocket for another match, but Moll stilled his hand.

'Wait. I think there's a sort of light in here.' She screwed up her eyes at the shadows. 'A glow like the water in the well. Follow me.'

She stepped off the staircase with Gryff and ran her hand over a knobbly root that lined the chamber wall; it was cool to touch – so cool it felt to Moll like it might never have been warm. They edged further into the darkness. A flap of wings rushed towards them and Moll felt the cold breath of a creature rustle through her hair. She shivered and Gryff growled as the bat screeched, shaking the silence with its gristly flapping. Then it was swallowed by the dark.

'Don't like bats,' Siddy muttered, caressing his pocket. 'Even Porridge the Second's scared. Maybe we should turn back.'

Moll scowled. 'Shut it, Sid, or I'll get Gryff to eat your worm.'

For a second, Moll's mind wandered to the Dream Snatch, to Skull and Hemlock clawing for her mind. Her heart beat faster, drowning out the near-silent sound of Gryff's footsteps as he padded further away from her. Moll blinked. She wasn't imagining it; they were shrouded in darkness, but further ahead the chamber ended and it was hazily lit by a bluish light, like a winter mist.

'Look at the walls at the back of the chamber there!' Oak cried.

Jutting out from the earth wall, the tree roots twisted into incredible shapes. And, although every root was different, every shape was the same: the mighty head of a stag.

Moll gasped. 'Sixteen points on each of the antlers – just like you said, Oak! They're carvings of the silver stag, aren't they?'

'The oldest and wisest beast in Tanglefern ...' Siddy whispered. 'The beast whose bones make up the Oracle Bones!'

Oak reached out and ran a hand over the pointed tip of an antler. 'All this lying hidden underground.'

Siddy peered into the mouth of a roaring stag. He shivered then stepped back.

'The blue light – where's it coming from?' Alfie asked.

But Moll hadn't heard him. She whirled round and her heart quickened. 'Gryff. Where's Gryff?'

'*Brrrooooooo.*'

Moll jumped. 'Gryff! Where are you?'

'*Brrrooooo.*'

Moll scanned the wall of stag heads, feeling her way towards Gryff's call.

And then she saw him, sitting very still beneath a head carved from the roots.

'This one – the one Gryff's found!' Moll cried, running towards it. 'It's glowing inside! That's where the light's coming from!'

'Moll,' Oak said quietly. 'That isn't a silver stag's head.'

Moll looked up at the head twisting out from the tree roots. It was much bigger than all the others and the neck was craning over her in a mighty arch. But there were no antlers. The head was rounder, the ears larger, and the mouth opened wide, bearing row upon row of razor-sharp teeth.

This was a wildcat and its eyes were blazing with turquoise light.

Chapter 32
The Missing Lines

The eyes were orbs – big and round, burning bluer than the sea amid the roots. Two clawed paws jutted out from the chamber wall either side of the wildcat's head, and beneath them sat Gryff, staring up at Moll with wide yellow-green eyes.

Moll's breath fluttered. 'Do – do you think the amulets are *inside* the wildcat? Are they what're making the chamber glow?'

Siddy peered closer. 'But the roots are wrapped round each other thick and fast. You wouldn't get your hand inside one of those gaps. Not even you, Moll.' He turned to Oak. 'You'll have to cut them—'

Alfie gasped. 'No, wait! There are letters carved into the root above the wildcat's head. None of the stags have that. Look – here!'

Moll sprang up on to her tiptoes and scanned the words: 'It says: EMBUR.'

Siddy shook his head. 'EMBUR doesn't sound good – like *dismember* only shorter.' He shuddered and looked hopefully towards the exit.

234

'We should try mixing the letters up,' Alfie said. 'Remember, Moll? That's what Mellantha did; this might be another clue!'

Moll's mind raced with letters until they became meaningless squiggles. She shook her head. 'I'm no witch doctor; I can't crack it just like that!'

Gryff padded towards Moll and rubbed against her knees. She closed her eyes and tried again. The letters floated before her; she moved them back and forth, arranging them into different places, and then suddenly she opened her eyes.

'I've got two words!' she cried. Her eyes were sparkling and there was a tremor in her voice. 'EMBUR backwards – it's RUB ME!'

Everyone looked at the wildcat made of roots.

'Rub me?' Oak murmured.

He ran a hand over the neck of the wildcat. The chamber was silent, as if sucked of air, but nothing happened.

Siddy tilted his head to one side and looked at the creature's eyes. 'Maybe you've got to do it, Moll,' he said quietly. 'Like with the coin in the door. You're the next Guardian of the Oracle Bones after all.'

Moll lifted her hand and ran it very slowly over the wildcat's head. Almost immediately, a tingling sensation prickled through her, as if every hair on her body was standing on end. Although the fur had only been carved out of roots, Moll could *feel* each individual strand beneath her fingers – and it felt soft and warm, like Gryff's coat.

Gryff curled his tail round her leg and, at that moment, Moll felt more wildcat than girl. As if she and Gryff were linked up in something so tight not even the Bone Murmur could explain it.

She let her fingers slip over the wildcat's nose and instead of rough tree roots the nose felt warm and alive. The warmth spread through Moll's body and, for the very first time in her life, she felt as if she was actually holding magic in the palm of her hand. She edged her hand into the fur of the wildcat's throat.

Then something extraordinary happened. With a loud crunch, one of the wildcat's front legs moved. Quick as a flash, it clamped down on to Moll's wrist. Oak, Alfie and Siddy jumped backwards, but Moll didn't flinch. Neither did Gryff.

The wildcat's eyes were blazing, then from inside the tree roots there came a voice – deep, soft, like it was part of the tree itself. And Moll recognised the voice. Because it carried with it half-forgotten memories – memories of her beginning.

'Moll? My darling, Moll,' it said.

Moll trembled. *Could* it be?

'I'm here, Moll. It's your pa. And I'm here for you. *Right here.*'

Moll blinked in disbelief.

Again the voice sounded. 'I've missed you, my girl – *so much.*'

Her pa's voice was so real she could almost touch it. Moll

glanced at Oak who stood beside her, his hands clasped over his mouth.

'You're bigger now.'

And Moll could tell that the voice was smiling. Because this was more than just a voice somehow. This was a voice that carried a person with it: a broad-shouldered, strong man with dark hair and a wide smile.

Moll leant hungrily towards the voice. 'Are – are you *real?*' she whispered.

The voice laughed. 'Real?'

Moll nodded.

'I'm real, sure enough.'

'But—'

'Real isn't what you see, Moll. It's what you *feel* – what you know deep down to be true even though you've got no proof.'

An ache swelled inside Moll – part happiness, part terrible loss. 'Then you must be real,' she said quietly, 'because I *can* feel you.'

The voice was smiling again. She could tell.

'I've never stopped watching over you, Moll. I've been in the leaves when you've been climbing trees; I've been in the river when you've been swimming; I've been by your side when your sleep's been troubled.'

Moll willed her voice forward. 'It was the Shadowmasks who – who took you and Ma away, wasn't it?'

Her pa's voice was silent for a second. 'We knew it would come.'

Moll felt angry tears rising inside her. 'You knew! And you didn't stop them?'

'It was written, Moll – written in the Oracle Bones before we died . . .'

Moll shook her head. 'The Bone Murmur says nothing about you leaving.'

'There are two lines missing from the Bone Murmur as you know it, Moll, lost over the years as it passed down through the generations. And it was the missing lines that my dear Olive read in the Oracle Bones. There was a reason she didn't reveal them:

> There is a magic, old and true,
> That shadowed minds seek to undo'.

Here Moll's pa paused. And then he spoke the missing lines:

> **'They'll splinter the souls of those who hold**
> **The Oracle Bones from Guardians of old.**
> And storms will rise; trees will die,
> If they free their dark magic into the sky.
> But a beast will come from lands full wild,
> To fight this darkness with a gypsy child.
> And they must find the Amulets of Truth
> To stop dark souls doing deeds uncouth.'

Moll's voice was smaller than a whisper. 'You knew all along? And there was nothing you could do?'

'Both your ma and I thought we had more time. We thought we could fight back and find the amulets before the Shadowmasks struck.'

Oak shook his head. 'You should've told me, Ferry. I would've helped; I would've fought with you and Olive.'

'We knew it had to be so,' Ferry replied. 'The only way the Bone Murmur could go on was for us to die. The old magic had to stir and fight back.'

'But the message you read in the Oracle Bones,' Moll said, 'the one to find the amulets: *Dew Hill Maiden*. We followed it. We searched for the heart of the forest, for the amulets – and we found *you*.'

Ferry laughed. 'When you look for one thing, you often find another.' He paused. 'And then you realise it's the unexpected thing you were looking for all along.'

Moll leant closer to the wildcat so that only her pa could hear. 'I think I've been looking for you all along – even in my dreams I've been looking.'

'I know, my girl.'

'What happened that night by the river, Ferry?' Oak asked. 'There are things we still don't know.'

'The Shadowmasks summoned their Soul Splinter and, though it may've killed me and Olive, it didn't splinter our souls like they'd hoped. We believed in the Bone Murmur and we died for it, so our souls fought back and became the very things the Shadowmasks fear and hate. Our souls *became* the Amulets of Truth.'

'*You're* the amulet?' Moll murmured. 'And my ma ... is she here too?'

'It's only me here, Moll – I'm the first amulet. Your ma's the second and the third is an unknown soul.'

A sudden dread washed over Moll. 'Aren't the amulets all together?'

'No. The search will take you much further afield than Tanglefern Forest, Moll – over wild seas and across the remotest mountains. The Shadowmasks' power is growing and their darkness is spreading across the lands; the Ancientwood here is just the beginning ...'

Moll's heart sank. The task was widening before her into a dark, forbidding valley.

Alfie shifted in the shadows. 'How can we find the Amulets of Truth like the Bone Murmur says? You're – you're a soul – a voice in the dark ...'

'Before amulets become coins, jewels, pendants and the like, they have to have had a *story*. They have to have counted for something.' Ferry paused. 'Each of the Amulets of Truth contains a soul and each of these souls is searching for a virtue needed for the old magic to triumph – virtues that define us as human beings. Once you've shown that virtue, the amulet'll be yours.'

'What's the first virtue?' Moll asked glumly. 'Because if it's being polite or thinking before speaking or dressing proper then we're not going to find these amulets fast.'

240

Ferry laughed. 'The first amulet stands for courage. For being brave no matter how bad things get – because you're not going anywhere in life without bravery.'

Everyone was silent. And then Ferry said, 'Oak, you've been brave fighting to keep Moll and the whole camp safe since the day I left. Alfie—' Alfie leant in closer, '—you've been brave helping Moll when it meant risking everything.' Ferry's voice became a whisper so that only Alfie and Moll could hear. 'And in finding the amulets you *will* learn the truth about your past.' Alfie's eyes widened. 'And Siddy—'

Siddy bit his lip. 'It's not my fault I'm scared of bats – Ma borned me that way.'

Ferry laughed. 'Siddy, you showed courage taking my bone reading and leading everyone to the heart of the forest when no one would believe you. Gryff's protected Moll's every move even though there are Shadowmasks out there waiting to take him too.' He paused. 'And Moll, my own Moll, you've shown bravery in so many ways. Sneaking to Skull's camp, then escaping, following my bone reading, fighting the Dream Snatch and keeping going every single day, no matter how frightening things have been.'

Moll felt the tears rolling down her cheeks. The wildcat's paw squeezed tighter on her wrist and, for a second, the turquoise eyes flashed brown – a deep, dark brown like polished leather. Moll looked into her pa's eyes and smiled. And then the burning blue eyes of the wildcat returned.

'All of you – you've won the amulet fair and square and in a few moments it'll be yours.'

'What've we got to do to beat the Shadowmasks?' Moll asked through gritted teeth.

'Find the last two amulets and destroy the Soul Splinter. You do that and you crush the Shadowmasks and the Bone Murmur is saved – the old magic will keep turning.'

Moll clenched her fists. 'There's something else, Pa. Why did the Shadowmasks shave your heads when they came for you? There's something important about that, but I can't work out what!' But at that moment there was a crunch and the wildcat's paw lifted from her wrist. Moll could feel her pa slipping away. 'Don't go!' she cried.

Her pa's voice was quieter now. 'You haven't much time, Moll. The amulet'll be yours in a few seconds and later you'll know what to do with it.' He paused, his voice quieter still. 'Moll, never forget you're part of Oak's camp – you *do* belong. I loved you more than any father could love a daughter, but I wasn't given much time. The others have time and they're longing to give it to you. So, for me, let them in.'

'But – but I only just got you back!' Moll stammered, fresh tears welling. 'Don't leave me now!'

'You've a journey in front of you, and a journey's two things: a moving away and a moving towards. In moving away there is only what is known, and in moving towards there is hope. This is a journey of moving towards. I'll never really leave you, Moll. I'm around you every day.'

And then the wildcat's eyes closed. The chamber blackened and Moll stepped backwards, feeling for Gryff. He snuggled close, then the carved wildcat opened its eyes and the chamber was flooded with blue light again.

A strange grinding noise sounded and, very slowly, water began to trickle from the wildcat's mouth into a wooden basin beneath it. It fell like rumbles of faraway thunder and then there was another sound, and it cut into the rumble as clear as a wind chime: the clatter of something hard dropping into the basin.

There, glittering under the carved wildcat, lay the most spectacular jewel Moll had ever laid eyes on. Cinderella Bull had rubies as red as royal robes and emeralds as deep green as the forest's leaves, but this jewel was something else.

'The amulet!' Moll whispered, hardly daring to breathe.

Every blue – sapphire, cobalt, cerulean, navy, indigo, azure, iris, teal – sparkled from the jewel and danced up and down the walls of the chamber, like a turquoise rainbow trapped underground. The jewel was encased in silver and not moon silver this time, but the *real* thing. There was a chain – with links as fine as spider's silk – fashioning the whole thing into a necklace.

Moll reached into the water and held it in her hand. It was cold and heavy, as if many untold secrets had been locked inside it. She slipped it over her head – a part of her pa right there with her.

Her eyes narrowed. 'Now we've got it, we're going for Skull.'

That's when the footsteps started: hesitant at first, then louder, faster, like a torrent of water rushing towards them.

Chapter 33
Cinderella Bull's Foretelling

Moll's eyes darted round the chamber. They were at the end of it. There was nowhere left to run. Gryff snarled through clenched teeth and Oak whipped out his dagger, pushing Moll, Alfie and Siddy behind him.

The footsteps charged on through the darkness towards them. Moll's pulse hammered in her ears and her skin crawled with sweat. It was over. There was no way out. She reached for Gryff and felt his heart beating with hers.

'Oak!' came a cry from the shadows.

Terror gripped Moll's throat. The Dream Snatch had started inside her again – slow and steady. She watched in horror as three dark shapes loomed out of the shadows. Skull? Hemlock? Gobbler?

'Oak!' the voice cried again.

Siddy had closed his eyes, prepared to be eaten alive by whatever was coming for him, and, beside him, Alfie felt for his dagger. Oak strained his neck towards the advancing shapes, his dagger outstretched before him.

And then he lowered it and smiled.

One after the other, Domino, Wisdom and Noah shot out of the shadows into the light.

'Sorry if we caused a fright,' Domino panted, hands on his knees. Though he was the smallest of the brothers, he'd outrun them both. 'Mooshie sent us after you as soon as she saw it.' He wiped the sweat from his brow. 'You're not safe down here.'

Oak took a step forward. 'Saw what? What's happened?'

'Skull's coming back,' Wisdom said, 'with Hemlock, Gobbler, Brunt – all of them. Cinderella Bull read it in her crystal ball. Skull knows we lied about Moll searching for the amulets far from the camp. He must've used some kind of dark magic now he knows her name, to find out where she is.'

Domino nodded. 'They'll come back to our clearing, Cinderella Bull says.'

'With the hounds?' Oak asked.

Noah shook his head. 'Cinderella Bull saw them in her crystal ball too. The Lull's healing properties worked, because when the hounds woke up they were just harmless strays. Skull let them loose when he realised, but we've wheeled the wagons out of the clearing and hidden them in the forest—' He paused. 'Because Skull means to burn Moll and Gryff out of Tanglefern.'

Gryff dug his claws into the ground, his fur bristling with anger. Beside him, Moll clenched a fist round the amulet.

'Well, Skull and Hemlock aren't going to smoke us out because we've found the amulet and – and . . .'

Moll uncurled her fist to show the glowing amulet, but her words crumbled into silence. And *what?* What did she think they'd be able to do with a necklace against the power of the Shadowmasks?

But Wisdom, Domino and Noah were staring at the amulet now, transfixed.

Wisdom straightened himself up, running a hand over his ponytail, and then he noticed the carved shapes of the silver stags all around them. He looked at Moll. 'You're right. Skull isn't going to smoke you out, Moll, because these stags and that amulet are worth ten times the power of the Shadowmasks.' His eyes shone. 'We got a chance now, Pa, haven't we?'

Oak nodded. 'Are all the camp safely away from the clearing?'

'They're up in the Sacred Oaks already,' Noah said. 'Most are armed with daggers and Jesse's got a pistol. When Skull comes, they'll let him have it.'

Oak took a deep breath. 'Then we've got to go fast because I won't let my camp fight Skull alone.'

Siddy glanced at Moll's and Alfie's daggers, then he tapped Oak's back. 'I haven't got anything to fight Skull with.'

'You can borrow my catapult,' Moll replied, handing it to him, along with a sharpened stone she'd kept tucked in her pocket since the night she'd been rescued from the heath. 'If the rocks are sharp and the aim's keen, it's as good as a dagger.'

They turned from the wall of stags and Moll threw a last glance at the carved wildcat, hoping that somehow, somewhere, her pa would feel it. Using the light from the amulet to guide them, they sped through the chamber, raced up the staircase, then hauled themselves out of the well.

The domed door was open just a fraction and beyond it there was darkness and silence.

Wisdom looked at his father. 'We need to climb this oak – from there we've got a better position to fight.'

Oak nodded to his sons. 'Use your daggers wisely on Skull's three lads – to wound, not kill.'

Siddy felt for Porridge the Second and muttered a last goodbye.

Fear snaked round Moll's throat. Inside the heart of the forest she was safe. But out there were Skull and Hemlock. And the Soul Splinter.

She thought back to her pa's words: *you're not going anywhere in life without bravery.* And, with that, she tiptoed towards the door and crept outside.

While they had been inside, night had fallen in the deserted clearing and the sky was full of stars. Gryff slunk in front of Moll and leapt up the Sacred Oak. Moll felt for the ridges, scoops and bulges in the bark and twisted up after him. The others followed, spreading out across the branches.

Moll clung to the trunk, her body trembling. In the distance, there were lights – and they were crossing the boundary, snaking through the river in a line of fire.

Oak clutched his dagger, then turned to his sons. 'Skull,

Hemlock and Gobbler are souls rotted in hell – do as you like with them. No one's going to mind them gone from Tanglefern.' He clasped each son by the hand. 'Now split up among the branches and take aim.'

Moll shuffled out along a branch, but Oak grabbed her arm and yanked her behind him. 'They can't be allowed to see you, Moll. You're to stay back. Understand?'

'But it's all because of me this is happening!' she whispered. She felt for her pa's dagger. 'I want to help fight back!'

'If we lose you, we lose everything, Moll: the forest and the Bone Murmur. That's what this is about.'

And so, flanked by Gryff and Alfie and shielded by Oak, Moll could only watch as Skull's gang drew nearer and nearer.

Oak cupped his hands to his mouth and let out an owl call. And, from every Sacred Oak around the clearing, owl calls answered. The camp knew Oak had come back for them and now it was time to fight.

Chapter 34
Up in the Sacred Oaks

Skull's gang rode into the clearing, holding torches that blazed with fire. The scars marking Brunt's face glowed in the torchlight and Gobbler's running eye gleamed like a beetle. But what frightened Moll most, what made the blood course through her veins, was not the two masks lit up beneath the hoods.

It was the strange creature that prowled between the Shadowmasks.

It moved like oil, stalking into the clearing with blazing red eyes and a scaled body. It was no bigger than a hound, but the head that hung from its black body was the unmistakable face of an ape.

Oak gasped. 'It *can't* be . . .'

Moll's face twisted with terror. 'What – what is it?'

'Cinderella Bull was wrong,' Oak said. 'Not all of Skull's hounds woke up as harmless strays; this one woke as – as— ' he gulped, 'an Alterskin. Witch doctors are known for cursing the spirits of animals in their power – and when they curse their spirits they shift their appearance too.' He aused. 'This Alterskin will have a mind of pure evil now; it'll do *anything* Skull commands.'

Moll clutched Gryff tight.

Gobbler hurled a torch towards the base of an oak and its light illuminated his broken smile. 'Come out of the trees and fight!'

Within seconds, a path of fire had ripped through the undergrowth and Skull's gang cheered. Oak's gypsies leapt higher within the trees.

'Hand over Moll and her wildcat or we'll see the clearing burned to the ground!' Gobbler shrieked.

Skull's boys spread out with Gobbler to face the oaks, where the wagons used to stand, but Skull and Hemlock hung back in the centre of the clearing with the Alterskin. They didn't need to fight; their curses were stronger than daggers and torches. The Shadowmasks' heads were bowed and their Dream Snatch flooded Moll's body, tearing through her with thuds of loathing.

We know you're up there, Moll Pecksniff. You and your wildcat. There's no escaping us now. Give yourself up and all this will stop – all of your camp will be spared.

Blood pounded in Moll's ears.

Your parents tried to fight us, but what good did it do them? If you don't surrender, we'll kill Oak . . . We'll torture the women . . . We'll tear the children apart . . .

Moll gripped the amulet, willing herself to be strong. But it no longer glowed and, hanging round her neck, it looked like nothing more than a small lump of metal. Doubt crept in as the Dream Snatch beat louder. Perhaps the amulet had never been magical at all. Beside her, Gryff was clasping the branch with his claws, shaking his head from side to side.

Sensing his panic, Moll stretched out a hand and squeezed his leg. 'Fight it with me, Gryff.'

The wildcat burrowed into her chest, his body shuddering.

Gobbler and Brunt had lowered another torch to the foot of an oak. Gobbler's hunched back swelled in delight as the flames crawled upwards, crisping the leaves to rust. More gypsies jumped within the branches.

'Give Moll and the wildcat up and your forest will be spared!' Gobbler shouted. 'What hope have any of you got against the Shadowmasks? Who's going to answer me that?'

And then Jesse emerged, darting out on to the branch of a burning tree.

Siddy gasped. 'Pa!'

'I'll answer you that, Gobbler!' Jesse hurled down a dagger.

It shot through the flames and sliced keen into Gobbler's neck. Gobbler yelled out in pain, his back humping over his face as he slid from his cob to the ground. He crawled a few steps towards the edge of the clearing, his running eye wild and wet, and then, after a few moments, he was still.

Skull looked up from his chant. 'Torch it to the ground,' he snarled.

Like unseen acrobats, the gypsies leapt within the oaks, from branch to branch, from tree to tree. Daggers showered down towards Skull's boys, but they sidestepped on their cobs, hurling their torches at the trees. The clearing blazed orange, a graveyard of scorched undergrowth.

Brunt urged his cob forward, towards Jesse's tree. Realising his ma and baby sister would be tucked up with his pa, Siddy fumbled for his catapult and drew it out. Roaring with fury, he pulled back on the pouch. The sharpened stone flew through the air and slammed into Brunt's head. He cried out and tumbled backwards off his cob.

Two more knives hurtled through the air; one slammed into the leg of a tall, lanky boy with ruthless eyes and the other lodged in the arm of the last of Skull's boys. He had a haunted look: purple, curled lips and dark shadows for eyes. The boys fell down off their cobs and stumbled between the roaring flames. Still more daggers showered down – towards Skull and Hemlock this time – but they dodged them with a sinister quickness, hanging back to perform their curse.

And, between them, the Alterskin's red eyes narrowed.

Wisdom flung down another dagger, then looked to Oak, who nodded.

'Stay here, Moll,' Oak whispered. 'So long as Gryff and Alfie are with you, you're safe.' And then he shouted out into the clearing: 'Down from the trees, men!'

Oak's sons, together with Oak, Jesse and Florence's father, leapt from the burning branches, spilling into the clearing like a raging tide. Moll watched, aghast, as they darted between the flames, brandishing their daggers at Skull's boys.

'You're outnumbered and you know it!' Oak cried. 'We'll spare you all so long as you leave the forest and never return!'

Brunt was fumbling for something inside his waistcoat, then a pistol gleamed in the flames. 'Let them have it, boys!' he bellowed.

Several gunshots cracked into the air.

'Wisdom, Jesse!' Oak roared. 'Use your guns to wound not kill!'

Moll watched in horror, and yet, as she watched, the figures, the flames and the cobs were all becoming a blur. She felt the heat from the fire burn inside her, growing with Skull and Hemlock's chant. Her grip on the branch loosened, her balance wobbled, but Alfie seized hold of her. Beside them, Gryff's fur was wet with sweat and his eyes were wild. But Moll was oblivious to Gryff now. All she could feel, all she could hear, was the Dream Snatch clamouring in her ears.

'Leave Tanglefern!' Oak yelled from below. 'And we'll spare you!'

Skull's boys fought on, blind to Oak's words. Oak jammed his leg into Brunt's hand. The pistol dropped from Brunt's grasp, but he lashed out blindly with his dagger. Oak leapt backwards, then raised his own dagger. Jesse scampered forward and grabbed the fallen pistol from the ground. He raised it up, taking aim at another boy, but the boy ducked behind a tree.

Brunt jabbed his dagger at Oak's face. Oak jerked aside,

but the blade snicked his cheek. Blood trickled down to his jaw, yet still Oak jumped forward. Brunt was quick and he leapt aside. But Oak was quicker. He brought his dagger down on to Brunt's arm and it sliced through his clothing. Brunt howled with pain.

Oak drew out his pistol. 'Leave!' he roared. 'Or we'll shoot you all dead!'

Brunt's eyes were wide with fear and he faltered backwards. His jaw was shaking, but he raised his dagger again. Oak fired two shots into the ground before Brunt's feet. They ricocheted off a fallen branch and spattered against Brunt's shins. Brunt's legs buckled beneath him and he cried out. He looked at the dagger in his hand; blood had dribbled down from the wound in his arm and was now smeared over the handle. Grimacing, he let the dagger fall to the ground and, clutching his arm to his chest, he limped away, out of the clearing, into the darkness.

'Come back!' Skull roared.

But Brunt had already disappeared into the forest.

'He won't come back for you!' Oak cried to the last of Skull's boys. 'Leave and we won't fight you any more! Find other lodgings and work; Skull's dealing in a magic far darker than you realise!'

Skull's boys stumbled backwards, clutching their wounds. Bent double and fighting for breath, they looked at each another with panic-stricken faces. Oak's men gathered together in a cloud of anger, shouting and wielding their weapons. Beaten and bloodied, Skull's boys heaved themselves away from the clearing. Skull and Hemlock kicked their cobs in pursuit of the boys, howling for them to return.

'The Soul Splinter's been summoned!' Skull shouted after them. 'You want to miss out on dark magic like that?'

The Alterskin flicked a glance up to the very branch Moll crouched on, then followed.

Moll blinked several times, trying to understand what she was seeing. They were winning, surely, but then why did everything in her body tell her that Skull and Hemlock were stronger than all of this.

The Shadowmasks were lost in the trees for a moment and, in the commotion, no one noticed Gobbler's misshapen body haul itself up with a gun and take aim at the back of Oak's head. No one except Alfie.

The barrels of Gobbler's gun loomed like tunnelled eyes, but Alfie's arm shot back and, with one eye closed, he hurled his dagger. It spun through the air, a glint of leather and metal, and sunk into Gobbler's hand. The gun fell to the ground and Gobbler edged backwards, cursing. Alfie's eyes widened in shock as he realised what he'd done.

As Oak's camp fought to quell the flames, Skull tore back in the clearing, pausing for a second by Gobbler.

'Help me,' Gobbler rasped. And Skull fired his pistol into Gobbler's heart.

He raised a cloaked arm and pointed at the branch Moll and Gryff crouched on. 'That one,' he hissed. Then he turned from the clearing and rode back towards the Deepwood.

Moll shook her head, burying it in her knees. 'They're calling for me, Alfie! Make it stop!'

Beside her, Gryff clung to the branch, his whiskers trembling, his growl weakened to a whimper. Then he threw his head back and yelped.

Alfie held Moll by the shoulders. 'They've gone, Moll. It's just us!'

Moll shook her head, her body rigid with fear. 'They're here, Alfie. They're *here*!' She shuffled nearer to him.

And, like ghosts in the darkness, Hemlock and the Alterskin waited, stitched into the shadows beneath the Sacred Oak.

We know you're up there, Moll – with your wildcat. We can feel you. We can hear you breathing. Give yourselves up.

'Can you hear it?' Moll whispered, her eyes wide.

But, before Alfie could answer, something black and sinuous bolted up the tree towards Moll. Gryff leapt in front of her, his claws splayed. The Alterskin's red eyes throbbed and its scaled limbs thrashed out at Gryff. Moll scuttled backwards, pressing herself against the tree trunk with Alfie. Gryff yelped in pain as the Alterskin's claws sank into his fur, then he twisted free, gnashing his teeth, lashing at the ape-like face with razored talons. The Alterskin bellowed in anger and hurled itself at the wildcat.

Time shrieked to a halt.

Moll caught Gryff's terrified eyes, just as he fell from the tree. Limbs scrabbling, the Alterskin hurtled to the ground after him.

'GRYFF!' Moll yelled.

Gryff darted away from the Alterskin, but a net shot out from the shadows, hissing through the air. It whipped against Gryff's face and he swerved left, into the clutches of the Alterskin.

Moll struggled against Alfie, feeling Gryff's pain tugging inside her.

'GRYFF!' she yelled again, her eyes filling with tears.

'If you go after him, the Shadowmasks get you both!' Alfie shouted.

Hemlock slid out from the shadows, hurling the net again. It sucked Gryff backwards, cutting into his fur. Snarling, spitting, tearing at the ropes with his teeth, Gryff fought inside the net. The Alterskin thumped a claw on Gryff's back and Hemlock pulled the net tighter, strapping the ropes to his cob.

Oak and his men were rushing towards Hemlock now, but he leapt on to his cob and spurred it on, back towards the Deepwood with the Alterskin.

Moll twisted and shrieked within Alfie's grasp.

'No! Not Gryff!' she howled, great sobs ripping through her body.

Jesse fired his pistol at the Alterskin. It stumbled and then he fired again and again until it slumped down, dead.

But Hemlock rode on, wrenching Gryff further and further away from the clearing.

Chapter 35
Darkness Stirring

M oll scrambled down the tree, her eyes blinded by tears.

The clearing was a blackened wasteland, the Sacred Oaks charred with ash, but Oak's gypsies ran back and forth from the river beating down the flames with pails of water.

Oak rushed over to Moll. 'OK?'

And she knew what that meant: they were going back for Gryff.

She watched as Siddy tended to his father's wounds, then she scoured the clearing for Alfie, but he was nowhere to be seen. Dread crept in. Perhaps he'd realised they didn't stand a chance now and the thought of returning to Skull's camp had thrown up fresh fears.

It was Raven that Moll spotted first, entering the clearing ahead of Alfie as he led Jinx and Oak's cob towards them.

'Figured there's not a chance we're letting the Shadowmasks take Gryff so I fetched the cobs.'

Moll tried to smile, but an emptiness was growing inside

her, filling the space where Gryff had always been, even if she'd not known it until now. They swung themselves up on to the cobs.

'Wisdom, get the last of the flames out, then see to the wounded with Siddy!' Oak cried. 'Ma'll help you!'

Driving the cobs through the trees, they galloped through the river and raced into the Deepwood. The stars above them seemed to fade, one by one, as the darkness grew. Moll clasped the amulet around her neck tight as they galloped through the beeches, past the dead owl and the pierced rat.

There was no sign of the vapours this time, but somehow the air felt heavy, not with rain, but with something much, much darker.

Alfie's body was hunched with fear and Oak had cocked his pistol, but Moll didn't notice. Gryff's absence burned within her; she'd get him no matter what. They pulled the cobs back to a trot, then picked their way through the last of the trees before Skull's camp.

A low, almost strangled laugh escaped through the branches towards them. 'Tie him up on the ceremonial table, Hemlock!' Skull shrieked with pleasure.

The three of them edged forward and peered into the clearing. Enormous torches lit up a long wooden table. A giant bat had been carved into it, its painted black wings unfurled across the surface. Only then did they notice the trees ringing the clearing. Moll gripped Jinx's reins tight.

They were unmistakably *alive*.

Their trunks leered forward, their branches twisted into

drilled arms, their roots knotted into mangled feet. But the worst thing of all was the faces. Gruesome heads bulged out of the gnarled bark: troll heads with bat wings for ears, goblin faces with wild boar snouts, werewolves with snake tongues, warlock heads with wolf fangs. And they were snarling, growling, licking their lips in gleeful expectation.

Moll seized Oak's arm. 'They're tree ghouls, aren't they?'

Alfie froze. 'Tree ghouls?'

Even Oak's body was rigid with fear. 'The vapours – Skull must have trapped them inside the trees. And when you trap the broken hearts of witches their curses are said to seep into the vessel that carries them.' He urged the cobs back several paces and then in a low whisper he said, 'Stay well away from them.'

'But . . .' Moll's words fell short.

Skull and Hemlock were approaching the table, wrestling with a bundle of rope and fur. Moll watched, her body tearing inside as she remembered what Oak had said about Gryff years ago: *'Wildcats will fight to the death for their freedom; they are what it means to be really free.'*

'PAAHHHH!'

Gryff was stamping his forelegs and hissing through his teeth. He flung himself against the ropes and the tree ghouls cackled and groaned around him. The ache inside Moll grew, pounding inside her throat. But the tree ghouls moaned on and into their cries Gryff began to yelp.

Hemlock tossed the bundle of wildcat and rope on to the table, then, seizing a hammer, Skull drove several nails into the ropes, fixing Gryff fast. Bound on his stomach, his limbs splayed, Gryff gnashed his teeth and jerked his head from side to side.

And then the chanting started, low and deep, as Skull and Hemlock circled the table, their masks in shadow, their hands held high.

Moll clenched her teeth, ready to fight their Dream Snatch. But it never came. What followed was different, darker.

'Tonight we summon you to finish our chant,
Master of the Soul Splinter, do what we can't.
Come from the shadows, the gloom most dim.
Use curses of power, deadly and grim.

For here lies the beast, the one we all need.
Join with us now and make this cat bleed!
Believe us, the girl is not far away.
She'll come for him soon, the last of our prey.'

Somewhere in the night sky far above them something was stirring. The darkness seemed to thicken and the tree ghouls screeched with pleasure.

Alfie turned to Oak. 'We go – you and me – into the clearing to fight for Gryff!'

'And leave me here?' Moll hissed. 'I'm not sitting by while—'

It happened so quickly they could barely draw breath.

A tree ghoul ripped its roots from the soil and lurched towards them, swiping out with a withered claw. Moll screamed, ducking beneath it. It crunched down, rupturing the soil, and she fell from Jinx. Oak and Alfie spurred their cobs forward, towards the clearing.

'Use your dagger on Gryff's ropes!' Oak yelled to Alfie.

But the tree ghoul lumbered forward, wrenching them from their cobs, stringing them up in the air like puppets.

'Run, Moll!' Oak screamed. 'Get away from here!'

Moll scoured the trees for Jinx, but she was gone. She looked towards the ceremonial table and then she met Gryff's eyes. He blinked hard at her.

There's still hope, Moll, he seemed to be saying.

Hope? Moll thought. *What hope is there in all of this?*

Gryff tried to raise his head, but the ropes held him fast. And all the while Skull and Hemlock muttered round the table. The summoning was almost complete.

'*Come to us, Darkebite; the child is near.*
Drop from the darkness, feed on her fear.'

Moll cowered in the shadows of an ordinary beech. Just metres from her, a tree ghoul grunted as it overturned the undergrowth in search of her. Alfie and Oak wriggled and slashed at it with their daggers, but it wound them over and over again in its branches, like a spider binding a fly.

And, above the clearing, the darkness was gathering, conjuring a high-pitched screeching of its own.

Bats, thousands of them, swarmed overhead, swelling, growing, bulging into a terrifying shape. A figure was materialising, made entirely from the bats, and it throbbed high above them: Darkebite, the third Shadowmask and the Master of the Soul Splinter, had been summoned.

Tears streamed down Moll's cheeks. If she ran in to try and save Gryff, the Shadowmasks would kill her and the Bone Murmur would be broken forever. Everything her parents had fought for would have been in vain. She caught Gryff's eyes and the tears fell faster.

You're going to be OK, Moll, he was saying. She could almost feel his thoughts.

Silent sobs wracked Moll's body. Maybe this was how it was meant to end. Gryff's life for her own . . . He'd saved her once before and now he was doing it again.

The figure of bats was throbbing with screeches – hollow, like a dead man's call – and it was sinking towards the table.

Moll clutched the three feathers inside her sheath: luck, protection and, she looked up at Alfie and Oak, friendship. She gripped her pa's dagger tight, then, throwing one last glance at the tree ghoul crashing through the undergrowth metres from her, she darted into the clearing. Another tree ghoul thrust down its claws, but Moll leapt between them, racing on towards Gryff. Hemlock and Skull looked up at her, laughing behind their masks. Above them, the bat figure slid nearer still. Gryff looked at Moll, his yellow-green eyes large and scared.

Embur, a voice inside Moll called, almost so weakly Moll

ndered whether she'd heard it at all. *Embur*, it said again. And somehow Moll knew that this was her pa willing her on. Her mind whirled. And then she remembered the carving above the wildcat's head in the heart of the forest. She gripped the amulet for all she was worth, rubbing her thumb over and over the jewel. She felt a surge of hope, a hope so strong she could practically taste it.

But the descending figure, still more bat than human, was settling on the ceremonial table. Two enormous leathery wings unfurled over Gryff.

The amulet seemed to tingle inside Moll's fingers and it was glowing again, as it had done in the heart of the forest, coating the whole clearing in a turquoise veil.

Skull's eyes locked on to the amulet. 'Stupid child! You think that's going to help you now?'

Moll swallowed. What did she expect would happen if she rubbed the amulet?

Hemlock glided towards her, his mask a wall of stone.

Moll stumbled round the clearing, closer and closer to Gryff, gripping the amulet and her pa's dagger tight. The turquoise light was brightening now, crushing the darkness back. Clinging to a shred of hope, Moll tore the necklace off and held the amulet high.

'You can't take Gryff away from me!' she shouted. 'Because we've got things more powerful than the Shadowmasks ever dreamed of!' She shook the amulet for the Shadowmasks to see. 'We'll never give up on the Bone Murmur – we'll save the old magic!' Moll was trembling, but she could feel her pa's voice inside her, urging her on.

Hemlock ran towards Moll and she rubbed the amulet harder and harder. She looked at Gryff, the longing bursting up inside her. Hemlock advanced still closer.

All at once there was a thunderous crash followed by a tumult of screeching as the winged figure on the table crumbled into thousands of bats that tore off into the shattered sky. Hemlock stopped, his eyes suddenly wide with terror.

The ceremonial table had split in two and Gryff was scrabbling out of the net. Tearing back the ropes, he shot free and bounded over to Moll, flinging himself against her. Moll held him tight and their hearts clamoured together, beating with love and pain.

'The amulet!' Oak roared as the tree ghoul that held him bashed him against a branch. 'Hold it up again, Moll!'

Skull's and Hemlock's heads were bent low. Moll raised the amulet high and staggered backwards, her dagger ready. Gryff limped in a circle round her; he was cut and battered, but his teeth were bared. The two Shadowmasks edged forward while muttering their curses and, with every step they advanced, a terrible pain split through Moll. Gryff growled and spat; he could feel it too.

'You – you won't win,' Moll stammered, rubbing the amulet harder. 'Nothing good can come now you've cut away your souls!'

There was another deafening crash, followed by another then another. All around them the tree ghouls were itting down their centres, smashing forward in crumpled heaps, like giant stacks of bones. Alfie and Oak, finally free, raced towards Moll and Gryff.

The Shadowmasks were centimetres away from Moll and Gryff now, but their bodies couldn't fight what came next. The blue light from the amulet seemed to thicken into mist and it curled round Skull and Hemlock, tearing at their masks, ripping them away to reveal their faces. And they were the most terrible faces Moll had ever seen. The skin was a sickly grey and it hung in shrivelled folds, writhing with maggots. The mouths and noses were slits, like gashes in rotting skin. Moll recoiled in horror.

Then the turquoise mist began to claw at the Shadowmasks' necks. Their bodies contorted in vicious spasms, cringing backwards.

Skull clutched at his face, almost tearing the skin from his scalp. 'Get away from me!' he howled. 'Get away!'

'Darkebite!' Hemlock cried. 'Come back to us!' His body jolted into another spasm.

Moll's eyes widened. But Darkebite didn't come. The Shadowmasks' eyes were bulging whites, rolling within sunken skin. Moll's stomach churned.

Beetles, large and black, were spilling from the Shadowmasks' mouths and, as the mist tore at them, their bodies began to shrivel. The mist grew, brightening and thickening, until all that was left of the Shadowmasks were two masks: a skull and a face of slate. And then two rasping voices hissed through the clearing towards Moll:

'*Darkebite will come back for you . . . The Master always does.*'

A shooting pain pierced through Moll, sharper than anything she'd felt before. She stumbled to the ground, clutching Gryff and the amulet to her. The voices muttered on, knifing at her skin.

'*You can take our bodies, but you can't ever take our souls. We're locked inside the Soul Splinter; we'll never really die!*'

Summoning the last of her strength, Moll crawled forward and stabbed the masks with her pa's dagger. The voices crumbled into hisses, like thousands of tormented snakes, before dissolving into the dawn.

Pain seared through Moll. The forest around her was fading, Oak's and Alfie's cries just voices in the distance. But the clearing – it was *changing*. The mist was glittering now and – it couldn't be . . . it was melting into water, settling as a sparkling lake.

Moll could feel herself slipping further away.

The amulet was wriggling inside her palm again. She tried to hold it, but it struggled free. She seized the chain, trying to draw it back, but it tugged against her fingers and, as it did so, Moll heard her pa's voice somewhere deep, deep inside her, beyond the pain inflicted by the Shadowmasks.

'My Moll, you've done it! You've won the first amulet and beaten back Skull and Hemlock!'

The amulet pulled harder and the chain dug into Moll's fingers.

'I love you, Moll, and I'll be with you always.' The voice

s silent for a second. 'But there's a time for everything. So long as my soul is down here with you, it's trapped by the damage the Soul Splinter did to it. You must let me go.'

'Where – where will you go?' Moll sobbed.

'The stars, Moll. Every star is a soul watching over us and I'll be looking down at you – always.'

Moll felt for her pa's words and held them close. 'I love you, Pa,' she whispered.

'I'll never really leave you, Moll.'

'I know.'

Clinging to the echo of his whisper, Moll let the amulet slip through her fingers. She felt a strange lightness, as if a weight had suddenly been lifted from her. The amulet floated upwards, hanging above the lake like a miniature moon. And then one by one, like falling stars, lilies whiter than snow dropped from the sky on to the sparkling water.

The amulet, dazzling blue, hovered for a few seconds more and then it drifted upwards. Up, up, up into the sky – higher than the forest, higher than the furthest mountain peaks, higher than the moon – until it rested up in the heavens, the brightest of the glinting stars in a gathering blue dawn.

Moll tried to cling on to what she was seeing, but she was falling too fast now, tumbling down into bottomless black . . .

Chapter 36
The Secrets of Dawn

A low, rolling sound rumbled into Moll's sleep. Gone were the drums, gone were the rattles and the chants. This noise was different and she'd recognise it awake or asleep. Her eyes flickered open a fraction.

Two wide yellow-green orbs hovered in front of her face. They were lined with black circles and dashed with vertical stripes.

She blinked.

The rumbling noise again. '*Brrrooooooo.*'

Moll blinked a second time, then opened her eyes. 'Gryff,' she smiled, folding him into her arms and hugging him tight.

She looked around her: at the red velvet curtains drawn back from her bed; at the morning sunshine streaming through her shutters; at the polished pine walls; at the kingfisher feathers and giant fir cones scattered on her wardrobe. Someone had restored it all. And, for the first time in weeks, Moll felt a surge of happiness. She buried her head in Gryff's fur and laughed. He purred contentedly.

We did it, Gryff!' she whispered. 'We found the first amulet and we set my pa's soul free!' She tickled the wildcat's ear. 'And somewhere out there is my ma,' she said. Her heart beat excitedly at the thought. Then she sat upright in her bed and gasped.

'Oh, all that?' said Oak, who was sitting on a chair before a collection of strange objects strewn across the end of Moll's bed. 'Lucky charms from the camp – to make sure you woke up in good health. The stones with holes in them are from Hard-Times Bob. He thinks they'll be lucky.' He pointed to the largest stone, one that would have taken hours to haul inside the wagon. 'The daft old man thought he could squeeze his body through this one, but he got it stuck round his ribcage and he's had the hiccups ever since.'

Moll giggled.

Oak picked up a jam jar full of minnows. 'Siddy's lucky charm – except no one in the camp agrees it is a lucky charm. He wanted to chuck it in your face to bring you round, but Patti warned him that was one step too far.' Oak held up a cluster of red berries. 'Holly berries from Mooshie, I'm afraid; she hoped if a fertility charm was the first thing you saw on coming round you might start acting more like a lady in the future.'

Moll squeezed out the air from inside her cheeks and it made an unladylike squelch. 'And that?' she asked, pointing to a black plaited bracelet which looked as if it might have been made from animal hair.

'That's from Alfie,' Oak replied. 'Said he didn't believe in lucky charms so he made you a bracelet from Raven's tail. He said if Raven carried him away safe from the Deepwood, maybe he could help bring you back too.'

Moll didn't need to ask what Oak had given her. Her wagon was as good as new and it was clear he hadn't left her side since the Deepwood – and that kind of loyalty was more important than any present or charm.

'How long have I been sleeping?' Moll asked.

'Four days. The Dream Snatch – it almost sucked the life right out of you.'

'I've never slept that good and long!' She paused, her eyes widening. 'Does that mean it's stopped coming for me? The Dream Snatch won't twist my dreams to nightmares any more?'

Oak smiled. 'You and Gryff broke the Dream Snatch. You shattered it to pieces once and for all when you lifted that amulet up.'

Moll leant into Gryff. 'I don't understand though. What happened back in Skull's clearing?' she asked. 'Why did the amulet release all its power then? Why not when the Shadowmasks came to our camp?'

Oak's eyes sparkled. 'I'm not sure, but the old magic first stirred when time dawned. So magic's at its strongest when light changes: when daylight drops to dusk or night drifts into dawn.'

'You're just saying words that begin with d.'

Oak shuffled on to the bed and ruffled Moll's hair. 'I'm

271

't lying, Moll. Magic's at its strongest when light changes. So I think when dawn came to Skull's clearing the amulet was at its most powerful.'

'But didn't the Shadowmasks have curses and chants to break the amulet's power?'

'There's nothing stronger than the powers locked inside the Amulets of Truth. Your pa said the first amulet stood for bravery, so when you raced to help Gryff you gave it even more power. The Shadowmasks may've brewed curses dark enough to splinter souls, but they were broken in the face of your courage.' Oak smiled. 'The amulets are part of a deeper magic still and, so long as we find them all, the Shadowmasks can't touch our souls.'

'The last four Shadowmasks'll come for me though, won't they?' Moll said quietly. 'They haven't gone for good.'

Oak shook his head. 'I don't think so. Not gone. Weakened maybe – forced back for a while – but they'll come again.' He paused. 'Which is why, in a few days, we'll be leaving the Ancientwood.'

Moll shook her head. 'Leaving? But—'

'It's no longer safe, Moll. Darkebite knows where you and Gryff are.'

'But – but where will we go? This has always been home.'

Oak squeezed Moll's arm. 'We'll live as outlaws down by the sea.'

Moll's eyes grew big. 'By that big puddle of water leading out to the edge of the world?' She shivered then looked around her wagon. 'We'd have to leave all this...' She paused. 'And what if Gryff doesn't like the sea?'

Oak smiled. 'I've been over the heath and down to a cove by the seashore, Moll, while you've been resting.' He paused. 'And if you thought living in a wagon was good wait until you see the cave I've found.'

A ripple of excitement flickered inside Moll. She nodded to Gryff. 'We might quite like caves, actually.'

'You're the Guardian of the Oracle Bones now, Moll,' Oak said. 'Soon you must throw the bones and then we'll follow the bone reading to find the second amulet. With it, we'll destroy the Soul Splinter.'

Moll's body tingled. 'But Skull and Hemlock – they said their souls're locked inside the Soul Splinter and they're never going to die. How can we kill someone who can't die?'

Oak shook his head. 'We just have to hope that, if the first amulet destroyed Skull and Hemlock like that, the last two will have the power to destroy the Soul Splinter. Then the Shadowmasks' souls will die and the Bone Murmur and all it stands for will be restored for good.'

Moll groaned. 'That's heavy that talk. I was better with the jar of minnows –maybe even Mooshie's holly berries.'

Oak wrapped her up in a bear hug. 'Come and see every- one; they've missed you. Siddy said that even Porridge the Second's taken your absence hard.'

Once Oak had left, Moll bounced out of bed, filled with an energy she'd almost forgotten she'd ever had. She pushed Alfie's bracelet over her wrist, then threw on a dress.

And then she remembered. The clearing, the Sacred Oaks, the blazing flames. She edged out of her wagon with Gryff.

Her mouth fell open. 'But – but …'

Oak smiled. 'Turns out that amulet of yours had a healing power – same as the water in the well. Cinderella Bull said the Sacred Oaks twisted up stronger, bigger and greener than ever before when we were fighting Skull and Hemlock in the Deepwood. We think it was your pa's way of saying thank you.'

Moll's gaze dropped to the centre of the clearing where a haphazard jumble of spotted neckerchiefs, ruffled skirts, brightly-coloured waistcoats and glittering rings were assembled. Every member of Oak's camp was there – with Siddy and Alfie in the middle waving an enormous banner which only included one word spelt correctly:

WELLKUM BAK MOLL!

They'd drawn a picture of Moll and Gryff next to the writing, but it was hard to tell which one was Gryff and which one was Moll. Both were a mass of cross-looking squiggles with lots of fur and hair.

Hard-Times Bob struck up on his accordion and in moments everyone was cheering and shouting and even Cinderella Bull was shaking her shawl in an excited dance. Moll jumped off her wagon steps and, for a reason that was too difficult to explain, she shuffled over to Florence and

hugged her tight. Florence smiled and Moll knew that somewhere her pa would be watching. Mooshie bustled over,
sobbing loudly and embracing Moll with her favourite tea
towel, then Wisdom hoisted Moll up on to his shoulders. In
a single leap, Gryff sprang up on to Moll's wagon roof to
watch while Siddy clambered on to Alfie's back and they
charged about the clearing, trying to wrestle Moll down.
The cheering grew louder, the beats faster and the dancing
and wrestling wilder.

'Mind you don't make those wrestling towers any higher,
Moll!' Mooshie shouted. 'The skies're full of strange birds,
including great eagles that'd snatch you up and eat you
whole!'

Moll looked over at Gryff and laughed. 'Snatch *me*? Not
likely.' She glanced back at the fire and suddenly noticed
what Mooshie and Patti were preparing. 'Doci baci balls!'
she screamed, swerving Wisdom to the left.

Beside the fire, Mooshie and Patti had laid up two rows of
stools, logs and fallen branches and down the middle, on
tree stumps and upturned boxes, were bowls of one of Moll's
favourite foods: small balls of crisped-up bacon, wrapped in
roasted dock leaves sprinkled with vinegar.

Before long, the entire camp was scoffing down doci baci
balls and raising toasts of forest fruits tea in the summer sun.

Moll sat with Siddy and Alfie, while Gryff nestled
beneath one of the boxes they ate off, gulping down the
food that Moll tossed to the ground for him.

Moll turned to Alfie. 'So you're a member of Oak's camp

now and you'll learn our ways and superstitions soon enough.'

'Like you must never wash a blanket in May because you'll be washing away your family,' Siddy added excitedly.

Alfie shrugged. 'Haven't got a family.'

Siddy tried again. 'If you're pregnant, you mustn't wear shoes because it's like putting your baby in a coffin before it's even born.'

Alfie raised his eyebrows. 'Not likely to have a baby either, Sid.'

Moll threw her hands up. 'We'll go through the super-stitions another time. What's more important than all that is the Tribe. That's something you want to get into if you're in Oak's camp.'

Alfie took a swig of his tea. 'Who's in the Tribe then?'

Moll and Siddy drew themselves up very tall.

'Us two. We're the Tribe.' Moll paused. 'And I may ask Florence in a few days – if she promises not to make me go hawking with her.'

From Moll's feet, there came a growl.

'Oh, and Gryff. He's in the Tribe too.'

'What does the Tribe *do*?' Alfie asked.

Siddy lowered his voice. 'Breaks rules mainly. Avoids chores—'

'—tells lies on Tuesdays and Thursdays,' Moll said.

'And does brave things like rescuing trapped otters and mending owls' wings.'

Alfie considered. Moll leant forward so that only he could

hear. 'I'd do it, Alfie, because you've got to remember that I'm not buying into Skull's stories about your past and I know you don't believe them either. I reckon there's stuff you're still not telling us – like why you thought the amulets could help you …'

Alfie leant back on his stool and then, to Moll's surprise, he winked.

So there were secrets he was holding back.

Alfie held Moll's gaze. 'I'm in.'

Siddy jumped up, sending Porridge the Second flying into a nearby cup. 'I've got to tell you, Alfie, there are a number of tests you have to do before you're allowed in.'

Alfie raised his eyebrows. 'Like what?'

Moll lowered the last of her doci baci balls down to Gryff. 'For a start, you'll be monkey-barring across the river using the alder branches.'

'Then you'll be gurgling the rudest song you know to Mooshie and Ma with your mouth full of river water!' Siddy said.

'And after that there's the midnight dance to the tree spirits on top of Hard-Times Bob's wagon!' Moll grinned. 'Oh, and you've got to take a bath in the mud swamp beyond the glade – then roll in the clean washing!'

Alfie's eyes were wide. 'You two did *all* of that to get into the Tribe?'

Moll's eyes sparkled. 'Course.' Then she slipped off her stool and buried her head in Gryff's fur to hide her smirk.

*

The camp celebrated all through the day and long into the night, and, with Skull and Hemlock gone from the Deepwood, no one thought to keep watch.

But set back from the clearing, tucked into the knotted branches of a yew tree, a figure squatted. Two enormous leathery wings forked up out of its back, folded for now, like giant hands in a darkened prayer. Jet-black eyes shone through the mask of burnt wood, following every move that the girl and the wildcat made down below.

The eyes blinked once and then, like some huge insect, the figure crawled higher up the tree, right through the canopy, until it was looking out over the forest. It waited for several minutes and then it took off into the velvety darkness, shredding the night with each thrust of its wings.

Down in the clearing, Moll glanced up and frowned. The stars glittered back at her as they always did, a puzzle of shimmering lights.

But somewhere not so far away, inside a house lit only by candles, a snakeskin mask looked up. Its owner crossed the room to the window and looked out at the night. And then it smiled darkly as the leathery wings beat closer.

Acknowledgements

For a long time I feared that my greatest life achievement might end up being the junior long-jump record at school or playing Trixie Martin in *Daisy Pulls It Off* when I was twelve. And then *The Dreamsnatcher* happened. But it wouldn't have been a book at all if it hadn't been for some very wonderful people . . .

Thank you to my brilliant agent, Hannah Sheppard, for seeing potential in the book when it was still rough round the edges. You kick-started everything and your editorial advice has been invaluable. One day I promise I will write you a pug. A huge thank you to everyone at Simon & Schuster – to my über-talented editor, Jane Griffiths, for making the book so much better with her editorial comments. You helped bring Moll and Gryff to life and you gave the story structure where it was wobbly. Liz Binks, you nudged the title in the right direction and together with Elisa Offord, you guys are the most enthusiastic and impressive Marketing & PR team I could ask for. Thank you also to other S&S superstars: Elv Moody, Laura Hough, Sam Webster, Tracy Phillips, Stephanie Purcell, and to Jenny Richards for such an awesome cover and Jane Tait for a pretty epic copy edit.

grateful to all the wonderful children I've
ver the years who constantly inspire characters,
sations and plot lines. Thank you to the dazzling Sara
er for playing Moll so brilliantly in the film trailer for the
book, to Annika Arora for advice on the cover and to May
Stanton for following Moll and Gryff from the very start.
And I owe a massive thank you to my friends, to everyone
who kept on believing I'd get there despite the setbacks.
Thank you to Thomas Webb for never doubting; to Cat
Graham for reading and editing early drafts; to Harriet
Agnew for loving Lyra and Pantalaiman with me all through
school; to Hana Geissendorfer and Vic Glendinning for
inspiring me to work as hard as they do; to Heather Holden-
Brown for wise advice throughout the process and to the
Angus Girls (Georgie Majcher, Lucy Walton-Rees & Eleanor
Howse) for all the memories that inspired Moll's life in the
wild – camping up the glen, swimming in the rivers, walking
over the moors. Thank you also to the incredible Salvesen
Clan for all their ongoing love and support – to Vesen, Lica,
Hal, Emily and, of course, the totally wonderful Steph.

To Pete Ingram, my Romany pal and author of *Wagtail
Tale*, thank you for talking to me about the Romany ways –
for carving chrysanthemums, dancing wooden puppets and
chatting gypsy recipes. And thank you so much to Dave
Peacock, from Chas and Dave, for letting us film the trailer
for the book in such an incredible setting. Sitting in your
Romany wagon and riding your gypsy cob bareback through
the forest was nothing short of magical.

But the book would never have happened had it been for my parents who gave me a childhood filled with adventure and wonder, and let me grow up as wild as Moll. Thank you to my father for roaming the hills with me in search of eagles' eyries, for setting up ridiculously competitive obstacle races in the garden and for building tree houses perilously high up in the branches. And a monumental thank you to my wonderful mother, who read and edited countless early drafts, and who is the reason I love reading and writing as much as I do. Thank you for teaching me to dream – and to dream big – and for telling me never to give up. Thank you to my brothers, Will and Tom, for finally admitting I'm funny, for endless teasing (Moll is as punchy as she is because you taught me to be tough!) and for your love and support. Thank you to my little sister, Charis, for sending me anything remotely magical you get your hands on (you have Moll's eyes) and thank you Tron for offering me the most shrewd business advice I've ever heard from a thirteen-year-old.

Last of all, thank you to my husband, Edo, for telling me to write in the first place, for being overly enthusiastic about early drafts (when I see now that they were a bit pants), for giving me a Roald Dahl writer's shed at the bottom of the garden and for being as patient, loyal and loving as Gryff. You made me write the book I did.

·˙About the Author·˙

Abi Elphinstone grew up in Scotland where she spent most of her childhood running wild across the moors, hiding in tree houses and building dens in the woods. After being coaxed out of her tree house, Abi studied English at Bristol University and then worked as an English teacher in Africa, Berkshire and London. *The Dreamsnatcher* is her first book and a sequel will be published in 2016. Abi's favourite book is *Northern Lights* by Philip Pullman and if she had a daemon it would be a wildcat with attitude.

Website: www.abielphinstone.com and www.moontrug.com
Facebook: www.facebook.com/abielphinstone
Twitter: @moontrug
Instagram: @moontrugger